HELL TO PAY
· THREE ·

FLAME UNLEASHED

JILLIAN DAVID

Crimson Romance
New York London Toronto Sydney New Delhi

C R I M S O N
R O M A N C E
Crimson Romance
An Imprint of Simon & Schuster, Inc.
1230 Avenue of the Americas
New York, NY 10020

ISBN 978-1-4405-8949-2
ISBN 978-1-4405-8950-8 (ebook)

Acknowledgments

As always, thank you to fabulous editors Gwen Hayes and Bev Rosenbaum. Their kindness and support have made all the difference in my growth as a writer. Thanks also to Crimson editor Julie Sturgeon, whose attention to detail and excellence has made this series shine. She's also very patient with this naive, anxious, and possibly OCD writer. I've learned more from her about the business of writing than I could ever have imagined.

I must sincerely apologize to my hubby, who is holding out for a spot on a novel cover. Short, bald guys don't sell books, at least not yet. But one day, honey, I promise. One day.

CHAPTER 1

Holy hell, she needed to kill someone.

Impractical stiletto leather boots snapped against concrete as she strode up the chipped sidewalk near the Warehouse District of New Orleans. Dilapidated, abandoned buildings clashed with garish bars that depended on sports fans, college students, and tourists. This section of Port Street wasn't a main road or a well-to-do area of town. Good. That meant fewer tourists but more denizens like her—beings that worked best in the shadows.

Tonight, there must have been a football game or another equally inane reason to imbibe, judging from the amount of people out. Of course, drunkenness was not a crime, despite what she might think of her former husband, God rest his bastard soul. No matter, she would find some kind of louse among the lushes before this night ended.

Farther down the street, the quality of the architecture deteriorated. Dozens of motorcycles were parked outside one raucous establishment. No peppy zydeco tunes here. Instead, tired metal beats drifted into the street. Yes, this area would do nicely for her evening's goals.

Just another night in a city, obtaining her requisite kills. The macabre had become routine. How sad.

A few men leaned against the cinderblock storefront, faint light illuminating the tips of their cigarettes. When she sauntered by, paused, and pretended to contemplate entering the bar, she had their attention. Let them take note, lulled into a sense of security.

Enjoy the view while you can, boys.

One man caught her knife's interest—the blade craved criminals. What remained of the man's bone-straight hair had been pulled into a thin ponytail, and a leather vest strained over his belly. Its fringe was overkill, along with silver detailing that glinted on the new motorcycle boots. He probably owned one of those souped-up custom Harleys parked front and center.

Leather-clad motorcycle guys were generally sexy, but not tonight's fare. Too bad.

Despite his ridiculous getup, her knife began to pulse on her leg, begging for her to reach into the slit on her leather pants, slide the knife from the sheath beneath her boot, and shove it into ...

Got a criminal. Now to reel him in. Might even get the Meaningful Kill tonight.

Tossing her fake hair back off her shoulders, she reveled in the waist-length blond waves. She rarely wore her natural hair down, so this wig brought her to a whole different state of being. Part of her costume was designed to attract certain types of criminals. Part of the costume freed her spirit. So long, mild-mannered nurse. Welcome back, Ms. Blond Bombshell.

Hell, if she had to spend eternity killing criminals, she might as well look good doing it. She had read all the popular books. Who didn't love a sexy demon-slaying chick?

Beside the victims, of course.

She caught the man's eye and licked her lips, a deliberate act that would have been socially unacceptable in her previous life. But this evening's wardrobe veered away from the taffeta, crinoline, and hoops of antebellum evening soirees. Even her torso confined by the black bustier felt like freedom tonight. In a disguise, she could become any woman. The better the disguise, the faster she could forget her real self.

Cursed to kill for hundreds of years as an Indebted, at least she could dictate her attire and the method of carrying out her job. Small victory, but it provided a modicum of control.

When his friend nudged him, the balding man drained his can of beer, crushed it against the wall, and dropped the crumpled metal on the concrete. Despite his nonchalant stance, the glint in his narrow eyes gave away his lust.

He pushed away from the wall. "What's a honey like you doing down here?" His voice sounded like nasally gravel and instantly grated on her nerves.

"Seeing if there's any action."

She glanced at his groin and raised an eyebrow. His Adam's apple bobbed once, twice. With the heels, she topped him by several inches, so his line of sight naturally came to rest on her ample bosom.

Keep looking, nasty guy. It'll be the last thing you see before this night is over.

"What'd you have in mind, beautiful?" His voice oozed over her like sewage slime.

"Let's see where the night takes us." Trailing a hand over her hip, she drew his attention, just like the demon-stalking heroines in the popular novels. Ironic, really, if one considered who was the true demon here.

"I do like a woman who knows what she wants," he drawled, adjusting his jeans.

"Try to keep up ..."

"Right behind you, babe."

Babe. Yuck. Anything but "babe."

She strolled away, giving the man time to contemplate her leather-clad backside. He couldn't help himself. Her heart pounded in anticipation as she led him down the street for a few minutes in search of a location far enough away from the bar. Spying an open gate between two dilapidated buildings, she slipped in ahead of him, giving her backside enough of a wiggle to complete the seduction.

Summoning her best thespian skills, she acted delicate and wilted but still enticing while she leaned against the cement wall inside the abandoned building's courtyard. The man took the bait and boldly placed one hand on the wall next to her head.

As he leaned forward, she tilted her head away. "What's your name, big guy?"

He wetted his lips and leered. "Decker."

She trailed a finger down his chest. "All right, Decker. Now, I'm sure you're not a good boy. Am I right?"

"Uh, yeah." He flicked his gaze away and down.

Guilty. Excellent.

"Anything you've ever done that's particularly bad?"

"Like, sexually?"

Good grief. These men thought about nothing else with an attractive woman in front of them. That single-mindedness in her prey was why she excelled at her job, why her disguise helped her accomplish her goals. The possibility of sex worked every time. So predictable, these men.

If not for the need to stay ahead of her quota of kills, she'd have walked away and tried again tomorrow night. This man was that disgusting. But this criminal would do for her knife's needs.

Twirling a long, flaxen strand of hair around her finger, she giggled. "Oh, Decker, I'm sure you're into all kinds of kink. But what I'm talking about is other naughty things. You ever been in jail? Or maybe should've been in jail?"

He snorted. "You the police?"

"Not even close. I like bad boys. They turn me on."

He put his hand on the wall on the other side of her head and pressed his groin into hers. She resisted the urge to curl her lip and kick him in that offensive yet small bulge. Even though she might enjoy playing the temptress, she was never tempted, especially by a guy like this.

"What do you want to know?" His chest rose and fell more quickly now.

She batted her eyes. "Tell me the worst thing you've ever done in your entire life."

"You don't want to hear it, babe."

Babe. Seriously. "Oh, yes I do. It turns me on—"

She froze.

What was that? A brief flicker of movement high on a nearby building distracted her. Seeing nothing, she dragged her attention back to the balding biker.

"Well, once I ..."

His stale cigarette breath offended as he put his lips to her ear and whispered the sin. Or sins.

The hot air crawled over her neck as he spoke. "... and she might have been fifteen years old, but she acted eighteen. I mean, how was I supposed to know? But her mother, now that lady was tasty ..."

The knife throbbed, hungry, as her intense need to consume criminal blood escalated. Repugnant didn't even begin to describe this monster. What a delicious feast for the knife.

It might even qualify for the Meaningful Kill, the one act that could release her from the eternal, hated contract. A girl could hope.

As an Indebted, her boss was Satan in human form, Jerahmeel. Such a nasty, horrifying creature. Her life had boiled down to killing felons to feed Jerahmeel's appetite for the evil amassed in these sinners.

How she would love to be done with this hellish quasi-existence, to be done with disguises and hiding. And was it asking too much to ask to be left alone?

To do what? Rot? Beyond her ever-present duty to kill criminals and her mundane job as personal attendant for Barnaby, an ex-Indebted, she had nothing. No purpose.

She shoved the thought out of her mind and focused on the creep in front of her.

The minute his tongue touched her earlobe, she shoved him away, spun him around, and slammed him into the wall.

"Let me verify what you've told me," she said.

"What the hell?" He struggled against her supernaturally strong grip.

She dug her fingers into his arm, not caring how badly it hurt. Glancing around, she prayed Jerahmeel wouldn't take this opportunity to pop in. Jerahmeel fixated on people with extra powers, and he already had too keen of an interest in her—a bad combination. If he found out about her additional mind-reading skill, her life would be a living hell. Actually, her life already was a living hell. It would simply become worse than now. Hard to imagine.

Pay attention. Get this job done and get out.

With one more quick glance to ensure no one approached, she steadied the biker's goateed chin, entered his consciousness, and did something no creature alive today—human or otherwise — knew she could do. She *pulled* the thoughts from his mind.

Digging past the mental curtains where he thought about sex and beer, she pushed deeper into the glowing ember of his crime. His horror at the inner invasion coated her own thoughts like cold, wet cobwebs. She mentally gripped the image of his crime and dragged it into her own consciousness, while adjusting his perception to reduce his sweaty panic. Good. Now he believed that her exploration of his mind was all part of fabulous foreplay.

"That's nice, babe," he murmured, trapped in her thrall.

Forcing a smile, she held him in place as she teased out the details. A few years ago, he had done horrible, unspeakable things. Brutal, drawn-out, bloody torture. His glistening, red hand on the ankle of—oh God, a child. A tiny figure hung from ropes that bit into thin, bruised arms. The grisly images flooding her mind wrenched at her stomach.

This man would suit the knife's need for a corrupt and tasty soul, to say nothing of her kick-ass alter ego's desire to deliver vengeance against everything evil. She hated confirming the crimes because of the after-images that remained imprinted on her memories, but her hidden talent was another way she could assert some control over her despised existence as an Indebted killer.

Of course, the knife signaled which criminal to kill, so why bother using her power?

An overabundance of caution, even after all these years. If she accidentally murdered an innocent, she might lose what sanity she had left. So she double-checked her kill. Every single time.

Also, if she picked only the worst sinners, maybe she'd increase her chances of obtaining the Meaningful Kill. Besides, she needed to flog her conscience with the horrible images of the criminals' deeds, to serve small penance for deserting her own children so many years ago when she became this Indebted killer.

Truth be told, she also enjoyed each small burst of vigilante retribution, bringing the crimes to light. Right before committing a crime herself. Because warped logic was better than no logic.

She shoved him harder into the wall. The idiot thought they were headed for wild sex.

"Oh yeah, baby. You like it rough?" He fumbled with his belt buckle.

You've got to be kidding. "You have no idea," she whispered. "Let me get some protection."

She bent down and reached for the knife, which rested in the sheath on her lower leg. Her night had gone from routine quota kill to an all-consuming need to kill in the space of mere seconds. Damned Indebted hunger drove her into a frenzy, despite her typical control.

"Yeah, do it, baby."

Another movement from the rooftop, like a moth passing in front of a light, stole her attention for a split second.

The movement distracted her. At the moment her fingers grasped the handle, Decker kicked her square in the chest. Despite fast reflexes, she didn't react in time and bent over, coughing. The knife clattered a few feet away, next to Decker. The blade glowed lurid green, hungry. Damn, it physically hurt not to touch her knife.

Thankfully, the damaged muscles and cracked ribs had already begun to knit back together.

"You gonna pull that shit on me?"

She edged toward the blade. Had to reconnect with it. Needed it. Now.

He followed her gaze. "You want this?" He kicked the knife into the depths of the courtyard. Then he pulled a gun from a side holster.

She crouched, ready to bolt over and retrieve her weapon. Longing for the blade threatened to drive her mad.

Before she could act, a dark figure landed in front of her with a heavy thud of boots on cobblestones and a long trench coat flapping around him, making him appear too large for life.

What in the blazes?

"Step away from the lady, *mon ami*."

"Who the fuck are you?" Decker sneered, pointing the gun at the man in black.

"Someone you don't want to cross." The man's voice, a rich tenor with a Cajun lilt, cut through the evening air. Although his voice held lightness, almost humor, he commanded attention, not by his giant frame looming out of the shadows but by a tantalizing charisma when he spoke.

No time to ponder how his voice slid over her like a satin sheet. She needed to get rid of this extra Musketeer, fast. Bless this hapless hero, but she was most certainly *not* a damsel in distress. Quite the opposite, and she was managing fine before he arrived. Now, if only he would leave her alone to complete her assignment. Then she could wrap this job up and go back to being inconspicuous.

"Get the fuck out of here!" Decker screamed as the gun shook.

When the man in the trench coat didn't move, the biker pulled the trigger.

The mystery guy moved faster than her eye could follow. The gunshot crack echoed through the courtyard. The sound was sure to draw attention. Not good.

Even though he rocked back a step, the unfortunate gallant remained standing.

No.

Still standing.

He brushed a hand over his chest, like a gnat had bit him.

She ducked into the shadows of the courtyard, found her knife, shoved it in the holster, and raced back. She had to get rid of hero-boy so her biker buddy could feed the blade.

With a gurgled grunt and wheeze, Decker crumpled to the ground.

What in the hell?

The large man stood over Decker's body as a pool of dark liquid stained the cobblestones beneath his feet. Soul's blood, wasted.

God, she had needed to let her knife drink that criminal's blood. Now her compulsion to kill had doubled, threatening to blind her. Ignoring the man, she knelt next to the dead biker. She took a deep breath, fought searing pain in her gut due to her missed kill, and wrestled her base desires back under control. Damn, citizens would be here soon. She had to move.

Was that green glint in the interloper's hand a trick of the light? With her knife lust, she couldn't trust her perception of reality. His weapon looked suspiciously like ... hers. That meant he was ... oh, hell.

If he didn't yet realize that they were both Indebted, it might give her a brief advantage.

Oh God, what if this was Barnaby's friend they'd come to visit? Surely not. How many Indebted could inhabit New Orleans without drawing attention? Several, right? New Orleans was a big city.

The would-be rescuer held out a hand, and despite her best judgment, she took it, noting his broad fingers and a hint of dark hair on the back of his wrist. She needed to get out of here, but something about him fascinated her. Another Indebted. How old was he?

With a wince, he drew her up in front of him. The small hole in his coat spoke to the gunshot wound beneath. The injury probably hurt like hell but would be well on its way to healing.

Standing in front of him now, her gaze rested right on his shadowed mouth, where she could make out a smirk of sensual lips. For a split second, she wondered what those lips would feel like on hers. Would they be warm and sensual or demanding and hard? Would they stay turned up at the corners?

Was he actually smiling like this ridiculous situation was some joke? She withdrew her hand from his heated grip and clamped down on her girlish thoughts. One hundred and fifty years old, and all of a sudden she felt flirty? Incredible ... and incredibly inappropriate.

"Why the hell did you do that?" She gestured toward the hemorrhaging biker.

Although the Indebted's face was mostly hidden in shadow, his one visible eye widened and he reared back. Dark hair curled beneath his fedora—were those strands as soft as they appeared? He rubbed the hair on his chin, less than a full beard but more than stubble. The scratchy sound sent a quiver of desire into her belly. While the knife pulsed with sick hunger on her leg, she itched with longing to touch the rough hair on the man's jaw.

"I don't understand. That man would have killed you," he said.

"I can take care of myself, thanks." She needed to feed the blade. Soon.

Voices drifted down the street, getting louder by the second. Damn it.

"*Pardonnez*?" His jaw dropped open, and the dark gaze bored into her. No, *through* her. She shivered.

"You ruined my evening." Probably not the most typical human response. After all, she'd just witnessed him murder a man. Sadly, though, she had become pretty blasé about the job requirements. Dead was dead.

Shaking with the effort to restrain the drive to kill, she clenched her hands into fists. The knife wanted her to wrap her fingers around the hilt and plunge the blade into a chest. Her hunger had risen to such a level, it would feed on anyone, including innocents and even her own kind. But this errant knight in proverbial shining armor shouldn't suffer because of her inability to focus.

She curbed her killing desires, just like she regulated other aspects of her life. Well, the areas she *could* control, that is.

With her efforts, the knife lust slowly ebbed. Sad emptiness took its place.

"You're ... unhappy that I saved you?" He grimaced, revealing square, even teeth.

"You wouldn't understand."

"Try me."

His mellow voice soothed her raw nerves like aloe on a wound. When he stepped forward, she jerked backward. Time to get away from this guy and from this scene, fast.

Shouts drifted into the courtyard. Citizens would be here in a matter of seconds.

"Sir, thank you for your help, however misguided. I need to be on my way."

"Thank you? That's it?" He gestured at Decker's body, motionless and silent in the cool night.

At the wry undertone, she pressed her lips together. Was he making fun of her?

Anger bubbled up. What did it say about her own humanity that the corpse at her feet disappointed her? Pissed her off. Not because he was dead, but because she hadn't been the one to kill him.

Here she stood in her ridiculous wig and urban fantasy getup, using sex to draw in her prey, like a warped black widow. For what?

Somewhere deep down, she wasn't this seductress, despite her fabulous disguise. All the air and energy left her in a rush. All bravado, no substance. She was a fraud, living in a shell of an existence.

Damn, how she wanted Decker's criminal blood inside of her knife. What if she just swirled the knife in the pool of cold blood? Maybe that would work.

No, it wouldn't. Had to be blood from the heart; the knife had to be in the chest. Damn it.

"Thank you. Goodnight, sir," she said in her firmest tone.

He stepped close enough that she saw his closely trimmed facial hair framing upturned lips, a mouth full enough to give a provocative smirk. A combination of cologne and Cajun spice blended perfectly around him. For a moment, she wanted to indulge, to taste, to experience a different life, to be someone else.

What the hell was wrong with her? With a dead body cooling at her feet, a handsome but still-clueless Indebted before her, and citizens on their way, she fixated on his mouth?

The damn blade pulsed again, again eager for someone's—anyone's—blood. It insisted on her complete attention, pulling her focus away from the man in front of her.

When she tried to evade him, he snagged her arm. He was strong, but of course, she was his equal. He couldn't budge her. At the display of her Indebted strength, shock crossed the visible part of his features. Yes, they shared the exact same secret.

"*Chèri*? What the—?"

Using his surprise to her advantage, she acted on pure instinct, stomping his instep with her spiked heel. He bit off a curse as his grip loosened. Dropping to a crouch, she rotated and swept an outstretched foot under the one leg he hopped on, and he fell hard onto the cobblestones. Unfortunately, when she rotated, her stupid wig caught on his hand, knocking it askew and covering an eye.

Not caring if he saw, she tugged her hair back in place. In one fluid motion, she leapt to the metal fire escape ladder and vaulted to a roof. Quite a feat in heels. How did those sexy vampire chicks in the novels manage? Never mind. No time to think about silly books.

She gritted her teeth and sprinted across the roof. Before descending the next ladder to the opposite street, she glanced back into the courtyard. She had gotten away in the nick of time. Patrons from the bar rounded the corner into the courtyard, followed by a police officer.

Decker's body was gone, a glistening puddle on the cobblestones all that remained.

The mystery man, too, was gone. Although he wasn't actually a mortal man but Indebted. Just like her.

He must have removed the body.

Why?

To protect her.

To take attention away from things in this world that could not be explained.

What a joke. Her entire existence couldn't be explained. Everything she did as a result of being Indebted defied logic. How would a dead criminal change that fact?

It wouldn't.

But a pattern of dead criminals could bring unwanted scrutiny to the Indebted that called New Orleans their home. Where had her consideration for others gone?

To hell, along with the greater portion of her conscience.

Jumping from the roof to adjacent buildings, she continued to the end of the block. There was no easy fire escape. She peered down the four story building and sighed. This was going to hurt.

She dropped off the roof, landing with an audible pop on one foot. A red wave of pain swamped her, and she gripped the edge of the brick to clear her head. Masonry disintegrated under her fingertips.

She pressed her lips together to keep from crying out.

Breathe.

Another few seconds, and she'd be functional.

With another crunch, her bones knitted back together enough for her to walk. Each step felt better than the last.

Once she reached the French District, she ducked into a dark corner behind a dumpster and pressed her fingers to her forehead. So tired. In the past, she had salvaged botched kills, but tonight was different. She still needed to kill, but the control she had exerted over that biker's mind took so much energy. Her fatigue would keep the desire to kill in check for a short period of time. The desperation no longer consumed her.

Sick consolation. For now.

Meeting a fellow Indebted had thrown her for a loop. True, some Indebted worked together, but Ruth operated in private, always had. She hated spectators of any kind. Ironic, then, how she'd given the man in the trench coat quite a show.

Like most of her kind, she avoided hunting in the daytime. More potential witnesses. So she would have to endure a miserable day until tomorrow night. Even though time technically meant nothing to her, twenty-four hours from now seemed like years away.

Maybe as a diversion she could indulge in a tiny fantasy about her hero's sensual lips.

CHAPTER 2

The next morning, she struggled to complete the duties of her mundane job. Helping Barnaby took little effort, yet she almost didn't pull it off thanks to her inability to focus.

For the past several years, she'd worked as a full-time nurse for the now aging Barnaby, attending to his increasing needs for assistance. As a former Indebted, he understood her urge to slake the knife lust periodically.

As a former Indebted, he represented everything that she wanted.

A normal, mortal life.

The opportunity to experience loving human companionship.

Freedom from the all-consuming need to kill.

She took a deep breath and blew it out. After smoothing her perfectly creased khaki pants, she patted her hair, secured in a bun at the nape of her neck. At least dressing professionally gave her a semblance of normalcy, as it had done for years.

Normal. How laughable. Just another damn disguise, really. At least this outfit kept people at a distance. Calm, conservative, reserved Nurse Ruth. With a stiff exterior appearance, she was less likely to be hurt, and that protection was all that mattered.

From all of the coursework at nursing schools over the decades, she had matriculated more times than she could recollect. For a time, giving solace to the sick provided her satisfaction enough. She even used her calling as a nurse to find the criminals among her patients and dispatch these evil patients to slake the knife's hunger.

She was pretty sure killing any patients, even bad ones, went against every word of the Florence Nightingale Pledge.

With a sigh, she turned back to her current day's tasks.

She pulled back the heavy brocade drapery, trying to enjoy the fine furnishings at the luxury Windsor Court Hotel. New Orleans's waterfront glinted in the morning light. Sunbeams streamed in the picture windows, bringing welcome brightness to the late fall day. Sunny weather normally gave her a sense of peace, but today the light annoyed her, unfocused her, like everything else this morning.

She hated leaving a job undone; it went against her core values. Worst of all, having to attempt another kill increased the potential for attention from her disgusting and terrifying boss, Jerahmeel. It was in her kind's best interest to avoid attracting his scrutiny whenever possible.

Her hands shook so badly that when she tried to lay out Barnaby's clothes, she couldn't make her hands arrange the clothes in a perfect row like she usually did. She couldn't think straight beneath the wave of desire to drive the blade into a criminal, combined with the fear of Jerahmeel's attention.

Hopefully she'd get her kill tonight without incident.

An incident. A good way to describe the man in the trench coat with lips meant for sin.

Recalling his voice and that sensual mouth sent a zip of excitement up her spine as she peered out the window. The thought of that man helped her forget the lingering knife urge.

Then a jolt of dread hit her. He was Indebted. He knew that she was Indebted, too.

The sunshine streaming into the room had turned to a harsh interrogation light. She wanted to close the blinds and hide.

At least that Indebted guy didn't know all of her secrets, a disastrous prospect.

But he knew enough to expose her guarded existence—an existence she'd worked hard to conceal from everyone.

Perhaps even herself. All those years of hiding had become second nature.

Who the hell was she anymore?

Barnaby shuffled out of the bathroom, his thin frame engulfed by the hotel's Turkish cotton robe. His kind smile creased hundreds of lines on his careworn face. A remaining few strands of hair straggled out from his bald head.

"Penny for your thoughts, my dear?" her boss asked.

"Just woolgathering," she said.

"Did you complete your assignment last night?"

Although his voice wavered, those pale blue eyes shone with sharp intelligence. His centuries-old strength and energy had waned, but his mind was as keen as when he rubbed elbows with Elizabeth, the last of the Tudors.

Ruth would never lie to him. She loved Barnaby, her mentor and her friend. He knew precisely what her job entailed, since he'd been an Indebted for hundreds of years until he broke his contract to be with his wife. He rarely mentioned that period of time forty years ago when he changed to mortal, but it had to have been momentous. No one broke his or her contract, right?

Not exactly. Barnaby did it, and his friends Peter and Dante attained their freedom, too. All right, so it must be possible to escape this hell, but how? By what rules? Damn it, she had no guidance, no idea of how to try to attempt her own liberation.

Breaking their contracts nearly cost those men their lives, but they'd succeeded. All three men had achieved the Meaningful Kill. Jealousy churned in her gut.

Maybe there was hope for her. Or maybe not, with Jerahmeel keeping closer tabs on his employees nowadays.

"No, I didn't get a kill." Damn it, she snapped at the one person she'd come to love and respect over the years. The man closest to a father and a friend.

Mean acid melted to muddy shame inside of her.

While she wouldn't lie, she refused to trouble Barnaby with her concerns. Ruth hadn't been a burden to anyone since 1864. She wouldn't start now.

"Couldn't find an appropriate candidate?"

She shrugged with a nonchalance that even she didn't believe. "It's okay. I'll find someone this evening."

"Of course you will, my dear." When he patted her on the arm, the bones in his hands stood out stark beneath his thin skin.

"Barnaby, how did you get the Meaningful Kill?" she blurted out. Hot guilt crawled over her chest. "I'm sorry. I realize that you can't tell me. Forget that I asked."

Staring at her for so long it made her squirm, Barnaby finally sighed. Anyone who knew him for a minute could see how he'd loved his wife, Jane. Sadly, her life had been cut short by illness, and Barnaby had carried on alone for the past twenty years.

He answered, his voice gravelly. "My dear, I would tell you if I could. Forsooth, I want for you to escape your Indebted contract. But I am bound by Jerahmeel's rules never to speak of it."

"You helped Peter and Dante."

"Not directly, and certainly not by telling them how I did it. To be fair, as I witnessed their changes and my own, I realized that the solution to the Meaningful Kill is different for each Indebted."

She brushed nonexistent wrinkles from Barnaby's clothes on the bed. "That doesn't help me, does it?"

His mouth pulled into a wry smile. "This existence wears on you, doesn't it?"

"I don't want to burden you ..."

"Nonsense. I think of you as the daughter I never had, Ruth." He coughed for a few moments until he caught his breath. "I so want you to have a good life, my dear."

"My life is good, working for you."

"But not good, right?"

"It's not ... what I would have wanted."

Emptiness weighted her shoulders every day—a black tunnel of death and murder with no end in sight. No one would want such a reality.

"No, I want you to have your own life, on your own terms. With someone who loves you, er, differently than I do." His grin folded his eyes into numerous wrinkles.

She ran a hand over her neck until she caught herself. "It's not in the stars. I had my family, years ago, and I ruined everything. But yes, it would be nice to live a life without the need to kill always pressing me."

"I understand."

Folding the remainder of his clothes, she laid them in a perfect, neat row. A useless exercise, considering he would wear these garments soon, but the precise activity and attention to detail calmed her. "Of course you do. And you did this job longer than anyone I know. What right do I have to complain?"

"You have every right, my dear. We all do." He cocked his head to the side. "But you are destined for great things one day. When the opportunity arises, you'll find your own path."

"And you know this information ... how?" Despite herself, she smiled.

"I've always had good instincts about life, my dear."

"Right." She brushed her hands together. "Well, my path right now involves making you presentable for the day so you don't lounge around like a society lady all morning."

He laughed. "Oh, you are good for my soul. Can't be allowed to be a slugabed."

Something odd, a tug of emotion from the knowledge that his mortal body would one day fail, turned in her chest as she slipped out of the room.

Before she could close the door, he asked, "Were you able to arrange brunch for Odilon's arrival?"

"I called down while you were in the shower. The food should be here soon."

"Very good. I can't wait to see him again."

"How long has it been?"

She peeked back in the bedroom. He stood at the bedside, staring up at the ceiling. The robe gapped at his neck, and his collarbones jutted out from beneath his skin. At the sight, her heart twisted. She'd helped many elderly patients in her nursing career but always maintained professional objectivity. With Barnaby, it was like seeing her own father aging right in front of her.

"My, how long indeed?"

He rubbed his freshly shaven chin. Barnaby still took pride in performing his own personal care.

"Let's see. I met Odilon in 1810, when he threw his lot in with that scurrilous Louisiana privateer, Jean Lafitte. I was on my tour of the New World, always on alert for shrewd investments. There was good money to be had in smuggled goods and supplies for shipbuilding to help the American military leading up to the War of 1812. We worked for Lafitte's company for a year, but the Indebted kills became too concentrated around New Orleans. I next saw him around 1975, after I transitioned to human, and then again in 1995 after my lovely Jane passed on. Time seems to move too quickly for our kind. I haven't seen him since Jane's death. The way time passes for the Indebted, it's as if only yesterday she left this world without me ..."

At his slumped shoulders and faraway stare, Ruth eased the door shut. Barnaby's wife had died much too young, a shame considering the immense risk he'd taken to be with her. Had the sacrifice been worth it?

She considered Barnaby's smile, both sad and joyous.

In the sitting area, she straightened the already neatly arranged furniture. Anything to distract her until room service delivered brunch.

At a knock on the door, Ruth rushed to the door of the suite, expecting to greet the waiter.

A tall man stood at the door.

As his intense stare zoomed in on her face, Ruth's stomach dropped out from under her.

To be more precise, he didn't stand, he nearly vibrated, such was the male confidence that radiated in all directions. A lazy smile spread across his sensual lips, which were surrounded by a closely trimmed scruff of dark beard and moustache. If his appearance veered toward handsome, the crooked nose likely from a prior injury pushed his features back to rugged. Even though she'd seen only half of his face last night, she'd recognize that jawline anywhere.

Beneath thick, dark brown eyebrows that slashed color across his forehead, his pale green eyes narrowed. His gaze, the color of backlit bottle glass, smoldered. Sooty lashes shadowed his eyes until his brows shot up.

Now someone else knew her Indebted status and how she used her body to lure in each kill.

How she had failed.

Even though Ruth was fully clothed, she wanted to pull a blanket around herself. Each sweep of this man's gaze virtually raked her bare.

Pressure mounted—fire against ceramic. She had to escape his scrutiny, or her protective shell would break.

She shivered.

Chapter 3

Mon dieu!

If the woman from last night did not stand before him, then this was her prim and proper twin. Today, instead of long waves of blond hair, gleaming auburn tresses had been unjustly confined to a knot at the nape of her elegant neck.

And her figure? Instead of those curves being poured into leather, she filled out plain tan work pants so as to bless the shapeless garments. A deep breath raised her ample breasts to strain the knit fabric of her forest green polo shirt.

Odilon couldn't help himself. He inhaled along with the woman, instantly in tune with her.

This mystery woman had haunted his thoughts since last night's encounter. At the demonstration of her strength and speed and her bizarre reaction to the dead man, Odie had realized she was also an Indebted. He, of course, empathized with her plight, trapped in his own macabre existence, compelled to perform murder. Perhaps she, too, had been forced to make a grim choice with a loved one, right before becoming Indebted. That's normally how it worked. That's how it had happened for him, at least.

God, what he'd give to destroy Jerahmeel once and for all.

Enough. Time enough for plotting later. He needed to concentrate on the beautiful woman in front of him.

The top of her head came to right below his eye level. How would this glorious woman fit against him? Odie needed to know. His hands itched to reach for her.

He had to know what she'd feel like beneath him, all that soft porcelain skin sliding over his skin. An image of her auburn hair, fanned out on a bed as he gripped those locks in his fist and drove into her body ...

Never in his centuries walking this Earth had he experienced such a rapid response to a woman. Sure, he was a lusty man in a general sense, but he always retained self-control.

Why the hell did she command his interest? Was it because she was an Indebted like him? He shook his head.

All he knew was this woman, as she stood there in such plebian clothing and subdued adornment, appeared even lovelier than the woman he met the evening before. Which woman was real? He had to find out.

Before he could open his mouth to speak, their gazes locked. Air left him in a whoosh. Long, dark lashes framed eyes with such a unique hazel the myriad colors glowed with an amber light. Flecks of green, brown, and gold swirled in the depths. Her winged auburn brows rose. Odie caught himself leaning toward her until he jerked upright.

Her full lips were moving, but he heard nothing except air rushing past his ears.

"May I help you?" she said. The tone of her voice, like an icicle plinking water from the tip, contrasted with the warm auburn hair and creamy skin. Concentrating on polite conversation became impossible as he attempted to reconcile the image before him.

Fire. Ice. Sexy leather. Khaki pants.

"How are you, um, after the ... man ... last night, *chère*?"

Her bland expression didn't change. "Unfulfilled."

That made two of them. He swallowed hard.

"Perhaps I could remedy that state?" The sudden tightness in his groin encouraged his imagination to devise several methods of fulfilling this glorious woman. Those curves on display as he drove into her soft ...

"Sir?"

Heat spread from below his belt to wrap around his neck until he couldn't breathe. "Ah, yes, about the kill. I had no idea that you were ..."

"Like you?"

"Well, yes. I haven't encountered another Indebted in town. It's been my territory for hundreds of years. I didn't realize Barnaby was bringing another ... you ... like us, me, or I would have helped you take care of your ... business. You know, er, welcome you to town, so to speak."

Mon dieu, he was babbling like a nervous schoolboy, squirming beneath her cool appraisal. He found he rather liked the idea of unlocking that constrained exterior, looking for the sexy, leather-clad spitfire that resided within.

Like the pull from a magnet, he leaned toward her again, satisfied by her sharp intake of air but ecstatic when that movement pushed her breasts up. So close, he could almost reach out and feel their fullness in his hands.

She backed up from the doorway and bumped into the wall, hands pressed against his chest. Her hot palms branded him, and he wanted more of that heat over every inch of his body.

Those beautiful eyes darkened as she looked up at him.

Certainly not an ice queen. The eyes gave it away every time. Any intense emotion turned every Indebted's irises black. The Indebted couldn't regulate that response.

Her now-obsidian eyes widened as she gasped. So. Not so prim and proper a façade as she might like to convey.

Not the leather-clad diva, either, though. Fascinating. She was neither character.

He lifted his hand until it hovered an inch from the skin of her neck.

Like a man about to jump off a cliff, he paused.

Damn it, he needed to touch her.

The vein pulsed at the base of her neck. That location would suffice.

He feathered his fingertips over the heated skin. Silk. Warm silk.

His existence boiled down to a two-inch square of this woman's neck. And he couldn't care less.

The sigh from her full, parted lips threatened his sanity. He inhaled, as if to absorb her breath, her scent of mint and lavender. The aroma made his head spin.

How in the name of God did the tiniest touch of his fingers on her skin create such boiling pressure in his groin? Delicious and painful, the electrical sensation shot from his hand to his hardening manhood. He wanted relief.

He shifted, trying to decrease the pressure of garments that were suddenly two sizes too small. Damn it, the movement only made things worse.

She licked her lips.

He had to taste. A scientific study only, to see if that lush mouth tasted as good as it looked.

"Ruth?"

His old friend's voice cut through the moment.

The woman, Ruth, startled and blinked those multicolored irises from onyx back to amber, and the spell was broken. She scooted away from him, back pressed to the wall, her cheeks flushed a delightful shade of pink.

"I'll be right there," she called over her shoulder.

The pulse in her neck danced. Good.

He took a step back, displeased that the heady scent of her no longer flooded his senses.

She licked lips too pillowy soft for conventional beauty but well proportioned within her sculpted face. "So you must be ...?"

"Odilon Pierre-Noir. At your service, *mon chèri*."

Odie lifted her hand to his lips, inhaling the light lavender perfume once more. Darkness swallowed the gold flecks in her irises as she watched him.

In contrast to her cool demeanor, the porcelain skin of her hand radiated heat against his mouth. When he reluctantly released her hand, the silky slide of her palm against his fingers shot a bolt of longing into his gut.

She frowned. "Your last name, it's different. We all take the surname of "Blackstone" when we become Indebted."

"It's French. Means 'black stone.' I prefer it to the English name."

"Odilon?"

"Yes, old Acadian. Very old. My friends call me Odie."

"OD? As in 'overdose'?"

One arched brow quirked upward, but the rest of her expression remained impassive. She would make a formidable poker player, and Odie did so enjoy gambling. Bet he could change her countenance in the bedroom from guarded to cosmic pleasure. He'd gladly ante up all his chips trying.

With effort, he dragged his imagination away from images of her glorious body laid out for him on a soft mattress, or floor, or any surface that allowed him to explore her curves, and refocused on the conversation. "My *mamam* would be hurt; she was proud of that name."

Just the tiniest quirk of a corner of her mouth. A chink in the defenses. Something for him to work on later.

"Hmm. All right, come with me then, Odie."

She turned on her heel, giving him a spectacular view of her heart shaped derrière. Even the wiggle as she walked turned his mouth to dry sand. And the fact that she was like him only intrigued him even more. What a pair they would make in the bedroom.

Turning a corner, they passed through a small dining area. Suspended above a cherry wood table, a small chandelier flung pieces of morning sunlight onto the plaster walls. The Mississippi River, sod-brown and lazily flowing to the Gulf, reflected the Crescent City Connection Bridge above. Ah, how he loved New Orleans.

They entered a well-appointed salon, complete with velvet upholstered Victorian chairs and settees. Seated in one of the plush chairs was a bald, wizened man. Odie wouldn't have recognized his old friend if not for the mischievous glint in those pale blue eyes.

"Barnaby?"

"Odilon, my old friend!"

He rushed to the old man but paused, uncertain how to proceed. Barnaby obviated debate when he held out a gnarled hand. His friend's fragile skin showed veins and sunspots, but the strength had not completely departed that grip.

"Help me up, you smelly Cajun."

Odie put a hand under his friend's upper arm to help him to stand. Ruth hovered nearby. Protective of Barnaby? Good for the old man. She was a lovely companion, and even if his friend had gotten on in years, Barnaby couldn't possibly be blind to her ... assets, even confined as they were under the staid attire.

Hugging carefully, Odie patted his friend's stooped shoulders. Barnaby's back was no longer straight. Bones ground together in the sockets, and the old man groaned.

"Getting old is not for the faint of heart, eh?" His friend chuckled and then coughed. "Sit, let's catch up."

Barnaby lowered himself back down, holding on to the ornately carved arms of the chair. Odie wanted to help, but the steely pride etched on the old man's face deterred him. His old friend, still stubborn after more than 400 years on this Earth. Amazing.

At a knock at the door, Ruth slipped out of the room. Odie couldn't help himself. He watched her leave, her smooth gait with those magnificent curves—it was impossible to look away.

Barnaby cleared his throat.

Busted, as they said in current parlance.

The old Englishman's devilish smile didn't help, either. But Barnaby knew the dance of attraction. Indeed, he had garnered the reputation as quite the paramour for hundreds of years. Barnaby was a legend. Hard to imagine, seeing his aging friend now.

Odie leaned back. "So it's been, what, about twenty years? Much too long, old man."

"Time has become somewhat fluid. But it marches on for me, now." The barest crease formed at the corners of Barnaby's eyes. Regret and ... relief?

Odie studied the rug pattern. "Sorry. You're right. Um ..."

"It's all right, my friend. I've been in your shoes. Ten, twenty, a hundred years? Means nothing when you're long-lived."

If he met his friend's probing stare, Odie would reveal his desperate hope. So he studied the fabric on the chair and forced a neutral tone. "You mentioned Peter and Dante when we last spoke on the phone. I heard some rumblings, but you know how I keep to myself. What happened?"

"Both contracts broken."

"How?"

"I can't say."

Two conflicting bursts of emotion fought inside of Odie. On the one hand, Indebted breaking their contracts would be a blow to Jerahmeel's power base and good for Peter and Dante that they succeeded. But on the other hand, it meant more work for the Indebted remaining on this Earth.

"Of course you can't tell me details. But was their experience like yours? Did they do it for a mortal?"

Barnaby's watery eyes twinkled. "For women."

"Figures."

Odie had met each man before. Peter had only been an Indebted since the 1940s. He'd never accepted the perks of having unhuman strength and power and instead dwelled on the guilt of being a killer. Understandable that he would want to break the contract.

Dante, on the other hand, the giant Swede born 300 years ago, had embraced his Indebted prowess and reportedly applied it with great enthusiasm, especially in the bedroom. It boggled the mind to consider Dante settled down with only one woman.

Odie crossed his ankle over his knee. "My own urge to kill has increased over the past year or so, which makes sense. Fewer Indebted left to keep He-Who-Must-Be-Fed satiated."

"You're right. And may I say that pissing off Jerahmeel is a generally bad idea? After losing Peter and Dante, he's sorely vexed, to put it lightly."

"At Peter and Dante? Or at you?"

Barnaby rubbed the backs of his arthritic hands. "All of us. You see, while I didn't exactly help, I might have had a tiny bit of involvement with each transformation."

Adrenaline shot through Odie as he sat up bolt upright, boots planted on the floor. No one wanted to attract Jerahmeel's interest. Ever. A mere mortal would never survive his boss's rage. So did that mean Barnaby was now a marked man?

"Exactly how tiny?"

A flicker of pain passed over Barnaby's face and then was gone. Fear? "Probably a bit too much involvement."

"Can Ruth keep you safe?"

"That's not her job, my boy. But yes, she does watch over me."

"You didn't answer the question."

The elderly man pulled a wistful smile. "I'm not afeared of death, you know. Not anymore."

"What are you saying, old friend?"

"I've said too much—"

At Barnaby's stricken expression when Ruth slipped in the room, Odie snapped his mouth shut.

Her eyes narrowed as she studied the suddenly silent men, and her lips thinned. "Brunch is on the table if you two are ready."

She turned to step out again, but Barnaby stopped her. "Dine with us, my dear."

"I couldn't. This is time for you to spend with your friend."

"Even more reason." Barnaby chuckled. "You keep yourself so cloistered with this old, rickety man all the time, you don't get to be around anyone else. Like us, I mean."

Ah, that particular shade of pink on Ruth's cheeks, the color of strawberry buttercream, had Odie's tongue watering. When she helped Barnaby up, damned if the tan fabric didn't stretch perfectly over her hips. He followed her to the dining room, where they sat around the cherry wood table.

The Indebted did not require food, but Odie personally enjoyed preparing and eating it, a simple pleasure that helped to maintain a thin connection to his humanity.

Between bites of poached eggs in tangy hollandaise sauce, he shared tales of how New Orleans had changed since he had first arrived in 1768, when the city was little more than a few streets of wood homes that blew down during each hurricane season. He and Barnaby shared with Ruth one of their more notorious escapades when they evaded the British military with the aid of a brothel full of lusty and loyal Creole women. By the time the ladies of the night had finished, the Brits couldn't walk straight, much less track down two suspected smugglers.

Ruth's eyes glowed as her mouth curled up in reluctant amusement at the misadventure. How Odie would enjoy finding new ways to make her smile.

"So, are you still dabbling in genealogy these days?" Barnaby's question caught him off-guard.

"Why, yes. I find it fascinating. With the advent of the Internet and an unlimited supply of free time, I've created new programs to trace family trees."

"To what extent?" Ruth broke her silence. Her cool but sensual voice caught his attention like someone grabbing his balls.

Damn, but he wanted to focus on the fork sliding over her lips, not genealogy work. "I like to know what my daughter's family is up to, to know that my progeny carries on successfully. It also helps that they have a secret benefactor now and then, as the situation presents itself."

"Presents itself?" Her tapered fingertip tracing the rim of the juice glass challenged him to remain calm.

"Well, not many in my extended family had a lot of money. But after hundreds of years of compounded interest, I, of course, have plenty. If a hardworking kid dreams of going to college or needs help creating a better life, he or she might suddenly find himself or herself the recipient of grants or donations. There's a whole legend in the Turcot family about a ghostly force that helps deserving people when they are most desperate."

"That's you? Turcot?"

"Yes, that's my old name before I became Indebted. Now I'm the Turcot ghost, occasionally saving the day by sprinkling family members with a little money."

"You don't feel you're interfering?"

She pulled apart a buttermilk biscuit, neatly popping small pieces into her mouth. He employed immense willpower not to fixate on her full lips as she chewed.

"Odie?" she said, arching an eyebrow.

Barnaby also looked up at Odie with a bemused smile.

The back of Odie's neck fired up like a guilty schoolboy. He couldn't remember the last time he'd been embarrassed. Or infatuated.

He swallowed a bite, but the food almost didn't pass through his tight throat. "No, it's not interference. I only give a gentle nudge in the right direction."

"Don't you feel strange looking up your long-lost family members, so many years removed?" she said.

Without that connection, he'd have long since become lost, mired in guilt, purposeless.

"Not at all. It keeps me connected to the mundane world, my roots, my own humanity. Why? Don't you know about your progeny?"

"No, that family is long gone."

Silence descended until Barnaby set down his fork and faced Odie. "Any other projects you're working on? You've always been one of the more industrious Indebted not only with philanthropy for your family, but also with your new ideas."

Odie had enjoyed discussing emerging theories and science with Barnaby over the 200-odd years they had known each other. They'd debated Madame Curie's research, motorized vehicles, space travel, and everything in between.

But Odie had never told anyone about his biggest theory.

For more than 200 years, he had quietly concentrated his rage, his all-consuming desire on eliminating Jerahmeel, to exact his revenge for the suffering rained down on Odie and his family. But Odie had lacked all of the information and thus never had a viable plan.

Until recently.

Now he knew how to destroy Jerahmeel and release all of the Indebted from their contracts. Freedom from their never-ending murderous existences.

Take Ruth, for example. A beautiful woman should never have to exist as this kind of slave, killing on demand and destroying her kind soul—one murdered human life at a time.

He speared a piece of Andouille sausage, savoring the pop of spicy meat as he chewed, stalling for time. But the savory juices clashed with the sour taste his knowledge gave him. Time to spill the beans, as they said, and start exploring the viability of this plan.

"Barnaby. Ruth. How badly do you hate Jerahmeel? How much do you hate the kills, the loss of your humanity?" He dropped the question like a lead weight. "Was the sacrifice you made worth it, as now, centuries later, everyone you loved has departed this Earth and left you here? Doing this?"

Agape, Barnaby stared at him like he'd grown a second head. "My God, what have you done?" The color drained out of his already pale face. His arthritic knuckles whitened as he gripped the table edge. He looked like a man struggling to remain upright. Maybe Odie had made a grave miscalculation.

"What are you doing? Stop upsetting him!" Ruth jumped up and stood next to Barnaby, faster than her chair could clatter to the ground. She checked his pulse and soothed him. *Mon dieu*, she was a gloriously protective lioness. Odie wanted that concerned gaze on him. Soon.

"What are you talking about?" Barnaby asked.

"Anyone can find the information, if they look hard enough," Odie said. "I've searched for a solution as long as I can remember. Current technology has helped my research. I recently put all of the pieces together. You know how much I want to destroy Jerahmeel. His annihilation is all I've ever desired, since I've become Indebted. I take it you've been privy to the secret, old friend, but perhaps ... never told anyone?"

"There's no reason to tell. What you're suggesting is impossible. It's insanity to consider such a thing."

"What secret? Barnaby, what's going on?" Ruth's gold-glinting eyes darkened to black as her cheeks flushed. "Stop scaring him! It's bad for his heart."

"No, my health doesn't matter. It's all right, dear." Barnaby's gnarled hand shook as he patted her on the arm. "Well, you've opened the door. So go on, Odie. Share what you know. But do so at your own risk."

Odie rolled his hands into fists. "I know how to get to Jerahmeel. To his lair. With some help, I believe I can destroy him." *Mon dieu*, if they would only believe him.

"Destroy him?" Ruth whispered, leaning forward, palms on the table, color high on her sculpted cheekbones.

"Is this why you invited me to New Orleans?" Barnaby's voice cracked.

Odie studied the fine wood grain before him. "Only partially. I did want to see you before ..."

"Before I die?" Barnaby said.

The furious look Ruth shot Odie made molten lava seem chilly.

He flinched. "My apologies, but yes. I also wanted to discuss my plan with the one man who might have more insight into this Jerahmeel problem than I do."

Ruth's harsh intake of air split the tension in the room. "Jerahmeel problem? Like it's an equation to work out? An irritating thorn to remove? Are you kidding me? He rules our lives, owns our souls. It's not a problem to be solved. It's hell."

"Look. With help, I do believe I can destroy him." He uncurled his hands and turned them palms up. He didn't want to hope—couldn't hope—that they would help him. But some support would be welcome.

"You believe? Don't you know for sure?" Ruth whispered.

"I'm not sure. But if it works, you could be free of this curse. We all could be free."

CHAPTER 4

Free? No more servitude to the devil? No more wishing that the next kill would be Ruth's last? Holy hell, wasn't that what she had wanted all along? Her head spun with possibilities and raw hope.

"You said you believe you can destroy him." Barnaby folded his napkin and pushed the plate forward. "Please elaborate."

At his nod, Ruth righted her chair and sat back down. She watched Barnaby while also studying the man across from her. Odie didn't appear unhinged. As a matter of fact, the handsome man appeared calm and collected. But the idea that an Indebted could destroy Jerahmeel and break the curse for all of them? Pure madness.

But an intriguing idea nevertheless.

Odie took a gulp of coffee and set the cup down with a too loud clink. "As you may know, there are vortices in this world that cannot be fully explained. Places like Mount Fuji in Japan, Mount Shasta in northern California, even Glastonbury in your beloved England. These vortices are more than destinations for crystal-worshipping oddballs. They have a real purpose: Jerahmeel."

"I don't understand," she said.

"These vortices don't exist for people to ascend to a higher plane of existence or board the mother ship. These are portals to Jerahmeel's domain, his lair. Enter any one of these sites and you will find our boss."

Her heart skidded a beat. "Truly?"

He rubbed the trim hair on his jaw. "Research suggests it's true."

"Suggests?"

"I believe it's true."

When he raised his dark eyebrows and shrugged, her knees went to jelly and she almost believed him. Exactly like she'd trusted another handsome man years ago.

Trust. Odie hadn't earned hers, not yet and possibly never. Fine, she'd play along with his insane theories for now, if for no other reason than to prove that he was lying.

"Let's presume for a moment that you're correct. How does this help us?" she asked.

"Odie, don't answer that," Barnaby snapped. His watery blue stare locked on to Odie with an intensity Ruth had never seen before.

"I'm sorry, my old friend, but others need to know the solution. If we can get to Jerahmeel at his lair and overpower him, he theoretically can be destroyed."

"Lair?" Ruth asked.

Odie rubbed his chin. "More like portal to hell, to be accurate."

She bit her lip as a sinking feeling hit her in the midsection. "So, 'if'? 'Theoretically'? 'We'? May I presume the risk is substantial?"

"That presumption is logical, *madame*."

"Dear God, Odilon. You cannot actually suggest walking through the gates of hell and attacking him." Barnaby's voice quavered and cracked.

"Possibly. But there is no other alternative. What he's made me do to my family ... I won't be a slave anymore. I hate killing mortals, especially to serve a master with an insatiable appetite. As our kind dwindles without replacements, the urge to kill will be so bad, I'll have to murder every day just to keep him fed." He squared his broad frame to Ruth. "Don't you hate what you're forced to do every week? Don't you want to be free of this?"

"Of course I hate it, but not enough to commit suicide. Or worse. What do you think Jerahmeel will do if he discovers we're trying to destroy him? Simply let us go? Kill us quickly? No. He needs us to continue working for him." She studied him. "Why now, Odie? Why not 100 years ago? Why not 100 years in the future?"

"Why not before? I didn't have all the pieces of the puzzle figured out. Why not in 100 years? Because Jerahmeel's at a weak point. He's unable to make more Indebted because his power has waned for the last century. I'm not certain if it's because he's about to be replaced or if it's a temporary weakness. Doesn't matter. I want to take advantage of the opportunity before I attract too much attention from him and incur his wrath."

On instinct, she glanced over her shoulder. "Some of us have attracted too much of his interest as it is."

"What do you mean?" Odie leaned forward, his entire frame tense.

The bites of biscuit churned in her belly. She didn't want to talk about Jerahmeel. Quite the opposite.

Barnaby rubbed his bald head, fatigue lining his face. "Ruth has a bit of an admirer in Jerahmeel."

"What?" Odie gaped. "Impossible. Jerahmeel only admires himself."

She squirmed beneath the unwanted attention, preferring to disappear. However, that didn't appear likely to happen any time soon. "It's true. Jerahmeel shows up at some of my kills and kind of ... flirts ... with me." The act of speaking the words made her insides knot again.

"Flirts?" Odie's brows drew together as his eyes darkened.

"He likes to, um, hang out with me. Right after I perform a kill," she mumbled, staring at the polished tabletop.

A muscle in his jaw jumped. "What?"

"He usually arrives right after I've completed the job. I believe the knife signals my location."

"And he wants ...?"

"More than I'll ever give him."

Odie snorted.

Face burning, she glanced at Barnaby. He nodded for her to continue.

She whispered. "He's made some … propositions."

Odie banged his fist on the table with a loud crack. "Sick doesn't start to describe his behavior. How about unholy and disgusting?"

Barnaby held up his hands. "Simmer down, my friend."

She cringed beneath the waves of anger blasting across the table. Odie had gone from rakishly genteel to unhinged in the space of two seconds. The fabric on his denim shirt strained over tense muscles. Tense cords in his neck framed his rapid pulse.

Barnaby rubbed his forehead. "That's why Ruth keeps a low profile. Disguises herself, tries to kill efficiently and quietly. It helps, but only to a certain extent. He finds her most of the time. He's fixated."

"I've never heard of Jerahmeel acting this way before," Odie said.

"Neither have I."

"We might be able to use that interest in her to our advantage."

Irritation made her scalp crawl. "I'm still right here."

"Oh, I know, *chère*. We haven't forgotten you. And what you can bring to the table." When Odie smiled, his lips curved upward, but the emotion never reached his eyes.

"No!" Barnaby shouted.

"Yes. This could be the key." No longer sensual, Odie's gaze now felt more like an evaluation. And he found her lacking. "You still live in Portland?"

"Yes, why?" Dread hung like a cold hand on the back of her neck.

"That's how he gets to you so easily. Mount Shasta and Mount Hood are connected vortices. I bet his main lair is Shasta. Going a longer distance takes much more energy. By living in Portland, you've made it very convenient for him to check in on you. A short commute, as it were."

She rubbed at goose bumps that rose on her arms. All these years, she'd been playing right into Jerahmeel's hands.

Odie jumped up. "But don't you see? His unnatural interest in you—that's our in."

"No, it's not." Icy fear spiked through her arms and legs. Handsome or not, she didn't like where his thoughts were headed.

"You're the bait."

Damn it, if his rakish grin didn't melt her insides.

But how could he even propose such an idea and hope that she would go along with it? By using charm to convince her to join him. Oh God, she was being used. Yet again.

Anger made her hands shake until she clasped them in her lap. "This conversation needs to end. Don't involve me. What you're suggesting is worse than suicide."

"What could be worse than that?" Odie asked.

A shudder rattled up her spine. "What Jerahmeel proposes for us to become. Together. For eternity."

"You mean?"

"Yes. Forever. With that thing."

"Unacceptable. Even more reason to get rid of him."

She slapped a palm on the tabletop, surprising even herself. "Stop. Stop it! I would rather attempt to escape Jerahmeel's clutches by getting the Meaningful Kill than try a ridiculous scheme with a high probability of failure and worse."

Barnaby bowed his head into his hand, then squinted at Odie. "This plan of yours is but a dream, my boy. Let it go. Other Indebted have reached similar conclusions. What you don't know is that they have tried and failed. When they failed, they lost whatever free will and happiness was left to them. Their eternal torment made this standard Indebted existence look like an island vacation. Your solution is impossible. The consequences of failure are worse than deadly. I'm sorry to disappoint you."

Odie slumped in the chair, the very picture of defeat. If it weren't for the glint remaining in his eyes, Ruth might have bought the act.

A lock of wavy hair the color of black coffee fell forward over his brow. She fought the urge to smooth that hair back. How would his skin feel beneath her fingers? And how could she think about his hair during a conversation like this?

After 150 years of self-induced celibacy, her hormones had gone off kilter. Maybe it was because he was Indebted. Or maybe the part of her that craved intimacy had been hidden for too long. Whatever had her attention, she didn't need the distraction right now.

He took another bite of sausage and eggs, and damn it if Ruth couldn't stop staring at the oil shining on his lower lip. So much for self-control.

Odie dabbed at his mouth with the napkin. "Well, maybe later down the road then? Forgive me for mentioning anything and spoiling your meal. Let's enjoy the day." Although his words conveyed concession, his passion to destroy Jerahmeel spoke otherwise. He fairly vibrated with barely contained, righteous indignation, even now.

She wouldn't bring up his plans again. No need to add more fuel to the fire of Odie's interest. Or Jerahmeel's.

Odie sipped the coffee as they finished their brunch. What small appetite she typically possessed had left her, and she pushed the food around on her plate as she glanced at the man sitting across from her.

For his part, Odie chatted with Barnaby about events from hundreds of years ago and their adventures together. Light, harmless conversation. As if the topic of the ultimate destruction of evil in this world had never arisen.

So why did guilt crawl up her neck?

Because she wanted the safe option. She wanted to try to get the Meaningful Kill herself and be done with her personal hell, once and for all. To consider Odie's plan risked too much. Besides,

Barnaby made it obvious that such a plan had failed in the past. Surely, it would be foolish to try again.

Guilt prickled her skin again. What about all the other Indebted? All of the mortal victims?

Damn her compassion.

Okay, fine. Perhaps Jerahmeel could be defeated, but she wasn't the person to do it. All she wanted these days was to avoid Jerahmeel's unnatural attention—do her job and get on with life.

What life?

What would she do when Barnaby was gone? What purpose did she have? Could she simply get another job? Helping another ... what? Human? Indebted?

No former Indebted was elderly at this time. Any other ex-Indebted had departed this Earth centuries ago.

Assisting mortals no longer piqued her interest as it had for the past century.

Maybe some kind of mission work? She could hunt evil mortals while helping innocents. The very definition of conflict of interest.

She shook her head. When she tried to visualize her future, only a black hole appeared. The bottomless pit of her life, sucking scant hope into an abyss.

"What about a tour of New Orleans?" Odie startled her out of her dark thoughts.

"Pardon?" she asked.

"May I take you and Barnaby on a tour of New Orleans? Complete with cultural activities and fantastic food?"

"That sounds lovely, old friend. I'll be ready in a moment." Barnaby pushed back and shuffled back to his bedroom.

Odie stood as well.

Ruth walked to the window. Citizens strolled in T-shirts and pants. Maybe she should make Barnaby put on a sweater. He got chilled so easily these days. Damn it. Her boss was aging in front of her, and there was nothing she could do about it.

"What about you, *chère*?" Odie had caught her staring toward Barnaby's room.

Oh, how her bones melted when he used that word. *Chère*. No one had ever called her that, and the way he said it both soothed and riled her nerves, like fingers trailed down her spine. Too bad they had no future.

Too bad she didn't trust that lopsided grin. Or any man's smile, for that matter.

She'd had a partner, 150 years ago. He had used her and then discarded her, ripping away her children in the aftermath. She never saw her beautiful son and daughter again. That disaster had turned her into the Indebted killer she was today. Since then, she'd avoided any emotional entanglements, and today was no time to break that rule.

"My apologies, but no, I will decline." Moving back to the table, she gripped the back of a chair.

"Why?"

"Well, someone took my kill, so I need to prepare for this evening ..."

"But it's daylight, so you have plenty of time."

His quick grin managed to be both chagrined and sexy at the same time, and something fluttered deep in her stomach. An emotion she had never experienced before. Something restless, like a bird on the verge of taking flight.

Her love for her husband had been simple, affectionate, but unrequited, and ultimately used against her.

But being around Odie felt like she'd punched her ticket on a grand adventure and was about to depart. Soaring hope and fear. She wanted more of that sensation, and at the same time, she wanted *none* of that feeling.

"Thank you. No." Hopefully, he would get the hint.

"My humble apologies for disrupting your work last night, *madame*."

"You didn't know." She tried to paste a kind smile on her face and hoped she succeeded. "It's not every day you find a damsel in distress who gets mad at you for gutting her murder victim."

"You're correct. It's not every day such an opportunity as this one presents itself."

Shivering beneath his ice-green gaze, she tried not to climb over the table to fix that errant curl of hair that brushed across his forehead. Never in her prolonged life had she felt that compulsion, and she laced her fingers together to hide the sudden shaking. Blinking to focus on anything but the man sitting across from her, she spun around to leave the room.

He mirrored her movement with two quick strides around the table, and then stopped, a heartbeat away. When he stood right in front of her, all she saw was his sensual lips, surrounded by the close-trimmed beard and moustache. What would those whiskers feel like on her mouth, her neck, her ...

She studied his dark, wavy hair, worn long enough to tempt a woman to run her fingers through it. What intrigued her even more was how the fabric of his untucked denim shirt fabric strained against those broad shoulders. How his thick thigh muscles flexed beneath the dark indigo jeans as he shifted his weight from one black-booted foot to another. She couldn't stop staring.

"*Magnifique.*" Less a word, than a caress, coming from his lips.

Her breath caught in her throat as the heat from his large frame washed over her in waves, like her skin had become hypersensitive to the temperature changes coming from him.

It only took an instant to bridge the space between them. When Odie leaned in and brushed his lips over hers, the smell of spicy Andouille and his cologne surrounded her, sending delicious coils of pleasure deep into her belly.

As he pulled back, an emotion, like laughter and panic, cracked open inside of her.

Rigid control shattered.

Ruth surged forward, pressing her lips to his, heat against heat.

Odie's big hand snaked around her neck, pulling her even closer as she reveled in how his strong mouth slanted over hers, each angle sparking delicious quivers through her limbs.

He braced his legs apart and leaned into her, nudging her lips open with his. The hardness at his groin had her breathing faster. Or was it him?

Ruth slid her hands around to the corded lines of his back and squeezed. The groan in the back of his throat vibrated through her torso until her nipples tightened in response.

His scratchy beard sent lightning bolts of desire into her gut. The sensation swirled and grew until she wanted those lips and that deliciously rough beard on the rest of her body. Immediately.

As if he knew her thoughts, he parted her lips further, and she opened for him, savoring the sensation of his hot tongue on the inside of her mouth. Their tongues tangled in an eddy of torrid passion. The touch of his hand on the back of her neck, the caress of his fingers over her cheek, transported her. For this small space in time, his kisses took her away from this life as an on-demand killer. And for this small space in time, she no longer felt the distance of being hundreds of years removed from her beloved children and from her husband's still-raw betrayal. She could happily exist here, safe in this sexy man's arms.

No, this Indebted man's arms.

Unhuman. Just like her.

Indebted. With a harebrained plan to try to destroy Jerahmeel.

If he could only charm someone into helping with the plan.

Someone like her.

Bait.

Holy hell, how could she be so naive?

Had it truly been so long since she enjoyed a man's touch that she succumbed the moment Odie showed any interest in her? For a second there, she would have done anything he asked. Putty in his hands. He was much too dangerous and much too enthralling.

A man had used her years before.

Fool me twice.

Right now would be a perfect opportunity to use her secret gift. Unfortunately, after she'd used her power on her husband 150 years ago, she now tried to tiptoe the fine line between verification of crimes and avoidance of psychic invasion for her own personal gains. Tempting as it might be to confirm Odie's intentions, her principles held fast. She'd have to do this the old-fashioned way.

She placed her palms on his muscled chest, waves of heat searing her hands. When she shoved against him, his hands gripped her neck and back, keeping her close.

"Odie."

He trailed his hand over the sensitive skin at the nape of her neck, and Ruth shuddered.

"Odie, stop."

She dipped her head, turning away from another kiss. Unfortunately, all this did was encourage him to brush his lips over her neck and jaw, each touch swirling exquisite sensations down her spine. He nipped at the sensitive lobe of her ear, eliciting tiny waves of happiness. His scent of warm, spicy man nearly undid her resolve.

"Enough. I get it."

"*Pardonnez?*"

His eyes had turned the typical jet black of an Indebted with heightened emotion.

So what if he felt something? She refused to be seduced into participating in his risky plans.

Pushing harder, she stepped away, and his arms dropped to his sides, pulling the fabric tight as his chest heaved. He blinked several times, and his iris color changed from endless night to luminous green again.

His brow furrowed. "Did I do something wrong, *chère*?"

"I might be an easy mark, but you won't lure me into your scheme with this ... coercion."

"What?"

As he held his hands up, Ruth backed up, bumping into the chair. She grasped the back for support, waving off the hand he offered.

"I understand your motives, sir."

"What?"

"Don't play me the fool."

"But I didn't—"

She wanted to believe the lost, wounded expression on his tanned face, where lines of concern wrinkled his forehead. Almost gave in again. Almost believed that a sexy rogue might have wanted her without strings attached. If she had lived any different life, she might have fallen for it. But not in this life and not today. She would never trust a handsome man again.

"You'll have to seduce someone else into helping you." She brushed a fingertip over her lips before the action registered, cursing herself as his hungry stare locked on to her mouth. "Now if you'll excuse me, I need to attend to my work."

Now that she had succeeded in breaking his spell, however, the hated knife began to throb, clouding her mind. Every thought focused on obtaining her next kill. When would this sick insanity stop?

"*Madame*, I didn't mean to imply that—"

With a sharp movement of her hand, she cut him off and dropped back into ingrained society manners, erecting an instinctive barrier, as she had done for years, even while her world crumbled all around.

"Why don't you wait in the sitting room for Barnaby? He'll be ready soon for his tour. Please enjoy yourself today, and keep him safe. If he has any fatigue or problems, would you bring him back immediately?"

"Of course, but—"

"Thank you, sir. It was a pleasure to meet you, and I wish you every success in the future."

For a moment, he simply stood there, mouth open and eyebrows raised. Then his features turned dark and hard, making him appear larger and more dangerous. He inhaled and then snapped his jaw shut, pressing his lips into a harsh line. Turning on a heel, he stormed out of the dining room.

Damn if she didn't study how his thigh muscles bunched under the blue jeans, and damn if the air didn't cool twenty degrees as he departed. She had gotten her senses all addled by this man with a plan. A plan that would never include her.

CHAPTER 5

That evening, she asked the concierge at the hotel's front desk about which section of town to avoid. Then she went directly to that area: Central City.

Amazing how New Orleans changed only a mile or so south and west of the French Quarter. No tourists here, just pockets of old homes interspersed with blighted, run-down buildings. Poverty and sadness permeated the air and pressed down on her shoulders, sapping energy and hope. Flickers of movements in the boarded up homes hinted at squatters living there. Ruth had already seen drug deals in the dark side streets this evening.

So basically, a perfect location for her work.

As a general rule, she tried to spread out the placement of her kills so there would be no pattern and to engender less curiosity from local law enforcement. More importantly, changing the location of the kills made it harder for Jerahmeel to anticipate her whereabouts. Normally, too, she would vary her costume, but she'd brought only the one blonde wig for this trip. She hadn't planned on needing multiple attempts to achieve her kill quota while on vacation.

Due to a sheltered upbringing in Rockville, Maryland, her upper-class family had raised her to have genteel manners. Now, however, as an Indebted killer, gone was the woman who loved dinner parties and dressing in taffeta, the woman who lived for her children and her husband and helping others. Gone was the woman who believed in love and faith in her fellow man.

Amazingly, her marriage ended not because she had become an Indebted, but because of her other power. The power that had nothing to do with her unhuman state.

She had discovered her husband's betrayal through her gift of reading minds, the same ability she used now to verify the crimes of each kill.

First the Civil War, then her conversion into an Indebted, and finally her husband's deception had all but driven away any hope for humanity—her own or others'. She couldn't trust her husband, and every kill increased her lack of faith in mortals. Who did that leave? No one.

Barnaby's presence helped, but when he finally passed away at some point in the future, she would be adrift again, searching for purpose, clinging to ... nothing. Fine, she could nurse someone else, but it wouldn't be the same. The meaning of her life had lost all substance, like trying to grab hold of air. Panic raked her lungs raw, and she had to lean against a light pole to catch her breath.

Nothing. She had nothing left, she had no purpose, no family. Oh, God, there was nothing.

She might have used her gift on Odie, but she hated invading someone else's deepest sanctuary and, as a general rule, refused to use her power in that manner.

She had no idea where her ability came from, only that it had fully manifested in a time of desperation, her darkest hour—or so she had thought. She had hints of her power prior to that black moment, but the final straw came with the terror that she would lose her children. A weird, high-pitched teakettle-type whistle in her head had nearly split her skull in two. Then bang! The power to read minds—specifically, her husband's—emerged. After that, the power became a part of her.

And she had no intention of sharing the details of it with anyone. Her ability was her most guarded secret.

But if she had looked into Odie's mind, she would've seen the truth. Did she really want to know what he thought about her?

Even now, a niggling sense of him in the back of her mind remained. Strange. Like he stood right outside of her line of sight, a ridiculous idea, since she hadn't even told Barnaby where she was headed tonight. Maybe her lust for the kill had gotten confused with her lust for ... other things. Damn Odie's sexy mouth. She brushed her fingers across her lips before she could stop herself.

Quit it. Finish tonight's job.

Rifling in the empty purse she used as a prop for her disguise, she smiled when a group of men on the opposite corner nodded in her direction. She turned down another street, searching for a safe location to stage the kill. Her goal: Draw attention as a single white woman, lost and possibly drunk, who had wandered over from the tourist sections of town.

These men would see exactly what she wanted them to see.

Pushing blond hair off her shoulders, Ruth glanced around again.

Almost midnight. Most citizens had settled in for the evening. Anyone who remained out at this hour had a higher chance of being what she, or rather the knife, needed.

To help create her alter ego, she had dressed in stiletto heels. The black slacks and a black wrap top were suited more for a dinner party than a walk through the rough section of town. By adding the flaxen wig, she completed her transition into the right frame of mind for the kill. Now she felt more alluring, more in touch with the other aspect of her personality. The deadly seductress created such dissonance with her normal character.

"Normal character." What a joke. Even daily life had become an act. Holy hell, what a nightmare she had become.

"Hey, mama, whatcha doin' out here tonight?"

With some encouragement from his friends, a black man approached. As expected, when she glanced back, additional men closed in behind her. Now she needed to see whether this guy would suffice as a criminal about to die or if another of his friends better fit the bill.

Too bad the man wasn't alone. She hated witnesses, but she wasn't in a position to pick and choose. She had to make this kill work tonight.

"Ah, can you fellas tell me how to get back to the French Quarter? I'm a little lost."

She stumbled and giggled, ignoring the knowing smirks as the men formed a loose circle around her. The knife's relentless hunger began to heat her leg, and her heart pounded.

When she pivoted back to the first man who had approached her, the knife nearly keened, its desire for a corrupt soul was so intense. This sneering man reeked of evil. Good. The more corrupt, the better, as far as her chances of getting the Meaningful Kill went.

He stared at her chest, oblivious to the danger she presented. Perfect.

"Maybe you want to give me ... directions. Over there." She pointed with her chin toward a parked car on a side street.

"You know I do."

He followed her fifty paces away, next to a car without front wheels. He was a big guy, dark as night, with a gold tooth that glinted in the streetlight when he grinned, and all pumped-up muscle and swagger.

She staggered once again for good measure, and the idiot did nothing to help. Not that she expected chivalry, but his lack of couth only added fuel to the knife's hunger.

"Let me tell you a secret." She hiccupped.

"What you wanna tell me, baby?"

The knife wanted him. Now. "Lean closer, sugar," she said.

He licked his lips, grinned, and preened like an overstuffed peacock. As a lover would, she took his face in her hands, almost caressing the arches of his cheekbones. The hoots from his friends faded as she entered this guy's mind.

"What the—"

He pulled back, but she pressed her hands tighter to lock him in place. "Shush. Just enjoy it."

She effectively shut down his speech center with a thought as she parted the curtains of his mind. Since he hadn't admitted to a crime, she would have to find it.

His friends walked toward them, restless and punching each other on the arms as they watched their mute buddy. To them, he appeared riveted on Ruth and about to get some action.

Which was exactly what she wanted them to see.

Her scalp beneath the blond wig itched. *Concentrate.*

Into the deepest recess of his conscious mind she went, filtering past images of a woman whose gray-laced, curly hair surrounded a careworn face. Ruth pushed past glimpses of babies, all smiles and outstretched arms, each perched on a different woman's lap. This guy was a real winner.

She found the crime. There, buried deep down and abutting his subconscious. Although he had done a remarkable job suppressing the memory, if a person had a past, Ruth could eventually find it. When the man made a guttural sound as he fought against her control, she tweaked the mental pressure so he could no longer move.

"Let me see what you've done there, handsome," she crooned.

Part of her wanted to ease the indignity of the mental invasion. Part of her no longer cared; she only wanted to complete this kill and move on.

His eyes widened into two terrified whites hovering in a dark face. She pressed deeper to unlock the memory of his crime. Or should she say, crimes? Where to start? Good God, was he a sociopath? How had he suppressed this much evil? During a robbery, he shot a convenience store worker at point-blank range. She watched blood spread over the clerk's shirt as he crumpled to the floor.

What about breaking and entering into a little old lady's house? Ruth couldn't stop the flow of images slamming into her mind, one after another. Damn it, the lady's screams and the impact of his booted foot shattering brittle bone echoed in Ruth's head, an aftereffect of the images. She would have that sound in her head forever, damn it.

Mentally backpedaling, she couldn't exit this man's mind fast enough. When she withdrew, her restraint over his speech center ceased.

"Shit, lady, what the hell? Get the fuck away."

He lashed out, likely expecting to knock her to the pavement, but she absorbed the impact and didn't budge. Before he could reach for the gun hidden in his waistband, she slid the knife, glowing lurid green and starving, out of the sheath. It guided her hand toward the man and she plunged the knife to the hilt, right below the man's xiphoid process, angled toward the heart, right where it liked to feed. As the knife consumed the man's disgusting soul, languid and delicious relief flowed through her limbs. Sweet, sick satisfaction. She didn't want more, she only wanted to finish and get out of here.

"Shit ..." He would have crumpled, but Ruth pressed him against the car, hiding the knife from his friends.

A shot rang out, whizzing by her head so close her hair moved. Holy hell. To be fair, she wouldn't die from a gunshot, but a direct hit would leave her vulnerable until she could heal. Not only did the bullets hurt like the blazes, but it would raise questions if she returned to the hotel dripping blood.

She swung her gurgling friend in front of her like a shield to absorb the bullets that thudded into his flesh and knocked her back a pace.

"Shit, you hit Deshawn," one of the men screamed as he reloaded his gun.

When her victim drew his last breath, she yanked the knife out of his ribcage and stuffed it back into the sheath. She'd clean it later.

For an instant, relief from obtaining the kill made her weak in the knees. This man had been so utterly evil.

Had she done it? Did he qualify as the Meaningful Kill?

She stared at her bloody hands. Nothing had changed.

Anger deflated her soul until all that remained was suffocating disappointment.

Then remorse flooded her like a dam had broken. Damn it, every time she killed, it was like reconciling two ill-fitting halves. The daytime Nurse Ruth and her murderous alter ego didn't mesh well. She collapsed to her knees, spent, guilty, and relieved. God, she hated killing and she loved killing, thanks to the damned knife and Jerahmeel.

Hearing footsteps, she glanced up in time to see a gun leveled at her head. Then a flash of light and a bang.

But not from the gun.

Sulfur fumes burned her nose.

Not him. Not tonight. She only wanted to get the heck out of here and pretend to be normal for as long as possible, until the next urge to kill.

"Delicious dining, *mademoiselle*. Much appreciated," Jerahmeel said. "I almost didn't recognize you."

He blew smoke off his smoldering fingers with an air of satisfaction. The other men, or what remained of them, had been reduced to blobs of charred flesh, the only indication of their passage from this Earth. The odor of singed hair and fried entrails turned her stomach.

Sure, she had worked in burn units before, but this horrific scene was altogether different. It had taken about two seconds for Jerahmeel to roast them alive. Holy hell. What could he do to a perpetually healing Indebted?

Ruth scrambled to her feet and turned to face her boss. Jerahmeel was unpredictable, not to mention disgusting, and she wanted her faculties about her every time he appeared. She fought the perverse urge to scratch the hell out of her head beneath the damned ridiculous wig.

He licked his lips, shaded dark in the poor streetlight, but she knew them to be an unnatural ruby red. When he raked his ember-glowing leer over her body, she wanted to cover herself, but kept her hands at her sides. Another whiff of sulfur and rotting meat taunted her nose, but she didn't flinch. She'd learned years ago that giving any reaction only fanned the flame of his desire.

"You picked a savory feast for me tonight. He's quite evil." With a pointy-toed shoe, he poked at the body crumpled at her feet. "Thank you."

She never said he was welcome. Ever. "Of course."

He adjusted the pouf of lace erupting from his jacket's velvet neckline. "You're looking delectable as usual, *mademoiselle*. I haven't seen a woman so grand since Empress Josephine. She was dedicated to her Napoleon, you know. They called her the power behind the throne. Ah, I do so love it when a strong woman supports a strong man."

The sensation of his gaze roving over her body made her almost physically ill, but she stood there and absorbed his interest without moving. The less response, the better. Maybe he'd grow bored of the sick seduction game and move on to someone else.

"But what is that unjust confection hiding your luscious hair, which I so adore?"

Acid churned in her belly. "Identification technology has improved in the modern times. I need to adjust my appearance so I can remain hidden, but still perform my work duties."

"I don't care. Take it off now, *mademoiselle*." His tone hit somewhere between a hoarse lover and a desperate psychopath.

Even though rules restricted him from physically forcing an Indebted to do anything, one never refused a command. He'd find another way to gain control, and it typically involved tormenting humans to force Indebted to his will.

The steaming organic material on the pavement attested to the power he could bring to bear without ever making contact with anyone. She unpinned the blonde wig with shaking hands.

"Drop it," he commanded.

She let it fall to the pavement. With a flick of his finger, the mass of hair incinerated in a flash of greenish light. The scent of burnt hair blended with the smell of fried humans in a noxious, sharp mixture.

"Take down the rest of it," he said.

Nothing good would come of this situation. She thanked her stars there were no witnesses to her humiliation. With sweaty hands, she removed the bobby pins from her chignon. The heavy weight of her long hair unfurled down to brush her lower back.

Silence descended as he stared at her; his fingertip, trailing smoke, pointed in her direction. She froze. *Do not attract more attention.*

A dog barked nearby, and she startled. The sound of cars a few blocks over on a larger street drifted toward where they stood.

At least her scalp no longer itched.

He licked those dark lips again and squinted his beady eyes.

Fighting the urge to glance over her shoulder, cross her arms over her chest, or flat-out run away, she maintained a rigid posture as he continued the perusal. A trickle of sweat worked its way between her breasts, and she resisted the need to wipe it away.

She broke the ungodly silence first. "So, if there's nothing else ..." Her voice came out high-pitched and shaky. Damn it.

The black stare locked on to her face, too eager, too hopeful.

"*Mademoiselle*, have you reconsidered my generous offer? I desire to rule with you by my side. But instead, I must watch you slog through this odious filth of humanity day after day, like a common servant. Join me in consuming the tasty evil life forces from the Indebted blades. You can decide when and whom those pitiful Indebted slaves kill. So powerful, you'll be almost as strong as I am."

God, how she hated this man—no, this thing.

All her kills. All those criminals. Thousands of horrifying images of death, rape, and violence—images she could never unsee.

And for what?

She remained Indebted to Satan.

When she inhaled, the humid bayou air hung heavy with undertones of burnt hair and death. A black future without end.

Might be worth considering an alternative plan, after all.

What should she do about Jerahmeel? Something in his demeanor had changed. Tonight, the way he frothed at the corners of his mouth while he propositioned her, the intensity vibrating out from his thin frame—he wasn't going to take no for an answer, which boded poorly for her own well-being.

As she opened her mouth to respond, a familiar denim-clad figure sauntered up the street and stopped a few feet away. Her heart jumped. The scent of Cajun spice and cologne wafted over and replaced the acrid fumes from the bodies on the sidewalk. Tension left her shoulders, but only just.

"Welcome to New Orleans, my lord. Anything I can help with tonight?" Odie asked. Bless his clear voice and easy stance, but this idiot had poked the sleeping bear.

CHAPTER 6

Blind rage had shorted out Odie's brain when the guys fired at Ruth. He had lurched forward to protect her, about to destroy the men. But then he'd planted his feet on the concrete. He knew. She needed that kill, needed the knife to stop consuming her every thought, needed to complete her job and remain under Jerahmeel's radar.

So he waited in the shadows.

Dressed in a tight, black V-neck blouse, Ruth's curves flowed into dark slacks and heels. His hands itched with the need to trace those lines to see if her hips and waist truly felt like a living hourglass.

What he didn't understand was why she had caressed her prey's face before using the knife. Or why an expression of mute terror froze on the man's face.

Odie understood gunshots, though. As the sharp noise had split the evening air, he dashed closer.

Until a brilliant flash lit up the night.

Odie ducked behind another car. *Mon dieu*!

Jerahmeel. Here?

Edging closer, the odor of burnt bodies and three lumps on the sidewalk told the tale. *Flambé a la Satan*. Bad for mortals and Indebted alike. There were creatures in this world more powerful than people like Odie and Ruth.

Like Jerahmeel.

Mon dieu.

After blowing the smoke off a fingertip, the Lord of Brimstone preened and patted his oily locks. If his boss weren't so damned terrifying, Odie would have rolled his eyes.

Even Jerahmeel's voice sounded smarmy. Too unctuous, almost like he was begging. How strange for such a powerful being.

At Jerahmeel's command, Ruth took off the ridiculous wig, only for Jerahmeel to incinerate it with another loud bang. When she released her dark auburn hair from the severe bun, Odie's own fingers spread out, reaching for those long tresses. How would those burnished locks feel sliding over him, covering her bare chest and shoulders? His mouth went dry.

Jerahmeel's slithering proposition to Ruth wormed its way to Odie's hiding spot. "*Mademoiselle*, have you reconsidered my generous offer? I desire to rule with you by my side. But instead, I must watch you slog through this odious filth of humanity day after day, like a common servant."

Ruth stood rooted in place, mouth agape. There was no good answer. Her boss had charbroiled three humans in a millisecond. He Who Makes All Things Crispy could pulverize Ruth just as easily.

Odie had to diffuse the situation before she tried to respond to his question.

Trying to project a casual air, he positioned himself slightly in front of Ruth. Right in the line of fire.

"What in damnation are you doing here, *pisse ant*?"

Vapors scented like rotten eggs wafted off of Jerahmeel's raised fingers. Like great Mount Vesuvius, The Lord of Damnation was getting ready to blow if they didn't play the situation right.

Odie shrugged. "Ah, I was out searching for an extra kill to serve you, my lord. But it seems you've reduced this group of candidates to dust. Too bad."

Jerahmeel growled.

In Odie's peripheral vision, Ruth stiffened. He prayed she would stay silent and let him distract Jerahmeel. For both their sakes.

"Since you've destroyed these criminals, my lord, I have no way to provide a feast for you."

"I was protecting her from these mortals," Jerahmeel barked.

"Since when does Ruth need protecting, my lord?"

She blurted out, "And thank you for helping, my lord."

Did she bat her eyelashes and sway on her feet? Brilliant.

"Hmm, well, it seemed the proper thing to do for a lady." Jerahmeel preened beneath her false adoration and ignored Odie.

Then, for a split second, Odie saw something he had never witnessed before in his boss: doubt. Jerahmeel's brow furrowed and a flicker of uncertainty crossed over those black eyes. He'd been caught doing something he never had done before—intervening in Indebted affairs on Earth. Maybe he questioned whether it was acceptable or not. Or he questioned the appropriateness of his flirtation with Ruth. Either way, Odie smelled weakness, however slight. Good information to have.

Facing Jerahmeel, Odie then pressed his luck. "I must be mistaken, but I thought the laws you are bound by disallow you from touching mortals?"

The growl got louder as the burnt egg odor invaded Odie's nostrils. On the edge of his vision, he saw Ruth's posture lock into rigid attention.

"How do you know that?" Jerahmeel demanded.

"Common knowledge, I'm certain."

Jerahmeel inspected his buffed nails and brushed his sleeves. "Well then. Technically, I did not touch them."

Odie's gut tightened. Jerahmeel had figured out a way around the restriction of having no contact with humans. This twist boded poorly for all humans. What limits did he truly have, then?

"Hmm. Must have taken a lot out of you to come all the way down to New Orleans tonight, my lord," Odie said.

He ignored Ruth's steady, painful stomp on the arch of his foot. The way she held her breath, she had to understand that they were literally playing with fire.

"It's no concern of yours, Odilon. Just continue your work. And get rid of these."

Jerahmeel waved toward what remained of the three other thugs. Black flakes drifted off of the drying blobs in the evening breeze. A strong gust of wind would surely take care of the mess.

"Of course, my lord."

The asshole purred. "Delectable Ruth, when you change your mind, I will be waiting."

And in a puff of sulfur, Jerahmeel was gone.

In stunned silence, Odie turned to face Ruth. She slowly ran her hands up her arms, as if trying to warm them, but didn't meet his scrutinizing stare.

"Is that courtship dance normal for you? And him?" Odie asked. "I've never heard of him tracking down other Indebted. I had no idea how bad his obsession was." He put a hand on his hip and wiggled, trying to break the acrid tension. It didn't work, as her frown attested.

After swallowing several times, she said, "I tried to explain it to you and Barnaby. This was the most forward invitation he's made to date. How the hell do I say no?" She gestured toward the disintegrating bodies on the sidewalk.

Even after a brush with a disturbingly amorous Satan, this woman managed to hold herself together. Odie's thudding heart slowed now that Jerahmeel had left.

Unfortunately, his attention turned to the … assets … of the woman before him.

One part of Odie wanted to tuck Ruth into his arms and comfort her. The other part wanted to rip off her dark pants and snug blouse and check out her curves firsthand. Somewhere between charity and lust, the tightness in his groin distracted him until he forgot the debate.

He had to stay focused. She needed his help, not his uncooperative dick.

Resisting the urge to cover his mutinous groin, he shifted his stance to relieve pressure. "So, when did he start acting this way?"

"Ah, around 1875, when I was trying to live a normal human life with my family."

"But you were Indebted then, right?"

"Yes."

"Staying with your family is against the rules."

"Thanks, I know that now. Apparently, he did, too. It didn't stop him from becoming much too interested in me and my family."

"Your family? Did he kill them?"

Somehow his hand had curled into a fist. He forced it to relax. He knew all too well about Jerahmeel's manipulation of families. A brief vision of Odie's own two dark-haired daughters floated before his mind's eye. *Mon dieu*, what he had sacrificed—and for what?

"No. But he might have interfered in the lives my family members." She shook her head, the dark tresses luminous in the streetlight. "Who knows? I'm still not certain what to believe. That was a long time ago, and everyone I've known has long passed on." Her tone turned flat. "It doesn't matter."

"But it does."

"No. It does not." She crossed her arms and glared at him.

Subject out of bounds. Message duly noted.

"So are you all right after tonight's ... events, *chère*? Did he hurt you?"

"I'm perfectly fine. Let's get these bodies cleaned up."

"That's not necessary."

"Why? Oh."

A gust of wind blew, and like burnt newspaper, the pieces drifted away on the breeze. Bizarre didn't even begin to explain the scene. A human life reduced to ash in a split second.

Two citizens stepped outside their house two doors down. One of them was on her cell phone and pointing.

"We should get out of here, *madame*."

"Agreed."

"Can you run?" He tilted his chin and winked. "You know, run, run?"

"Of course."

"Can you keep up?"

When she smiled, her entire face glowed like the light of the sun. "Don't hold back on my account."

"Then follow me."

He took off at preternatural speed, Ruth right behind him. They flew by homes, their feet barely touching pavement. He glanced back. Her hair streamed behind her like a glorious copper-glinting flag as she easily kept pace with what he knew humans would perceive as a blur or a rush of air. After a few minutes, he slowed to a walk, and Ruth followed suit. Neither of them panted, a side effect of their unhuman state.

"Where are we?" she asked.

Her wind-swept hair tangled around her shoulders. How good would it feel to draw a brush through those long luxurious waves, have those silky strands draped all over his naked body. Or over her body. Or spread out on a bed, like the rest of her?

His groin tightened. Again? He was like a teenager with his first crush. Ridiculous.

All day, he'd been distracted. When he'd held her in his arms earlier today, she had smelled like mint and lavender, tasted more delicious than anything he'd ever experienced, and those curves had fit perfectly against him.

And now she might be the key to his plan to destroy Jerahmeel.

With the unpleasant visitation from the Lord of Hell fresh on her mind, maybe he could press her for help. And if he got to run his tongue over her curves along the way? More the better. Right?

"I thought we might share a meal?"

He gestured toward the front door of a small restaurant where they had stopped. The scents of garlic, spice, and cooked meat wafted out into the street, and a warm glow spilled from the wavy glass windows onto the sidewalk.

"Do you always grab a bite to eat in stressful situations?"

One side of her full mouth quirked upward, and suddenly, he had little interest in restaurant dining and a heightened interest in tasting her lips.

He grinned. "After getting away from Jerahmeel, a fine meal seems like a great idea."

"Yes, but for how long will he stay away?" Sadness turned down the corners of her lush mouth.

"I don't know, but that's why we should enjoy tonight."

She countered, "You and I don't need food."

"Need and want are two different things. I *want* to have a meal with a fascinating woman. I *need* her to join me, or I shall perish."

She was a little prickly tonight, this beautiful, defiant woman. Perfect. A test of wills. Something he hadn't experienced in hundreds of years. He'd been with feisty women but none who could truly match him. He did love a challenge, especially if it concluded with her in his bed.

When she peered down the street, her sculpted face half hidden in shadow, the play of emotions over her features entranced him. She pinned him with those gold-flecked eyes.

Not only could she be the difference in success and failure in his scheme, but what a bonus if he could get those long, soft legs thrown over his shoulders as they made inexhaustible love. Odie simply needed to work a different angle until he had everything he wanted.

He waited for her answer.

"All right."

CHAPTER 7

Odie held the heavy door of Chez Herbert and motioned for Ruth to precede him. When he brushed his fingers over the small of her back, a frisson of electricity pulsed through the material and zipped up her spine. As they entered the opulent restaurant, she glanced at the tables set with crystal stemware and gold-rimmed dishes. The wood paneling gleamed, and pressed linen covered the tables. The scents of furniture oil, savory steak, and melted candle wax blended in a rich aroma. Although the establishment was small, its tables didn't crowd the customers. Comfortable and luxurious at the same time. And expensive.

Heat crawled over her cheeks as she smoothed her knit top and pants. She glanced at Odie in his jeans and denim shirt from earlier today. They were both underdressed.

"We can't eat here." She motioned toward the lingering customers, clad in elegant evening gowns and three-piece suits. "Besides, it's too late. The restaurant's closing down for the night."

"Don't worry. Besides, my clothing is more casual than yours."

He ran a hand through his tousled hair. Although his chest filled out the untucked shirt and rock-hard cords rippled beneath his jeans, she agreed with his assessment of their attire.

Ingrained decorum urged her to withdraw. Damn those old-fashioned manners, a holdover from the old Ruth. She needed to let go of that passive woman who cared about everyone's opinion and embrace the woman she wanted to be—the woman who might take a chance on a rogue like Odie.

"Let's leave. Please." She tugged at his muscled arm. He didn't budge.

"Nonsense." He waved at a middle-aged man who approached. "Ah, here's the maitre d'."

The tuxedoed restaurant host dipped his head and smiled. Ruth cringed in embarrassment.

Odie smiled. "Philippe, any chance you can fit in a late-night customer?"

"Of course, Mr. Pierre-Noir, we always have a table for you. And for your lovely companion."

Funny, but the host's eyes twinkled as he glanced at the two of them. Almost as if he truly didn't mind them arriving at his restaurant close to midnight.

"We don't want to be any trouble," she said.

"No trouble at all, *mademoiselle*, it would be my pleasure. Right this way, if you please."

The old Ruth took a backseat as the muscles holding her spine rigid finally relaxed. Damned if Odie didn't shrug those broad shoulders and wink at her. And damned if she didn't giggle like a schoolgirl. At a corner table, Odie held out a chair and scooted her forward, brushing her arms in the process, which released a tendril of happiness that flowed through her body. She hadn't enjoyed a gentleman's solicitous attention since those elegant dinner parties in Maryland 150 years ago. Barnaby didn't count; he was more like her father.

After Odie ordered a wine, the maitre d' left moist towels for them to clean their hands and faded away. Ruth tried to ignore the streaks of red on the fabric, folded the tinted fabric inward, and sighed.

The candlelight made Odie's green eyes dance with even more mischief, as if he had a joke to tell. Oddly, she rather enjoyed wondering about his thoughts.

Tempting as it might be to use her power, she wouldn't invade his privacy or risk exposing her secret. Normal communication would have to suffice.

When he reached out and took her hand in a feather-gentle grip, she jumped. He didn't move but watched her, eyebrows raised. Patient. Waiting.

Go away, old Ruth.

After a few moments, she did something foreign and relaxed and simply enjoyed the contact. Thick tendons beneath his tanned skin flexed with strength in that broad grip. Although his paw engulfed her hand, he cradled her like a piece of crystal, and she savored the delicious sensations that rolled up her arm.

"Thank you for doing me the honor of a meal together," he said.

His tenor voice, barely above a whisper in the hushed restaurant, sent chills down her spine. She wondered what that voice would sound like in another intimate venue, right next to her ear as they lay surrounded by soft sheets and pillows.

Shame on you. He's simply being kind. You have no business thinking differently about this man. Or any man.

"Thank you. I haven't had a nice meal out like this for a very long time."

"Nor have I. And certainly not with such a lovely companion."

The rough pad of his thumb caressing the back of her hand erased coherent thought. How did he do that? Did he have some sort of hidden power, too, an ability to control her mind or her emotions? Could he read her thoughts? Maybe he had something else in mind for tonight. Panic fluttered in her chest like a bird's wing, caught in a net. She stiffened.

"Odie, I don't want—"

"Shush, *chère*. Let's enjoy an extravagant meal together as though we were normal humans without a care in the world. For one night, we'll pretend."

Pretending. A skill she had perfected over the past 150 years. Whether human or Indebted, she no longer wanted to deal with the weight of maintaining a façade.

For one night, we'll pretend.

Fair enough.

She sighed beneath the slow rhythm of his thumb on her skin. Divine. The movement loosened muscles in her back and neck, and deeper in her core, something else opened up a crack that felt suspiciously like a chink in the armor around her guarded heart. Maybe she *could* let down her defenses for one night.

He eased his hand away when the maitre d' returned. After Odie tasted and approved, Philippe filled their glasses with wine and withdrew.

The sweet citrus tang of the red wine mixed with the oak tartness as the tastes danced over her tongue.

"What kind of wine is this? It's delicious."

"It's a 1961 Petrus. From a small vintner in the Bordeaux region that fermented very exclusive wines. Many consider this to be one of the best wines in the last 100 years. *Très magnifique*." He kissed his fingers. "Have you decided what you'd like to eat? I can call Philippe back over."

"I'm not sure what to get; it all looks wonderful," she said.

"Would you allow me to order for you?"

For a split second, she hesitated. The last time she'd ceded control to a man, the result had been disastrous. Frantic panic punched a fist into her gut. She finally nodded but couldn't meet his patient and eager expression.

He rattled off their order in French.

"Did you understand that?" he said.

"Some of it."

"Let me explain what delicacies you will enjoy this evening."

He proceeded to list the dishes he'd ordered in enough detail to make her mouth water in anticipation. It didn't hurt that the mellow voice passing through those strong and sensuous lips would make a hamburger and fries sound delectable.

She creased the serviette into a precise line. "My French is rusty. Learning it was part of my education, back in the day. Schooling was meant to make marriageable society ladies out of girls and such."

"Did the school help?"

"They married me off, so it must have worked."

"Interesting way to say it."

"Interesting time of life. A long time ago."

He chuckled. When he sipped the wine, a red drop clung to his upper lip. She leaned forward as if drawn like a magnet. The moisture disappeared as he rolled his lips together, the short whiskers nearly meeting in the middle.

After a moment, she remembered to breathe and continued. "And no, speaking French didn't help me one bit. Years after my change into an Indebted, I went to nursing school and got a real education. The matrons of Perry's School for Young Women would have been horrified that I aided the sick and the destitute. That wasn't part of the curriculum they taught us 'ladies of a certain station'."

Odie's grin mirrored her own.

"Oh well," she said, letting the wine slide down the back of her throat.

Their kind, the Indebted, never got drunk due to their supernatural healing ability, but she could at least enjoy the brief heat as the full-bodied red reached her stomach. After that, the liver regenerated too quickly for intoxication to occur.

"So you and Jerahmeel, huh?" Odie asked.

The slide of liquid stopped halfway down her throat and she coughed. Her hackles rose again.

She immediately went to her emotionless, polite expression.

No. Stop hiding.

Well, it certainly took guts to work Satan into casual dinner conversation. Odie's eyes twinkled.

She glared at him until he put up his hands.

Two could play this game.

"So you and Jerahmeel, huh?" She shot back.

"*Touché*. But mind you, *chère*, I'm not the enemy here. He is."

"I know. But what can we do? He's now bending his own rules. What's next?" She rubbed her arms.

"You're right. It's a disturbing expansion of his power. He cannot continue in this way. What would you suggest?" he asked.

Her toes tingled beneath the intense green stare, his focus not completely uncomfortable but not calming either. It stirred up uneasiness deep inside, something she couldn't quite name, like a big decision that remained out of reach.

"What would I suggest? I'm not answering that question. You never know when you-know-who will show up unannounced." The back of her neck prickled. Before she could stop herself, she glanced over her shoulder, cursing how Jerahmeel's unwanted attention had changed her, physically and emotionally. How could she, with all of her power and longevity, be scared of anything?

Easy, when that "anything" comprised the only creature who could make her life more hellish than it already was.

He sat back and rubbed his chin. "Doesn't it bother you? How he's got you back on your heels, off-balance?"

"Of course it bothers me. After a hundred years of his escalating come-ons, wouldn't you be tired of it by now? I expect him at all of my kills nowadays."

"Interesting."

"That's not the term I'd use for it."

"No, *chère*. What I meant was that it's interesting how he expends a great deal of energy to poof in and find you. Especially tonight. You're far away from the nearest vortex, yet he continues to show up. In Portland, you were right around the corner, energetically speaking. He probably comes from Mount Shasta or a secondary portal like Mount Rainier. But with all his traveling, that leaves him with less energy for other things."

"Like what?"

"Like security. Like taking precautions with his lairs."

"Doesn't he have minions for that?"

"It takes a lot of energy for him to make and maintain minions. And his recent ones have been destroyed."

Another Indebted, Dante, had destroyed a minion a month ago, which she didn't believe possible, given how strong minions purportedly were. Of course, Dante had been exceptionally motivated by insane rage and fear for his mortal love, Hannah. Ruth had arrived just in time to bear witness and ensure that Jerahmeel stuck with the rules. She could still recall the gruesome sound of the minion's bones snapping under Dante's crushing blows until he had annihilated the creature.

Jerahmeel stuck with the rules. That day.

She shuddered, imaging more nasty minions. "So who protects Jerahmeel?"

"No one. He leaves it to chance that none of us will get free of our knife lust long enough to track him down."

"What happens if we find him but we can't destroy him?"

"You think you're living in hell now?" His eyes no longer danced.

Suddenly, lightheadedness hit her. This conversation could not be headed in a worse direction. The wine turned metallic on her tongue, and her mouth went dry.

"What? Would you rather spend centuries more in this life of slavery?" he asked.

"I don't know which is worse—living a shell of an existence on Earth or diving straight into hell with him."

"Both are wrong. Both can be stopped."

She pressed her palms to the tabletop. "It's impossible. What you're suggesting has been attempted before. And they failed."

"We can do better."

"No. Don't look to me for help."

"Hey, I'm only making interesting conversation."

She didn't buy the innocent act for a minute.

He wrapped his fingers around the stem of his wineglass in a move that managed to be both elegant and strong at the same time. Swirling the wine, he studied the legs of the liquid on the glass and inhaled deeply. As he placed his lips on the rim, a bolt of desire shot into her pelvis, and she found herself enthralled by his sensual mouth. She caught herself running a finger over the edge of her own wine glass. When he swallowed the liquid, his bobbing Adam's apple riveted her attention to that spot on his neck.

His mellow voice startled her from the woolgathering, and her cheeks burned as she tore her gaze from his corded neck to his face. A sardonic quirk to the corner of his mouth told her she'd been caught looking.

"But what if you could do something about him? Would you?" he asked.

"It's a moot point."

"What if it weren't?"

"I'm not playing this game. Change the topic."

Fatigue lined his face as he exhaled.

She inhaled the Petrus along with a hint of his spicy, masculine scent.

"All right, *chère*. We can talk about other things." He sipped again. "How did you come to be Indebted?"

Sadness squeezed her chest so hard, it hurt to breathe, even after all these years. "I don't want to tell that story. Please. It would ruin the meal."

After several minutes of uncomfortable silence, Odie straightened up and cleared his throat.

"I did not mean to bring up such painful times," he said.

"Not your fault. I'm not one for bringing up my past."

The last time she had seen her son and daughter with their smiling, rosy faces, she had given them big hugs. Even now she could feel their wriggling bodies in her arms. A dagger twisted in her heart. Behind their beautiful faces, she could also visualize her husband, William, his cruel face purple with rage, probably counting the seconds until she was gone. A strange lump lodged in her throat.

She took another sip of wine in an effort to drive down the tightness in her throat along with her memories. Holy hell, how long had it been since she dwelled on this pain and explored her punishment? How about never? She refused to think about the past, much less discuss it over dinner.

Odie waited with a solemn expression. Beneath the curl of dark brown hair, the black slashes of his eyebrows drew together.

Before she had to produce an answer to the unspoken question, Philippe saved her by delivering their steaming appetizers.

Stirring the crab bisque soup, the tomato and seafood essence wafted up from the bowl. The tender crab pieces blended beautifully with beads of tapioca starch that captured the creamy liquid and transported it to her taste buds with every bite. For a moment, she lost herself in the enjoyment of the meal.

He leaned forward and whispered. "I didn't want to spoil your evening."

"It was already spoiled when I killed a man and then Satan stopped by to flirt with me."

She dabbed at the corners of her mouth with the soft linen and forced herself to relax her hands, one on top of the other, on the edge of the table. Manners first. No need to punish this man. It wasn't his fault, the mess she was in.

Odie leaned back in his seat. "Well, as penance, I would be honored to share my history with you. May I describe how I came to be this horrible creature you see before you today?"

Despite herself, the corners of her mouth lifted.

"Are you familiar with the origins of the Cajun culture? Acadia?"

"As in Nova Scotia?"

"Yes, exactly. I was born in Acadia, a New France colony. At that time, Acadia included much of Nova Scotia, some of New Brunswick, and Prince Edward Island. My grandparents wanted a more prosperous life than they could have in France, so they had established a farm holding. That's where my father was born and where I was born. Let's see, the year of my birth was ..." he studied the ceiling, "1731. Our farm was tucked into the woods off the coast, about a day's ride north from Halifax, if you have an idea where that is."

She nodded, enjoying his wistful smile as he reminisced.

"What was your home like?"

"Crowded. When I was young, our house contained grandparents, parents, and my siblings. Later, my brother and his wife and children lived with us until they had their own place. Every single day was full of activity and strong opinions."

"Sounds like a loving household."

Odie cut a piece of his roasted duck, closed his eyes, and swallowed. She followed suit with a savory piece of chicken in buttery béarnaise sauce. Time slowed as she waited for him to continue.

"I had a good family, and we all worked very hard. Father organized the planting and harvesting, which my brother, Gerard, and I did along with our grandfather. Then Father would go out fishing each day in the bay. Mother and my sister, Marien, preserved foods for the winter. It was a nice rhythm of life."

"Were you the oldest?"

"No, youngest. And oh, how I caught it from Marien—she loved bossing me around. It wasn't until I grew taller than her that she finally backed off. But by then, she'd discovered boys and lost interest in tormenting me."

Fine lines at the corner of his eyes crinkled with each smile as he told his story, and his strong hands emphasized points of his tale. His damp mouth, tinted red with wine, tilted her equilibrium.

Unable to stop herself, she licked her bottom lip and blinked hard to focus before continuing. "What happened to your brother and sister?"

"Gerard died of pneumonia while in the stockade awaiting deportation. Marien went to South Carolina with her husband. They left early in *Le Grand Dérangement*."

The way he said it as he gripped the knife and fork in his big hands contradicted his too-calm expression. His gaze had gone black as the muscle in his jaw jumped.

"What was that?"

"*Le Grand Dérangement*, otherwise known as The Great Deportation, was politically motivated by the British during the French and Indian War in the 1700s. The first wave removed thousands of Acadians to the thirteen colonies."

"So your sister ...?"

"Since she and her husband lived near the main settlement of Grand-Pré on the coast of the Bay of Fundy, they got rounded up sooner and were forced to move to South Carolina. They worked on a plantation for years, paying off ... debts."

"What debts?"

His black stare absorbed the candlelight. He set down the fork and kneaded his forehead, as though he wanted to rub away the memory. "They went unwillingly to South Carolina, which served as simply a place to live. It wasn't home. They had to work off fabricated debts for nothing that they wanted in the first place. Debt for the privilege of being run off of their own land."

"So they were slaves?" Her knife clanked against the plate, and she cringed. Thankfully, the few remaining patrons didn't appear to notice.

Percussive waves of anger flowed from him across the table. Even though he hadn't moved, somehow he had grown larger, as if every muscle flexed at once.

"It was called 'subsidized' work, meant to pay off their debt of passage and of resettlement. But when you figured in the lack of choice and the punishments? Yes, indentured slavery."

"And you?"

"By then I had a wife, Yvette, and two young daughters, Vivienne and Ada. We'd moved deeper into the southern forests of Nova Scotia, hoping to escape the British. Eventually, though, we too became part of the second wave of expulsion."

"Is that when you came to Louisiana?"

His strong hands now punctuated the story with angry chops. Each time he mentioned a family member, he became even more animated and his scowl deepened.

"Unfortunately, no. In this second wave of the *Dérangement*, all remaining Acadians were shipped directly to northern France. I suppose the authorities figured that our people came from France sixty years prior and we should all go back there. So I packed up my wife, our two daughters, my wife's parents, and off we sailed to France. The trip was misery, but even more so were the settlements there, which were nothing more than cold, muddy shantytowns.

"After a year of barely surviving, we had the opportunity to leave, encouraged by the French who wanted nothing to do with the lowly Acadians, and sail to Louisiana. There was no future for us in France. But Yvette's parents weren't in good health, and they stayed. The decision to leave was a gut-wrenching one, but I saw no other viable option at the time."

At Odie's sad frown, Ruth resisted the urge to reach over and stroke his arm. Her eyes burned, knowing how this strong man must have struggled to keep his family together, even as fate tore them apart.

"The real nightmare began two days into the trip. Yvette was five months pregnant. They packed all of the passengers into the bowels of the ship, stuffed in there like animals. Yvette got sick, lost the baby, and died a few days later of womb fever. *Mon dieu*, how she suffered. The fevers, her dry lips, the endless bleeding and pain. I tried to shield my girls from the worst of it, but they saw how their mother died. Yvette was buried at sea. Dumped overboard."

The solid metal handle of the knife gripped in his fist had bent into an angle. He dropped the deformed utensil to the table and his wide, black stare bored right through her.

She shivered. "Oh, God. So was that when Jerahmeel changed you?"

His laugh came out as a harsh barking sound. "No, even with Yvette dying, as much as I screamed to the heavens, Jerahmeel didn't answer my call. So we arrived in the small settlement of New Orleans. I, a shell of a man, accompanied by my two girls. All I wanted right then was to bury the pain of Yvette's death, but I had so much to do. I had to create a good life for my daughters. We had to survive. We rented a room, and a kindly lady watched my girls while I worked at any odd job I could get. Eventually, we moved into a place of our own outside of town. We lived off our garden and a few animals, and I built a small house."

"It sounds like hard work."

"*Oui*, but rewarding. I watched my daughters grow up. They were such sweet girls, so lovely with dark hair."

In response to the wistful smile playing over his sensual lips, the corners of her own mouth rose. Then his strong mouth turned into a frown, and Ruth's heart sank.

"One hot, hellish summer, the girls got typhoid fever." His strong tenor voice cracked, and a knot formed in Ruth's midsection.

She had treated typhoid during the Civil War. The relentless, bloody flux robbed young men of their lives. Years later, in the hospital wards, hundreds of patients suffered with typhoid, and in children, the disease was almost always fatal. She could only imagine what Odie had endured, losing his wife, then having his daughters fall critically ill.

"Vivienne was ten at the time and Ada was eight. I did every single treatment the doctor asked of me to try to help them. Their fevers were so high, and Ada constantly bled from her nose. Their delirium and suffering, as they called out for their dead mother, it destroyed me. One night, when both seemed close to death, I called out to the heavens for someone to help me, anyone. I finally got an answer, but not the answer I wanted. The Lord of Hell showed up."

"Jerahmeel." Although she'd never talked about it with anyone, she knew how Odie felt at his darkest moment. She understood his hope, sorrow, and the willingness to do anything to save a loved one.

If he clenched his jaw any harder, she feared the bones would break.

"At the time, I didn't care. Jerahmeel said he could help, so I signed the paper he held in front of me. Didn't read it. Didn't care. My life was forfeit without my daughters. I'd lost everything else I loved, and I couldn't lose them as well."

"Did he save them?"

"One of them."

"What?" Blood drained from her face.

"I had to choose."

CHAPTER 8

What kind of horrible parent could choose which child lived and which died? Odie rubbed his face, trying to erase the images of his gravely ill daughters, writhing on their beds, sweat and blood rolling down their sunken cheeks. Dry lips had pleaded with him to make the pain go away. Each weak cry ripped him like shards of glass on raw skin. Like it happened yesterday, damn it all. He pinched the bridge of his nose, desperate to push the memories away.

"What did you do?" Ruth asked.

Did she truly want his answer?

He leaned forward. Bad enough that he would speak of it to her, there was no need for anyone else in the restaurant to hear about his failure as a parent. An invisible knife twisted in his chest.

"I picked, damn it. What a sick shame. I picked a child to live. Hedged my bets. If one daughter could pull through on her own, it would've been my oldest, Vivienne. So I picked my baby, Ada. She was little more than a skeleton by this stage, except for her swollen belly. God help me, I chose Ada."

Ruth reached across the table, and he curled his fingers around her hand and returned the pressure. He didn't deserve it, but *mon dieu*, her very presence gave him comfort.

Her eyes glistened. "You did what you had to. Any parent would struggle with that decision, faced with the imminent death of both children. You had to make an impossible choice."

"*Merci*, you are too kind, but I question my fitness as a father every single day."

"What happened after Jerahmeel left?" Her reassuring squeeze of his hand spread warmth down to his toes.

"Ada slowly improved and returned to me. Vivienne fought valiantly and survived but barely. She remained frail for the rest of her life."

"You must have been protective of them."

"Of course. But you know the Indebted rules as well as I do. Per the terms of the contract with Jerahmeel, I was forbidden any further contact with my girls."

Even now, hundreds of years distant, the sucking emptiness when he had to leave his daughters caught him so unexpectedly that his lungs couldn't expand. The invisible band around his ribs finally relaxed.

He shook his head and pushed back the hair from his forehead with his free hand.

Anger played across her sculpted features as her brows furrowed. Then the tension faded into sadness and understanding. Yes, she, too, had given something up to become Indebted. They all did.

He rubbed a thumb over her elegant fingers. "I made sure the girls were raised in a good home and paid a lady handsomely to do so. Since I didn't need to sleep anymore, because of ... you know ... I worked day and night to support them."

"Did they grow to adults and have families of their own?"

His harsh laugh held no mirth. He withdrew his hand to knead tense muscles in his neck.

"Did they grow old? Not exactly. Ada, whom I had sacrificed my soul to save, died in the arms of her lady caretaker a few years later at the age of twelve. Yellow fever epidemic. Did you know we can only use our sacrifice once? If something else happens to a person we love, tough. We're simply out of luck. What a deal."

"My God. And Vivienne?"

"She became such a sad thing, all alone, pining for her sister, her mother, her father. Everyone had left her. The typhoid had made her so delicate. She did indeed marry a man, a teacher. He was a good husband. But Vivienne died bearing her second child."

Pop, pop, little simmering bubbles of outrage began to surface from Odie's crippled heart. Everything he had lost—his wife, his homeland, his children, his very humanity—and for what?

"What a tragedy." He curled his hand into a fist and thumped his leg. "Those were dark times for me. Darker even than when Yvette died on that damned ship. I still had to kill, I still was eternally Indebted, but it was for nothing. I never again could touch my girls' sweet faces, hold them as they cried, share their lives as they grew into adults and had their own families. Damn it, if I didn't feel robbed."

"I feel the same way."

"Of course, *chère*, I know you've had your trials. We all have, every last one of us, chained to Jerahmeel forever. How rude of me, all melancholy, ruining your dinner."

True, he was angling to get Ruth's help with his plan to destroy Jerahmeel, but with this hellish story, he didn't need to fabricate his emotions. He'd lived the nightmare, and his torment was the only true weapon left to him to fight with, God rest his daughters' beautiful souls.

She pushed her plate to the side. "You haven't ruined anything. Thank you for sharing that story with me." The intensity of her gold-flecked gaze swallowed him whole.

"You're too kind."

After a pause, she said, "If I may ask, earlier today, at brunch, what did you mean about helping your progeny over the years?"

The sucking pain beneath his ribs lessened. "Ah, yes. So Vivienne's second child indeed survived. My two grandchildren wanted for nothing in their lives. Vivienne's husband remarried a nice woman who raised the girls as her own and added two more sons. Their home was merry and loud, exactly what I wanted for my grandchildren. Except I had no part in any of it."

Emptiness poured into his belly like a pile of dry, lifeless sand.

She chewed her full lower lip. "Sad to say, I would never have thought to do that. What a wonderful gift you've given your family."

Her shared sadness tugged at him in ways he refused to contemplate. If only he could pull those corners of her lovely mouth upward.

"I hope my family feels the support is a blessing. Becoming a kind of fairy godmother gave me a semblance of completion, of purpose, that the decisions I made years ago, however awful, led to benefit later generations."

"You were a good father. You've managed to find something positive to accomplish with your eternal contract. I can't say I've done the same."

"Well, that may be true, but I'm finished with this existence. I've sacrificed too much. Being the family ghost no longer satisfies. Not if I have to kill mortals on a regular basis. I'm indebted to an evil creature that harvests power from human souls. No matter how much I try to compensate with good deeds, I cannot make up for my sins. I hate this life."

"Understandable, but what can you do? And don't give me this wild idea of climbing into a mountain and storming the lair."

He gulped down more wine. "No other options exist; believe me, I have searched. Besides watching over my family, my only other hobby for the past 260 years has been researching everything there is to know about destroying Jerahmeel. I've been through all manner of ancient texts and firsthand accounts. I have the information needed to bring him down, if only I have the right help."

• • •

Freezing beneath his dark scrutiny, Ruth said, "I'm not the right person to fight him."

"You are the perfect person. Can't you see why he must be stopped? How many more horrible decisions do we have to make about our loved ones?"

Her heart stopped. Ice flooded her veins. "Wait. You told me that story to play on my sympathies? To get me to join you?"

"*Non, chère.*" He extended his large hand, palm up.

She stood up, her chair ricocheting against the wall. "The hell you didn't!" Shame crawled up her neck as patrons looked up at her. Damn, she hated public scenes. All she wanted to do was cover herself with another costume or wig. Anything to help her disappear.

God, she was such an idiot. Drop the pretenses and enjoy his company? Put away the old Ruth, the woman who couldn't trust anyone, even herself. Just enjoy the evening?

So, how did that work out?

Lesson learned.

Clack, clack, clack. Like a ratchet pulling chains, she sensed her walls coming back up.

Secured. Protected. Isolated.

"I wanted you to know my history." He looked at the floor.

Her tinny laugh, on the edge of hysteria, rang false to her own ears. "You manipulated me. And to think I almost bought the tall tale."

Only an idiot would believe the sincerity glowing in those glass-green eyes, and damn it if she didn't waver again.

Stupid. When would history stop repeating itself?

"The story is true, *chère*. Please sit, and let's finish our meal."

She wadded up the linen next to the china plate. "Dinner's over, Odie." Ignoring the moues of disapproval from lingering customers, she turned on her heel and stormed out of the restaurant.

How naive could she be, nearly falling for his cock and bull story? Falling for the man? Even now, part of her still wanted to pretend that he didn't try to manipulate her, that the attraction was mutual and sincere.

Fingernails cut into her palms, she clenched her fists so tightly. No need to mince words: she'd been used by a handsome man. Again. Just like with her husband years ago. After 150 years, wouldn't she learn by now?

Damn and double damn, she should've known that Barnaby spilling her secret about Jerahmeel's unnatural interest would lead to trouble.

She'd become the best secret weapon for the worst laid plans imagined since the beginning of time.

Which hurt more: the fact that she believed there was a flicker of hope the curse could be broken or that she'd almost fallen for a winsome face who only wanted her for his insane scheme?

Odie caught up to her a block from the restaurant, his hair askew from running. Of course, he wasn't winded.

He gripped her upper arm. "Please, *chère*, listen—"

Cutting him off with a slice of her hand, she pivoted out of his grasp. It was like her husband's ultimate betrayal had happened all over again. The scab had not yet healed, and here was Odie, pulling it off to expose the fiery nerves beneath.

"Look, you had your fun. You tried pressuring me, and you tried rescuing me. Then you worked the sympathy angle. Congratulations, sir, you nearly had me, but as they say, I wasn't born yesterday. Far from it."

She walked again, preternaturally fast, but he kept pace, a large, silent figure at her side. For a moment, she indulged in a fantasy of Odie as her protector. For a moment, she flirted with the idea of letting her guard down and allowing him to be vigilant for the both of them, to cede control and finally relax.

But that required trust. In herself and in him. She had neither.

"I only wanted you to see the truth, *chère*."

If only his velvet voice didn't slide past her defenses. If only the hurt on his handsome face didn't appear so sincere, she might believe him. Might. But not this evening. Not ever.

"I see the truth, right in front of me, and it comes in the form of a charlatan."

"No. My desire to destroy Jerahmeel is real."

She hissed at the name and chanced a look around the dark streets, then took off again.

Odie swung his muscled arms as he matched her rapid strides. "The history, my two beautiful daughters, my wife—it's all true. Not a word is made up."

"You're telling that story to *use* me, though."

"I wanted you to know how I became Indebted. And I also believed that you have the same goals as I do."

"Well, I don't. And I don't plan to join your project any time soon. If you'll excuse me."

They arrived at the hotel where the marquis lights cast a too-bright yellow glow over the sidewalk. A few late-night patrons strolled through the doors, probably ready to lay their heads on the bed and sleep until morning, a very mortal human activity and one that she could never truly appreciate in her Indebted form.

He caught her arm in a firm grip that sent traitorous shivers into her neck. "I'll walk you up."

It wasn't a question.

Her breath caught. Her emotions switched from reverse to fast-forward.

Normally, she didn't respond to the caveman act, but frankly, she was weary of public scenes, of refusals, of conflict. A mutinous quiver of excitement flitted in her belly.

No. She refused to feel anything for this man. For any man. No more opportunities for betrayal.

Right?

He gestured toward the large glass doors, the hotel lights reflecting in his eyes. "So?"

Unexpected warmth crept up her face as she recalled their torrid kiss and those firm, passionate, demanding lips that tormented her earlier today. His offer held the promise of more than an escort, and God help her, that temptation replaced the anger she felt as he tried to coerce her into participating in his plan. But she hadn't experienced anger—true anger—in such a long time. She'd forgotten how the adrenaline surged and created other feelings.

Now she experienced a different sensation. Was it the man or the heightened emotion that piqued her sudden wanton curiosity? How would it feel to have sex with someone who made her feel this mad, this excited, this fearful of deception? A coil of interest heated her lower belly.

Would the risk of experimentation be worth the pain of betrayal?

How much life had she missed—would she miss—by continuing to hide?

Propriety be damned, she wanted to spend more time in this man's presence. She could enjoy physical intimacy without joining him in his lunatic scheme. She felt like a woman stepping off a cliff, one foot hovering over empty space.

Solid ground. Old Ruth.

Air beneath her other foot. New Ruth.

She could always send him away, right?

"Yes."

During the excruciatingly slow elevator ride to the top floor, their steamy sideways glances thickened the tense air. Her body thrummed in tune with this man. His every sharp breath, his every movement, set her hypersensitive nerves on edge. He personified danger to her heart, to her soul, to the entire world.

And her cloistered heart trembled at the danger. Risk avoidance no longer mattered. She wanted pleasure for herself.

She startled at the elevator ding, and then preceded Odie down the hall. Sensing his gaze on her body, her skin prickled.

At the door, she slid the electronic card into the lock. Odie's hand drifted down her lower back.

Hearing a muffled groan inside the suite, she froze. Another moan emanated from the within and panic flooded her mind. Meeting Odie's horrified expression, she darted through the door and into the salon.

When she flipped on the lights, the scene crushed her.

Barnaby, in his favorite linen pajamas, lay crumpled on the floor, gasping for air, his arthritic hands clawing at his neck. The scent of rotten eggs permeated the room. Jerahmeel stood to the side, a laconic smile on his red mouth as he twirled a lock of oily hair around a smoking finger.

"Hello, my dear. You took much too long to return this evening. I had to entertain myself until you arrived."

She drew back, right into the hard body of Odie, who wrapped his strong fingers around her upper arms. If he hadn't supported her, she would have fallen to her knees. Or worse, flew at Jerahmeel.

"*Mon dieu*," Odie whispered.

Barnaby's chest heaved as he wheezed, and his eyes rolled back in his head. He needed help and fast, but Jerahmeel stood in her way with a satisfied smirk pasted on his twisted face.

"Damn you! What have you done? Get away from him!" A piercing whistle, like that damned teakettle pressure sensation when her power erupted years ago, shot through her head.

For the second time in 150 years, rage consumed Ruth. She let loose her fury at the most deadly being on Earth.

And she didn't care one bit.

CHAPTER 9

At least the All Hellish One had the presence of mind to be taken aback.

Odie had never heard of a time when Jerahmeel was at an utter loss for words. Hopefully, Jerahmeel was at a loss for action as well, or Ruth, Barnaby, and Odie were at risk of immediate incineration.

Unfortunately, at some point, Jerahmeel would recover from the shock that his favorite employee, his precious, docile Ruth, had just laid into him. Jerahmeel's pride would not tolerate the hatred pouring out of her trembling frame. Soon, the Lord of Evil would revert to his go-to emotion: cruel rage.

Mon dieu, Odie would do what he could to make sure she wasn't anywhere near the line of fire when Jerahmeel snapped. As Ruth stepped to one side, Odie shadowed her, watching Jerahmeel, ready to absorb brimstone if the Lord of *Merde* exacted his revenge.

She pulled away from Odie and crouched over Barnaby. The old man gasped a painful, wet, rattling inhalation. When she ran her hands over him, he opened his eyes and moved his mouth, but no words came out.

Tears streaming down her face, she screamed again at Jerahmeel. "What did you do?"

How had she projected her voice so loudly? Even the windows rattled.

"I didn't touch him." Jerahmeel smiled, those lizard thin lips compressing into nothing, his black stare reflecting nothing.

"Damn it, you didn't touch those men a few hours ago, yet they're dead. So let's try again: What did you do?"

Odie cringed. He loved the vision of Ruth as an avenging angel, but she'd now pushed Jerahmeel far past what Odie had ever known his boss to tolerate. If she didn't back down, they'd all be worse than dead very soon, and then there'd be no one to take care of Barnaby.

Jerahmeel rubbed his narrow chin, mouth twisted into a moue of disappointment. "My dear, when you were unwilling to accept my proposition this evening, it seemed that stronger motivation was in order. Clearly, your reluctance to join me could only be tied to your duty to this ... mortal. Therefore I removed your duty."

"Removed?"

"You're welcome, I'm certain."

"Oh God. Barnaby?"

The elderly man's chest heaved with each word. "Dear ... can't breathe."

"Odie, call 911. Barnaby needs medical help. We have to save him."

"What?" Jerahmeel's eyebrows rose. "I thought you'd be happy that I cleared the path for us to be together. Unencumbered."

She rose and rounded on Jerahmeel, auburn hair tumbling over her shoulders, all glorious blazing rage, like a mother wolf about to take on a grizzly bear to protect her brood. Amazing. And so amazingly stupid. Odie lurched forward and pinned an arm around her as he pulled her away.

"*Chère*, this isn't wise," he said, willing her to hear him.

"Damn wise, I think."

"You can't win this round," he whispered.

"I'd like to try." She actually growled.

With her strength equal to his, Odie couldn't restrain her indefinitely.

"Please, *chère*," he whispered. "Think of Barnaby."

Something snapped in her fierce anger, her body sagged, and Odie slid his arms away from her arms.

But then she stiffened and faced down Jerahmeel.

Oh, *mon dieu*, she might be brave, but this bordered on foolhardiness of epic proportions.

"Get. Out." Her calm voice didn't fool anyone.

So hard was her trembling, Odie felt it in the soles of his feet. Nothing good could come of this confrontation. No one ordered Jerahmeel to do anything and survived.

Jerahmeel's fingertips glowed and smoked. "You command me?" he warned.

She jerked an arm toward Barnaby's curled form. "Look what you did. Yes, I command you. Get out."

While she didn't yell, her voice had amplified. Somehow Odie could hear her words inside of his head. Odd vibrations radiated out from her, like nothing he had ever experienced before.

"No one tells me what to do." Jerahmeel seethed.

"Do you really want a chance for us to be together?"

The double echo of her voice pierced Odie's ears and he winced. *What the hell?*

Jerahmeel patted his curls. "Of course, *belle*."

"Then get out." Her voice reverberated out of her body and drilled into Odie's mind.

"*Impossible*."

The Lord Most Vile pointed, and embers flared to flame on the carpet near Barnaby. This standoff was about to go south in a hurry. Odie had to end the confrontation without anyone being destroyed and help his old friend.

"My lord, the lady is overwrought." Odie used as soothing a voice as he could stomach. "Perhaps you should give her some time to consider the efforts you've made on her behalf. You know how women are, *non*? Hardheaded. They don't like to be told anything but instead want to draw their own conclusions."

Jerahmeel stepped back with a bizarre expression that might have passed as an attempt to look seductive. It was all Odie could do to resist shoving Ruth out of the room to get her away from this disgusting creature. At least Jerahmeel's fingertips had stopped smoking.

"Too true. Women are capricious and weak-minded, unable to see past what's in front of them. I will take your advice this one time."

When Ruth opened her mouth, Odie jabbed her hard in the ribs, and air whooshed from her lungs. For a moment, she was speechless. Jerahmeel needed to leave, for all their sakes.

Jerahmeel dropped into a courtly bow with a flourish. "*Mademoiselle*, I bid you *adieu* for this evening. I will call upon you when you've regained your senses. You will come to me of your own free accord."

Before Ruth could launch into a diatribe that might compel Jerahmeel to immolate the entire hotel, her boss simply disappeared. She stared, slack-jawed, as the residual smoke dissipated.

Odie shook his head to clear the ringing in his ears. "Um, *chère*? Barnaby. He's almost on fire."

"Holy hell."

She batted out the small flames with her bare hands. Although the blisters and open wounds would heal quickly, the burns still hurt. While she ministered to a gasping Barnaby, Odie thumbed on his cell phone and called 911 before opening the windows and fanning away the worst of the smoke.

The heavy silence was broken only by Barnaby's pained wheezes.

Odie was helpless again. He could do nothing for his friend. Barnaby's fate was in the hands of the medical personnel or God, if there was such a being. Just like a replay of his dear Ada's death, where he watched through a window as the lady caregiver kissed his dying daughter's cheeks. Ada's fear and pain—Odie should have been the one to comfort his child. But it made no difference if Odie'd been there; he couldn't have stopped her death. Just as he could not stop Barnaby's pain.

What the hell had Jerahmeel done to Barnaby? Whatever it was, although the man appeared critically injured, there were no visible wounds.

Medical personnel arrived and placed Barnaby on a stretcher. With oxygen running into his nose and IVs dangling from both arms, the old man's frame disappeared beneath the wires and lines. As quickly as they had come, the emergency personnel whisked Barnaby away.

With a quiet word and a palmed large bill, Odie encouraged the hotel's night manager hovering at the door to withdraw and remove concerned onlookers.

In the suite, silence descended. No movement, no voices. Nothing. Only a residual odor of burnt carpet and sulfur, acrid reminders of the consequences of contemplating hope.

Ruth knelt on the floor. For an instant, her eyes were a complete black. Not just the irises, which was normal for an Indebted, but totally black throughout. As the vibrations pouring off her body reduced, she blinked back to hazel and then stared into space.

"*Chère*?" He broke the deathly quiet atmosphere.

While he respected Ruth's desire to lay low, Odie's anger at this attack only served to fuel his determination to make his ultimate plan work.

Vendetta echoed louder and louder in his mind.

The image of his own two dark-haired daughters dying superimposed itself on the woman sitting before him.

"Ruth?"

He crouched behind her, wrapped his arm around her upper chest, and pulled her flush against him, holding her tightly. Her stiff frame eventually relaxed to the point where he appreciated how right it felt to have her in his arms. How good she would feel in his embrace for years to come.

Damn it. Not years. Where had that thought come from?

An evening or two of that curvy body beneath his, exploring the possibilities of sex with a being who possessed endless stamina. But no commitment. That was his goal, correct?

Besides, all of his past commitments had long since turned to dust. And if he coerced Ruth to help with his plan, he would be risking her life.

Therefore, attachments made no sense. Right?

Perhaps he'd begun to consider her as more than a luscious sexual interlude.

No. Not possible.

Unable to stop himself, he brushed his lips over the top of her head, inhaling lavender and mint in the silky strands.

When he stood up, she took his offered hand, got to her feet, and turned toward him. The haunted, empty expression on her sculpted features drove a spike of fear into his gut. She glanced around the room, to him, and back to the room again, like a soul searching for a home. Flickers of panic swirled in those golden-speckled depths and short gasps made her shoulders heave. He needed her to focus on something else before she lost her composure altogether.

He touched her arm. "We should clean up and check out of the hotel."

"Why?" That barely audible voice shook him more than her screams.

"It's not wise to leave any personal items here. I imagine neither you nor Barnaby wish to return to this hotel room after all that has happened."

She remained rooted in place, her gaze distant, looking through him. "No. Of course not."

"So let's pack up Barnaby's and your belongings. Unless you want me to take care of it so you can go immediately to the hospital?"

"No, we can be quick about it." Like a sleepwalker awakening, she tilted her face up to him and blinked. "Of course. We can be quick. We can be Indebted-quick."

They raced through the suite, stuffing items into suitcases. With their preternatural speed, they had set the room to rights within five minutes, even hiding the fire spot beneath another elegant throw rug and opening all of the windows. Odie would pay the manager generously for the burn on the carpet and blame it on candles and carelessness. Problem solved. Fewer questions later.

He took all the bags down and called for the valet to bring his car around. The tour with his old friend this afternoon seemed like a million years ago.

As Odie exited the hotel, the vision of Ruth standing on the sidewalk, alone, head bowed, her hands wrapped around her upper arms, hit him like a sucker punch to the gut. At least the blank expression had been replaced by sharp concern. Beneath the marquis lights, tears glinted in her eyes. Her full lips quivered in a frown until she clenched her jaw.

Not only did he need to focus on this woman's well-being, but he needed to help his friend. And how about the plan to destroy Jerahmeel? With his appearances lately, Jerahmeel's strength would be at a nadir. Odie had too much to do, too many proverbial plates to balance. Could he keep them all spinning without letting any crash to the ground? Had he become so heartless that he considered Ruth to be just another plate?

Absolutely not.

In this moment of crystal clarity, he came to a decision. Ruth took priority over everything else. "All checked out. Let's go see to Barnaby."

CHAPTER 10

After a ride across town in silence, the hustle of University Hospital came as a welcome distraction to Ruth. She and Odie checked in at the front desk of the ER, and a staff member escorted them to Barnaby's room. Ruth had been in every kind of hospital since the late 1800s, but this new facility impressed her. Every piece of equipment in this ER sparkled, and the monitors calmly beeped Barnaby's pulse and oxygen levels. A petite nurse made notes on a handheld computer.

Time had finally outpaced Ruth's skills. Because of the increased difficulty of hiding her identity, she hadn't used her nursing degree for twenty years. Of course, she could learn to operate the computerized machines, and surely the gentle art of nursing had not changed, but so much else had evolved. But if she were human? She'd be right here, fighting for the lives of her patients and giving them comfort as they suffered.

God, how she wanted to be human.

Anything but a killer.

Ruth turned back to her beloved mentor. His respirations were calm. On the monitor, his blood oxygen levels read normal, although he needed six liters of oxygen to sustain him at those levels. Not good.

"How is he doing?" she asked the nurse.

"Better, though we're not sure what happened. I'll let the doctor talk with you."

The woman darted out of the room and a few minutes later, a middle-aged physician with a gaggle of interns and medical students filed in. Ruth could tell which kids were at which level of training based on the degree of fear, uncertainty, and fatigue, not to mention the length of their bright white coats. Some things never changed.

"Are you his family?" The attending physician extended a firm handshake.

"Yes, I'm his caregiver. And this is his friend. We're the closest people to family he has."

The doctor crossed his arms. "Mr. Emerson has sustained damage to his heart, but I'm not certain what caused it. It's almost like he has been burned from the inside out, enough to injure a portion of his heart."

Damn Jerahmeel and his fingers of fire.

Odie's warm hand on her back centered her like an anchor in a rising storm.

"His heart is filling up with fluid because of the damage. But otherwise, we can see nothing else wrong with him. And no evidence of external injury. No medications that would cause this pattern. Do you know if he was doing anything ... odd before he got sick?"

"No," she lied. "Everything was completely normal. He just collapsed."

It was a grossly truncated version of the incident, leaving out the part where the manifestation of Satan tried to destroy Barnaby to claim Ruth all for himself. But the doctor didn't need that kind of detail to deliver medical care.

The white-coated crowd studiously tapped notes on electronic tablets.

Ruth forced a polite smile. "Will he recover?"

The lines around the doctor's mouth tightened, and he studied the monitor. She had seen physicians with that expression in the past, knew what it meant. A deep, sinking feeling threatened to consume her.

"It's too early to say; he's critically ill. I'd like to admit him to the cardiac ICU. They will do further testing and monitor him carefully. Ah, may I ask another question?"

She nodded, but the motion took effort.

"We like to make sure we have all the information relevant to each patient's stay. Does Mr. Emerson have a living will or a medical power of attorney?"

Ruth's heart flopped, but she clutched her iron will around her like a suit of armor. She understood why the doctor asked this question, and no, it was not for completeness. Not in this situation. They wanted those bases covered because they anticipated acting on the living will information. Even though she knew the drill, it didn't lessen the shock.

"I don't think he has a living will, but to the best of my knowledge, I don't believe he'd want to live on life support, if it came down to that. He's never put his thoughts in writing. That's my impression."

When she gripped the back of the vinyl chair, Odie's hand slid over hers and squeezed. Blast it, she would not crave reassurance from him. She was stronger than that.

"Very good. They'll move him to the ICU in an hour or so. Would you like anything? Water or juice perhaps?"

"No, thank you, that's very kind."

In a rustle of starched polyester, the group shuffled out of Barnaby's room. She pulled up a chair next to her friend. Odie rested his hand on her shoulder, and she relaxed for a brief moment.

What a change. A few hours ago, she was yelling at him for trying to coopt her into his scheme. Now he'd become considerate and supportive. And maybe his change in character was another ploy to get her on board with the scheme. She could make herself crazy second-guessing his motives.

At some point, she needed to take that leap and trust a man again. Maybe Odie was as good an opportunity as any. Not all men were like her husband.

Barnaby cracked open an eye and turned his head toward Ruth. She gently slid her palm beneath her boss's frail hand.

"Are they gone?" His thin voice rattled.

"Were you playing possum?"

"Did you know that one of those people who wasn't yet a doctor wanted to check up my bum! It's clear that's not where the problem is." He pursed his lips and slowly exhaled.

She loved the rare times when he slid into Elizabethan slang. "How are you feeling?"

He chuckled until paroxysmal wheezing took over. After a few moments of coughing, he sagged into the mattress. "Like hell."

"What happened in the hotel?" Odie asked.

Barnaby cleared his throat and winced. "Your Lord Jerahmeel showed up, spewing something about getting rid of me so he could have you all to himself, my dear. That odious creature has gotten madder over the years, I daresay." He inhaled through his nose, puffing the air out of his mouth. "He's right. He technically didn't touch me. He pointed a finger and zap, incredible fire in my chest." He panted until he could speak again. "It was like a hot clamp squeezing my body shut. I never knew he could do that."

"For how long?"

"Not long, as you came in right after he began. I fear I'd be dead if he'd continued."

"Are you still in danger?"

"If I'm alive and you're paying attention to me and not him, then yes, I'm in danger."

"He's a sick bastard," muttered Odie.

"He's getting worse," she agreed.

"You're both right." The muscles of Barnaby's chest and neck strained to drive air in and out. "I have a bad feeling about where things are going with Jerahmeel." He wheezed. "And my instincts have been correct for almost 500 years."

Barnaby paused to catch his breath again. His jugular veins were distended more than halfway up his neck, and Ruth fought to mask the dread that threatened to swamp her. Heart failure.

She glanced at the monitor's display of an increasing heart rate and decreasing oxygen levels, understanding the results but wishing to be ignorant of the medical facts.

As she opened her mouth to comment, he lifted a hand and dropped it back to the bed as though he no longer could raise it.

Odie slipped her hand into his with a gentle squeeze.

Barnaby puffed a few more times. "I originally didn't like the idea you presented yesterday, Odie. But I'm starting to see its merit."

"Thank you, my friend."

"You cannot be serious." She didn't buy Odie's wide-eyed, innocent expression one bit. He might be sexy as all get out, but this particular harebrained idea contained no hope for success.

He leaned toward Barnaby. "This is our best opportunity to finish Jerahmeel once and for all. It might protect humans as well as release our kind from their hellish contracts."

"And if it fails?" She clenched her teeth so hard her jaw ached.

Odie's grasp on her hand tightened, both reassuring and dangerous. "How could our existence be worse?"

"It could be plenty worse."

"My dear, consider it," Barnaby whispered.

"No. I'm sorry. I won't do it." She pulled her hand free of Odie's grasp and scrubbed at her face. "Barnaby, you're still alive. Jerahmeel might torture you even now. If I make him mad, he'll hunt for those who are most vulnerable. What about Peter and Dante and their families? They're all mortal." Horror washed over her as tears burned. "If Jerahmeel would attack Barnaby, what's to say he won't go after other humans? I won't put our friends at risk."

"Peace, my dear. No one will force you to do anything." Barnaby closed his eyes with a sigh.

Odie knelt next to the hospital bed. A muscle jumped beneath his beard. "So that reminds me. Would you like us to notify anyone that you're here? Maybe Peter and Dante?"

"That would be kind of you. But you don't need to trouble them. They've both been through so much. I do love them like my own sons."

"I believe they'd want to know what's happened," Odie said.

Something sharp twisted in Ruth's chest. She bit the inside of her cheek. *Keep control. Do not fall to pieces.* She wrapped her hands around the gurney side rails.

Barnaby's blue eyes snapped open again.

"If anyone can stop him, it's you and Odie, my dear. Just know that I believe in your strength. In your powers."

She gasped. Her powers? How did he know? She'd never told anyone. Not even Barnaby. And she'd never used her power around him.

And now Odie raised his eyebrows. Damn, he hadn't missed Barnaby's oblique comment.

"Why don't you rest?" If she didn't relax her grip, she'd bend the metal bed railing. With effort, she let her hands fall to her sides.

Barnaby smiled. "My dear, I know much more than you realize. And while I'm thinking of it, have Odie do a little of his genealogy research for you."

"I have no family left."

"You'd be surprised."

"What do you mean?"

"Not for me to say. As for your secrets ... not mine to share ..."

He drifted back to sleep as his pale, wrinkled lips relaxed. Whether he pretended to sleep or not, Barnaby needed his rest and possibly a miracle.

Odie hovered at her side. His ice-green gaze searched her and she shivered, but he wouldn't get any information out of her tonight. She resisted waking Barnaby to ask how he knew about her power. Later. It would have to wait until later.

Ruth felt all of her 150 years of age. "I'll go with him to the ICU. Do you have Peter and Dante's numbers?"

Odie nodded. "They haven't been human long enough for me to delete from my emergency call list. But I need to get on my computer at home and pull up the encrypted file. I don't like you being here alone."

"I'll stay with Barnaby. Besides, I can't imagine Jerahmeel would try anything where there are so many witnesses around."

"Possibly. But he's getting more erratic."

"I'll be careful."

"Please do. I'll return as soon as I'm able."

His caress down her arm to her hand triggered a gut-deep shudder. Then he lifted her hand to his lips and pressed a kiss to her tingling fingers.

"Stay safe."

"You too," she said.

When she turned back to Barnaby, she could swear the corners of her old friend's mouth had curled upward.

CHAPTER 11

The clock read 3:00 a.m. Peter and Dante would arrive by this afternoon.

Unfortunately, they were bringing their women, increasing the security risk. So Odie put two of his unhuman colleagues on alert. All of the Indebted knew Barnaby, either personally or by reputation. No one wanted him to be a victim of Jerahmeel. Help was easy to find.

But Odie had to avoid flooding New Orleans with the Indebted. Not only would the local kill rates go up, but each kill with a blade would alert Jerahmeel of the increased concentration in this area and raise his suspicion.

They all had to be careful, so very careful.

When Odie had gone home for a few hours to access the database and make arrangements for his friends' safety, he had also started the new genealogy program on his computer. In the past, he'd used the program to keep track of his progeny, but he changed the input to generate a new family tree.

There were only three Ruths who matriculated from the few nursing schools right after the Civil War. He pulled up archived graduation photos, and lo and behold, there she was with her high cheekbones and serious expression, her hair pulled up into a high bun topped with a neat white cap. Even in the grainy photo, she appeared ageless and elegant. And foolish in the 1870s, since she used her married name for this first diploma. He hadn't known her full name until now, but the image staring back at him in the faded photo was unmistakably Ruth.

After he traced that information back to her family in Maryland, the program began to populate the family tree. A few comments in archived family diaries and letters piqued his interest. *Mon dieu*, was this the mystery that Barnaby hinted at, a pattern perhaps? Something to do with his comment about her powers?

Damn it, Odie needed more time.

But he had to get back to the hospital. This research would have to wait.

Even if he floored it, it would still take over an hour to drive the sixty miles from Thibodaux to the hospital. Too far to run, even for an Indebted. Besides, running risked detection, so he saved that Indebted skill for special occasions.

For now, he craved Ruth's calm presence, needed to see her lovely face.

Why? Revenge on Jerahmeel, of course. The possibility hung like a fruit, tantalizingly out of reach.

To accomplish his revenge, Odie had to convince Ruth to join the mission. She was the lynchpin in the scheme; she could gain access to the lair of He Who Should Be Destroyed where no one else could.

What would it cost to convince her?

What would it cost if she said yes? How could he consider risking her life?

At noon, Odie arrived at the ICU waiting area. Families sat in small groups, holding hands, heads bowed, as subdued murmurs filtered through the tense atmosphere.

In the corner of the room was Ruth, her elegant hand pressed to her forehead, features carved in stone, the very picture of isolation. The twinge in his chest wasn't due to sympathy. It was because he knew precisely the feelings behind her expression. He had survived loneliness so profound it had changed the man he was.

As he approached, she looked up and a wan smile animated her sculpted face.

"How's he doing?"

"Worse. He's in and out of consciousness now. They're considering putting him on a ventilator."

"Oh no."

"I asked them to hold off intubating him. I don't believe he'd want to live that way." She pierced him with a bleak, hazel stare. "What do you think?"

"I've known that stubborn man for hundreds of years, and I agree. You did the right thing."

He sat next to her on the vinyl loveseat, ignoring the loud creak. She didn't move.

"Want to talk?" he asked.

She stared straight ahead, neck muscles working as she swallowed. "No. Thank you."

"Well, then I'll stay here with you until Dante and Peter get here."

"They're coming?"

"Left this morning. Chartered a private jet. Should be here soon."

"Alone?"

"No, Peter's wife and Dante's fiancée are with them."

"But Allie just had the baby."

"They don't care. They're coming. Remember, you're not the only one who loves Barnaby."

Her creamy cheeks colored. "I know. Of course it's their right to see Barnaby. But they're all in danger here."

Although the Indebted never required sleep, they sometimes enjoyed it. So it surprised him to see the deep circles beneath her gold-flecked eyes. Whether it was weariness or suffering, he could only guess.

He took her elegant hand in his and enjoyed the briefest pleasure when she didn't pull away. "I tried to make the women stay home. No one wanted to hear it."

She leaned forward, elbows on her knees, chin on her fists. "What if Jerahmeel shows up?"

"I have a plan B."

"Oh?"

"There are some of the Indebted from nearby states who will come here to keep watch—over everyone, if necessary."

"Wow."

"Barnaby has garnered a tremendous amount of respect over the centuries."

"I had no idea."

"He loved you, *chère*, that's for sure."

"He's not dead." Her intense scrutiny indicted him.

Ducking his head, he said, "Of course. I'm only saying that I can tell how he responds to your care. You're like the daughter he never had."

She sighed and pushed back the heavy fall of dark auburn hair. Odie caught himself before he reached out to do the same.

Ruth sighed again. "I knew logically that he'd be gone at some point in time. Didn't think it would be this soon, in this manner."

"As you said, he's not gone."

"I know enough about medicine to recognize a critical situation when I see it."

They sat for several hours, talking about nothing at times, sitting in silence at others. Occasionally, Ruth would go to Barnaby's room for a few minutes. Each time she returned, the circles beneath her eyes deepened. All of her pain manifested on her lovely face. There was nothing Odie could do but be present for her.

CHAPTER 12

"Ruth?"

A familiar baritone voice at the door of the waiting area drew her attention.

Never did she find herself so pleased to see such a meathead. Dante Blackstone entered the room, filling it with his presence. Even now, in his human state, he was still huge. He tempered his booming voice, but it nevertheless overwhelmed the space, causing others to look up.

"Hi, Dante." After giving him a quick hug, she peered around the room. Waiting family members glanced up at them. "Maybe we should go someplace else and talk?" This mountain of a blond man attracted attention wherever he went.

"Of course." He winked.

They filed out into an alcove at the end of the corridor and were met by Hannah, Dante's petite fiancée. When he stood behind the strawberry blond and folded her into his arms, the contrast between her fragile frame and Dante's big limbs reminded Ruth again how close to death Hannah had recently come. Behind her rectangular glasses, fatigue lined Hannah's gold-flecked, soulful brown eyes. Her cheeks remained too hollow, even a month recovered from her ordeal.

Nearby stood Peter, whom Ruth had met when he delivered medical supplies to save Hannah's life. The woman next to him must be Peter's wife, Allie. With her light brown hair pulled into a ponytail, nothing hid the glow of love for the infant sleeping in her arms.

Peter had done it. Broken the Indebted curse, found the love of his life, and created a family. An unheard of outcome for an Indebted. Previously unheard of, until Dante repeated the feat, that is.

Swift jealousy stabbed Ruth in the temple until she shoved a smile in place.

Decorum, like a suit of armor, encased her, insulated her.

"Thank you all for coming," Ruth said.

"Barnaby's important," Peter replied.

The lines on Peter's face and glints of gray in his dark, close-cropped hair testified to the fact that time had begun to pass for him now. Mortal now for over a year.

"Ruth, this is Allie and our daughter, Emma."

Although Peter was a calm, controlled man, his protective stance as he hovered behind his wife spoke volumes. Barnaby had hinted at some of the suffering Peter had endured to save Allie's life and transition himself to mortal. If the pride on his face as he gazed upon his baby girl served as indication, the struggle had been worth it.

Allie brushed strands of hair off her face without jostling the baby and glanced at Ruth. Allie's eyes were a rich emerald green but swirled with gold flecks. Somehow, her eyes seemed familiar. How strange.

Allie smiled. "How are you? I sent the bags of IV fluids and medications last month for Hannah, after the—her ... injuries. I heard you did a great job taking care of her."

Hannah nodded as Dante tucked her deeper under his corded arms. If his demeanor was any indication, he would never let her go. Who could blame him? The sweet woman had been close to death in a coma for more than a week after the attack by Jerahmeel's minion.

Dante *had* died to save Hannah's life. Those two had been willing to sacrifice everything for their love. His free hand cupped Hannah's cheek, as though he wanted to shield her. Obviously, their sacrifice had been worth the price.

Ruth's own cheeks heated. When she grasped Allie's outstretched hand, Allie recoiled as if she had been slapped. Alarmed, Ruth tried to pull away, but Allie held fast.

"Did I do something wrong?" Ruth asked, aghast.

Barnaby had mentioned that Allie could see death, an ability that had drawn far too much attention from Jerahmeel. That ability had almost gotten her killed. Of course it made sense that she sensed death within Ruth. Death was Ruth's specialty, after all.

In unspoken agreement, their companions formed a semicircle around the two of them, blocking them from view of any passersby.

Allie gripped her hand more firmly. "No. It's—this is so strange. Peter, please take Emma."

Once Emma was cradled protectively in her father's arms, Allie grasped both of Ruth's hands and gasped as her green gaze unfocused. An odd sensation filtered through Ruth's mind, similar to when she confirmed her kills by pushing into the criminals' minds. Intrigued, Ruth probed further, and Allie's mind seemed familiar, comfortable, like someone she'd known for years.

Which made no sense.

Connecting with Allie's mind was like having a phrase on the tip of the tongue, and Ruth couldn't quite find the words.

Ruth refused to delve deeper into Allie's consciousness. To do so would be intrusive, but her curiosity had been piqued. She gently withdrew from Allie's hands.

"What did you see?" Peter asked his wife, hovering next to her.

"What did *you* see?" Allie studied Ruth.

"I don't know," Ruth said. "But it felt ... comfortable."

"For me, too. So odd," Allie said.

"So, did you see Ruth's death?" Dante blurted out.

Peter glared at him, but the blond giant grinned sheepishly and stroked Hannah's shoulder-length hair. Such an odd couple, but somehow they fit each other perfectly.

Odie had remained a few paces back until Ruth motioned him forward, and he broke the awkward silence with a nod to the women.

"I'm Odie, an old friend of Barnaby's." He emphasized the "old," and everyone knew exactly what he meant. Old, old, like Peter and Dante had been. Like Ruth still was.

Beneath his short beard, Odie's lips curled upward. "You two codgers I know. How'd you two ugly mugs get such beautiful women?"

Dante and Peter grinned. Ruth sighed.

Allie tapped her chin. "Ruth, your mind feels a little like my sister's. It's strange, like I know you, even though we just met."

"I agree," Ruth said.

Allie glared at Dante. Turning back to Odie, she shrugged. "No offense, but I have this gift ..."

"Yes. Barnaby mentioned it," he said.

"Every time I touch an Indebted I see death. Because your job is, you know ..."

"Yes, we know." One side of Odie's mouth quirked and for a moment, he had the look of a boy in trouble, not a man who had been alive for hundreds of years. Even the wave of dark chestnut hair over his forehead gave him a youthful appearance.

"Well, we can explore what that was all about later." Allie commandeered her baby again.

Ruth turned toward Dante and Hannah. "It's good to see you again, both looking much better."

The lump in her throat hurt as she carefully put her arms around the frail woman who'd nearly died a month ago. On impulse, Ruth touched Hannah's face. With her mind still open from Allie, Ruth experienced another similar mental connection.

Hannah's mind felt like a comfortable pair of gloves.

"I thought your ability had short-circuited. Can you heal? Is that what I'm feeling?" Ruth asked.

"No, not since—"

Hannah's voice caught, and Dante glowered at Ruth.

"Back off, big guy, no one's hurting me." Hannah gave him an arch look, and the mighty Dante relaxed. "I can't heal anymore, Ruth, but I'll try again, if you want."

She closed her eyes, placed her hands directly over the remainder of Ruth's burns and, after a few seconds, cracked open one eye. Nothing happened. A red flush crept up Hannah's neck.

Ruth stepped back. "I'm sorry, I thought maybe it might have turned back on and that was what I felt."

"I'm not sorry," Dante interjected. "That healing stuff hurts her."

Ruth spied Odie rubbing his chin with a speculative set to his mouth, the appearance of a man working out a problem. The back of her head prickled.

She shook her head. "You're not all here to figure out my strange feelings, which are probably due to stress. Let me give you an update about Barnaby."

When she outlined the events leading up to finding Jerahmeel in the hotel room and Barnaby collapsed on the floor, Odie added a few details.

Silence followed the end of her story.

"So how is he doing now?" Peter asked, his mouth tense.

"Poorly. His heart has been damaged, from within. Jerahmeel did something to him, but it's not certain exactly what. Barnaby's been unconscious most of the last twelve hours."

"Can we see him?" Dante stepped forward, loosening his grip on Hannah.

"Yes, a few at a time," Ruth said.

"Why don't you take Dante and Peter back?" Allie offered. "I need to feed Emma before she wakes up starving again. I'll find a quiet spot and be back in a half hour."

"Are you sure that's a good idea?" Odie said. His grave voice commanded everyone's attention. "Jerahmeel may know that

Barnaby's here. If he finds us here, well, let's just say none of us are on his most-favorite list."

"I'm not letting you and Emma out of my sight." Peter's hands curled into fists.

"No, please, you should see your friend," Allie said.

"Why don't Hannah and I stay with you, Allie, if it wouldn't be too intrusive?" Odie said. "We'll get this hungry one fed and happy."

As if on cue, Emma squeaked and rooted around.

Peter handed Allie the diaper bag. "Stay close to Odie. Please."

"Ok, let's go find a nice place for a snack, then." Odie gently took the diaper bag and moved it to his own shoulder. Ruth's breath caught.

Odie, Hannah, and Allie strolled down the corridor. He towered over both the women and, by the way he scanned the hallway, was already taking his security job seriously.

Ruth sighed.

"You look like you could use a nap," Peter said.

"I don't need sleep. You know that."

"Need and want are two different things. Why don't we stay here at the hospital for a while and you take a break? You've been here since Barnaby was brought in."

"I don't know if it's safe for you to be here without protection," she said.

Dante bristled. "Number one, because we're mortal doesn't mean we're without skills. Number two, Odie has some colleagues lined up to help babysit us mere mortals. They should be here soon. Take advantage of the downtime. If anything changes, we'll call."

Peter nodded agreement. Funny. Here she was the indestructible one, and these mortals looked out for her well-being.

She had avoided exploring the full depth of the nightmare mess she was in with Jerahmeel and his lovesick fantasies. Better to leave it until later to think about that pile of manure. But soon, she'd have to reckon with him.

"Let's see Barnaby first, and we'll decide what to do later," she said.

In the ICU, a nurse ushered them into Barnaby's room. Over the past few hours, he had become a shadow of his former self, almost dissolving into the bedding. The two big men mirrored Ruth's sharp intake of air.

The men hovered near the bed, not moving, not saying a word, staring at the form lost in the sheets.

"You can talk to him. Even unconscious, he might enjoy hearing your voices," she whispered.

Peter tried first, placing his hand on Barnaby's upper arm.

"How's it going, old friend? You're looking a little rough." His voice broke. "Please get stronger, get better. I'd stab myself in the chest all over again, if it would make you get better."

"Ditto that, bro," Dante added.

A zing of realization ran through Ruth. "Hold it, you two. Is that the key to the Meaningful Kill? Take our own lives? Because if that's the case, I've been going about the task completely wrong."

The glance between the men could have frozen fire.

Dante shrugged and pointed. "You said it, bro."

"No. It's not that simple, and you know it." Peter rubbed his short hair. "The Meaningful Kill isn't the same for each person. Your solution may be different from ours."

"Yeah, how I did it was different from how Petey got his mortality."

"Maybe I should try it." She caught herself reaching for the knife.

"You can, but if you're wrong, all you'll do is draw Jerahmeel right to you."

"Damn it."

"You can say that again." Peter agreed, the corners of his mouth going white with tension.

"Can we maybe discuss this later?" Dante inclined his head toward Barnaby.

Heat flooded Ruth's face. How selfish could a person be?

Peter turned back to Barnaby and took the man's frail hand in his. "Where were we, my friend?"

"You were saying something stupid about stabbing yourself." Dante grinned.

"Ah, yes."

Dante pulled a stool up to the other side of the bed. "Barnaby, old man, you have to get better. What will I do without your advice? Just the other day, I was thinking, 'Man, I should call Barnaby for some help on an issue ...'"

Ruth stepped out and eased the door closed, giving the men time with their friend. No need to hog the time with Barnaby; she had sat with him as much as the staff would allow her since early this morning.

Maybe Peter was right. Maybe the journey out of this hellish existence required that each Indebted take a different path. If only she knew which way to go.

CHAPTER 13

Odie inhaled traces of mint and lavender as he handed Ruth out of his gray Audi coupe. Sunset brought a cool breeze that drew the scent of damp moss and dried leaves.

With the help of a few Indebted colleagues from Mobile and Memphis, Barnaby and their mortal friends would be watched over for the next few days. Odie's fellow Indebted had taken kills in their home territories before speeding down here, so hopefully Jerahmeel wouldn't know about the increased numbers of the Indebted in New Orleans.

When Odie had invited Ruth to his home, he didn't think she'd agree. But even an Indebted needed rest if he or she reached the limits of his or her emotional and physical strength. He could provide that rest for her. Watch over her.

Since when did he consider her to be something more than a pawn in his ultimate scheme?

He wasn't prepared to answer that question. Best to concentrate on driving the hour to his home.

After the first hundred years of toiling in New Orleans, he'd amassed enough money to purchase a large property. The rundown plantation had been abandoned after the Civil War, and he spent many years and thousands of dollars restoring the crumbling big house to its current beauty. The rows of live oaks lined the entrance to the home as he drove down the outside of the row around to the side of the house. Spanish moss drifted from branches in tangles, stirring in the slight breeze. A few prized pecan trees dotted the lawn, their branches spread wide and rounded.

Ridiculous as it might be, Odie hoped that Ruth would like his home. He refused to analyze why her opinion mattered. But it did.

When he pulled up to the entry porch and opened the door for Ruth, pride welled as he watched her eyes widen when she spotted the massive white columns and tall windows on both stories. Even in the waning light of dusk, his mansion had an imposing presence.

"You have a lovely home."

She walked up the front steps of the whitewashed plank porch, her heels punctuating each step with a solid tap.

"Let me."

He unlocked the front door, pushed it open, and preceded her to flip on the foyer and porch lights. When she gasped with that expression of wonder, the shadows of fatigue on her face faded.

That deep breath also enhanced the cleft between her breasts, as she still wore the black wrap top from last night. His mouth went dry. With effort, he dragged his gaze from that tempting valley.

Her lips formed a heavenly O shape. "This home is gorgeous. Look at the stairway curving up there. And the wood paneling on the walls must be original, right?"

"Yes, restored and varnished fresh. You know your plantation homes."

"Not particularly, but there were some estates and a few plantations in Maryland where I grew up. But they were nothing like this house. The architecture up north was much different. Here, it's grander, more open, more airy."

"Probably because it rarely gets below freezing here, unlike Maryland."

"Very possibly." She scanned the room from plaster ceiling to wood floor with an expression of awe.

Odie could easily spend a lifetime finding new ways to light up her face like that.

Ridiculous. He wanted help with his plan to get rid of Jerahmeel. If a taste of carnal pleasure came with the deal, more's the better.

Why did that conclusion leave a sour taste in his mouth? Why did the thought pinch something deep inside?

"Let me give you the tour."

"Do you give lots of tours?" Even when she sighed, gold glinted in her gaze.

He grinned. "Surprisingly, no."

Pink tinted her cheeks, and he had to make a conscious effort not to strut and preen.

He led the way past the grand foyer with its curved mahogany staircase. In the living room, leather and darker colors dominated the furniture and fixtures. Seeing the house through her eyes, it occurred to him that some lighter colors might improve the space. Maybe the house could benefit from a woman's touch.

He had been a bachelor for far too many years.

After strolling through the country kitchen, they entered the formal dining room. Despite the pecan wood table that gleamed beneath the grand glass chandelier, this room always felt cold.

"Use this room much?" she asked.

"I was just thinking that it doesn't get used at all. Too formal."

"You can tell a lot about people from which living spaces they enjoy the most."

He smiled. She had pegged him precisely, right in time to enter the library, the one area in which he found solace. Unfortunately, it also contained the computer that was running the genealogy program.

Odie's heart sped up as he saw lists of primary source documents on the screen.

She inhaled. "Smells nice in here. Old books. Furniture polish. I love it."

"It's my favorite room. But I've modernized it."

He gestured toward the carved wood light switches behind them to draw her attention, then flipped off the computer screen on the heavy oak desk.

"There's a bathroom with a shower on this floor. I mostly stay downstairs, since I converted this bedroom into my office. Upstairs are actual accommodations if you want to rest. In a real bedroom. Like a real person."

Her light chuckle lifted his soul like it had grown wings.

As they headed up the stairs, the view of her rounded derriere commanded his attention. The roll of her hips made his groin clench with desire. How he wanted to run his hands over those curves. *Mon dieu*, but he had been fighting the urge since the moment he had met the woman.

He pointed out the three bedrooms and a bathroom on the second floor, all with fresh bedding and linens at the ready.

"For a guy who lives alone and doesn't require sleep, you've certainly kept this house in guest-ready condition."

"Somehow it makes me feel ... human, if that makes sense?"

"It makes perfect sense."

"I even keep a few basic ingredients for cooking. You never know." He opened his arm up. "Please pick whichever room you'd prefer. I'll bring up the luggage."

Her faraway stare finally locked on to him. "Right. From the hotel."

"I'm not sure what's in which suitcase. We threw everything in together so quickly."

"Do I have to tip the valet?"

The moment those whiskey-gold and moss colored irises darkened with the double entendre was a piece of time Odie wanted to remember forever. This was the exact moment when he lost the ability to fight his desire. The exact moment when he no longer wanted her as a pawn or an accomplice. He wanted her as a desirable woman.

One taste and he would leave.

He closed the distance in one step and pulled her head forward to meet his lips in a crushing kiss so intense, his vision dimmed at the edges. Like fine ambrosia, she smelled delicious.

He tilted her face up to him, expecting her to pull back, to resist. The gods blessed him when she sighed and the corners of her lush mouth tilted upward. He rubbed his thumbs over her high cheekbones, her soft lips, and her porcelain neck.

Perhaps he could spare one more taste.

Unable to stop himself, he leaned forward again and brushed his lips over hers. The scent of his home with its wood paneling, the plaster walls and ceilings, the humid bayou air combined with lavender and her own exquisite fragrance.

Slanting his mouth, he roved over her lips, savoring them, nipping at them. When he plunged his hands into the silky fall of her dark auburn hair, he absorbed her answering groan with his mouth. He slid his hands down to settle at her waist. The heat where their bodies met could have burned the house down. An Indebted ran warm in general, hot when aroused, and Odie had no idea what happened if two aroused Indebted got together, but he was glad to have insurance against fire.

As he slid his tongue between her sweet lips, she yielded, sighing again as she opened to him. Desire clamped a vice around his ribs, and for a moment, he couldn't inhale. He braced his legs wider and drew her to him. The contact of her full breasts against his chest unlocked his lungs, and he sucked in her scent like a man surfacing from underwater.

A growl escaped him as he explored her with his tongue, loving her soft inner cheek, her pillowy lips. Their tongues tangled together, breaths mingled.

No longer tense, she now melted into him, sliding her hands over his shoulders. Her fingertips stroking the nape of his neck propelled him into orbit.

"*Mon dieu*, Ruth, you are like a fine wine. Like liquid velvet. So addicting."

Even though her strength matched his own, he easily walked her backward toward the nearest bed. He kissed her deeply, wanting to imprint her taste, the feel of her body against his, into his soul forever. Before he could reach for her, the buttons on his denim shirt all burst as she ripped open the clothing.

Her cheeks flared pink, but as she looked up at him from beneath her dark lashes, it was attraction, not embarrassment, that shone in those multicolored eyes. No, black eyes. Her irises had changed to the typical jet-black color of heightened emotion. Good.

"Oh, yes, *ma lionne*, my lioness, that's perfect."

She trailed her nails over his bare chest, and his hot rush of pleasure hardened him in a matter of seconds. Those sweet gasps near his ear didn't help, either. His jeans had become much too uncomfortable, too tight, and he needed to rectify the situation, fast. And if her frenzied hands told the truth, the feeling was mutual.

"What do you need, *ma chère*?"

"To feel normal. Make me forget what I am, what I've been through. Make me *feel*."

Flashes of his life—forced to spy on his own daughters because of the Indebted rules, hundreds of kills with the damned knife—flew through his mind. Normal. How many times had he wanted exactly what Ruth asked him?

"If that's what you want, I'll gladly provide it. And I'll never let you forget how sexy and beautiful you are."

"I need you. Now," she panted. Her beautiful lips, swollen from their kisses, parted as her dark stare searched him. *Oui*, the feeling was most definitely mutual.

"As you command."

When he gently pressed her against the side of the bed, she fell onto the mattress. With her arms spread out, she looked like an angel suspended in the clouds. He unclasped her black pants and slid them down with her panties, over the knife in the holster on her right leg.

The length of alabaster skin made his mouth water. The image of her half naked with her heels still on fired his desire. Raw need drove him like a horse being whipped into a galloping frenzy.

Now. He had to have her now.

He shoved his jeans and briefs down over his rock-hard erection without bothering to remove the clothing and pushed her knees up and outward. The view threatened his sanity, so temping was the pink skin revealed as she opened for him.

Standing at the edge of the bed, he tested her entrance, so moist and ready. As he teased her smooth nether lips, her little mewls of pleasure threatened to unravel his sanity. At the moment her fists began to rip the duvet fabric, he leaned back, a difficult task given that her strong legs urged him toward her.

Ah, yes, she was equally as unhuman as he. She had the same speed, the same strength. His match. But she was oh so feminine, so desirable. Unable to wait any longer, he drove his shaft into her softness, gritting his teeth as her inner muscles clenched around him.

Mon dieu, who had neglected to tell him that all Indebted muscles were stronger than normal? That would have been good information to know for the past 250 years. His cock had never been squeezed like this before.

He lifted her ample hips higher, palming the curves as if he'd never get enough in his hands. Seating himself more deeply inside of her, he tried to hold still and relax, to prolong the pleasure, but she grabbed his ruined denim shirt and yanked him toward her.

Relaxation be damned.

"Holy hell," she bit out.

That one phrase was all it took to obliterate his resolve to take things slowly. He pistoned hard into her heated sheath, wanting to be inside her body. Wanting to touch her soul. Odie had to brand her as his own, had to replace evil with pleasure, to moor her to this human world. He had to have her.

Not any woman. *This* woman.

His moans and her cries mixed in a crescendo of passion as he brought them to the peak together. He stroked her strong legs and thighs as his fast, pounding rhythm drove them both to the edge. They both came crashing down as her tight muscles held him while he spilled his sterile, Indebted seed inside of her. He rode her orgasm, teasing her to peak time and again as her pleasure continued. As he shifted, tiny aftershocks made her clench around him until he grew hard once more.

Drawing her legs over his shoulders, he leaned forward, pushed the hair off her face and kissed her deeply. Ready again, he moved his pelvis, seeking more release, and he shifted his stance to gain a better angle. The heels of her shoes bit into his back, sending him into orbit. With the indefatigable energy of his kind, Odie thrust into her again, this time with more deliberate intent. He rolled her hard nub with his thumb and finger as his erection slid in and out of her silky depths.

Against her lush body, he clung to what little control remained. He squeezed her buttocks, loving the voluptuous curves. Plunging deeper, he brought her to full fever again. She tossed her head back and bowed up to him as she ripped fabric from the duvet.

Snaking an arm beneath her, he kept her back arched and drove her further over the edge once more. She cried out, and he followed her over the precipice as their voices blended together.

Silence settled over their flushed bodies. Their breathing quickly returned to normal, another side effect of the unhuman state. She pushed her hair back off her forehead and smiled up at him. Having seen the satisfaction in her heavy-lidded, black gaze, he could now perish as a happy man.

Spent, he remained half crouched over her. Hell, his feet were still firmly planted on the floor. Unwilling to disrupt this perfect, crystalline moment, he held himself motionless, devouring the image of the sexy woman before him.

"Some valet service." She giggled.

"Consider your tip adequate, *madame*." He turned his head to one side and kissed a sleek calf.

She laughed again but watched him intently as he eased her legs to the bed and withdrew. Her inner muscles clenched, holding him inside. He groaned. How he wanted to stay here, like this, inside of this woman, loving her body.

She sighed and stretched, her full breasts straining against the dark wrap shirt she still wore. Bare from the waist down, her long legs splayed over the edge of the bed. Damn it, he should have done this differently, given her more than this centuries-starved half-clothed coupling. But he couldn't have slowed down if he wanted to, not with her beautiful body before him.

"*C'est magnifique*," he said as he fastened his jeans. He tugged the pieces of his shirt together then gave up and shrugged.

"Sorry about that. Hope it wasn't your favorite shirt." Her eyes had returned to the typical gold-flecked hazel, though they twinkled with mischief.

"It is now, *chère*."

She blushed as he helped her back into her pants, smoothing his hand and the fabric back up those shapely legs. He then pulled her to stand before him, rubbing his thumb over her hand, unwilling to cease contact.

"Why don't you relax, have a shower or bath if you'd like? I'll bring up the luggage, in truth this time. When you're finished, I'll see what's in the kitchen that might interest two unhumans."

"Sounds wonderful," she said, slowly withdrawing her hand.

Too wonderful. Too perfect. Damn this lovely interlude.

Cold lead settled in his gut. Soon, he'd have to convince her to join him, if they were going to destroy Jerahmeel.

CHAPTER 14

Odie's heavy footsteps paused outside of the bathroom. Ruth held her breath. Part of her hoped he would join her in the luxurious tub. Another part scolded her for the wonderful mistake it had been, having sex with him.

She sank to her chin in the steaming water in the clawfooted tub and blew out a full lungful of air. As she swiped the washcloth over her swollen skin, the rose-scented soap relaxed her while the rough fabric hit supercharged nerve endings. Blast it, she wanted him again. How was that possible?

Too bad they had zero future together. Just recognizing that truth cooled her desire faster than a bucket of ice cubes dumped into the bathwater.

Stark reality reared its ugly head. She could never put her trust in another man—not the way Odie probably wanted. Not the way Ruth needed. Until she could trust, she'd never consider any long-term relationship. What happened earlier this evening was simply a lapse in her otherwise solid, practical judgment.

What about their connection? They met on a level she'd never experienced before. That kind of intimacy couldn't be faked. Maybe he cared for her but couldn't commit. Maybe it had to do with his plan. God, had they made love as another of Odie's ploys to sway her to help with his scheme?

Not understanding Odie's true feelings created an emptiness inside her. Or was it her bleak future alone? She had no life, no purpose, outside of Barnaby. What could fill that hole? Or whom? She glanced at the closed bathroom door.

An eternity with a man like Odie?

Or even better, a mortal life with a man like Odie?

No. One roll in the bed did not an enduring relationship make.

God, what was wrong with her? Here she sat soaking in a tub, mooning over fabulous sex, while Barnaby languished in the hospital.

Barnaby. Her dear friend.

Eventually, he would depart from this Earth. If not now, then in a matter of years. Guilt assailed her like a slap to the face. Barnaby lay in an ICU bed while she rolled in the sheets with Odie. Some caregiver.

Thankfully, Barnaby wasn't alone. Friends surrounded him in his time of need.

A stab of jealousy and sadness made her wince. If she were in Barnaby's shoes, which friends would come see her?

No one. The theme of her entire life.

She hid behind the sex-on-a-stick costume that helped her score her kills.

She hid behind the prim and professional nurse uniform.

Where was the real Ruth?

Picking up a piece of her hair, she smelled residual sulfur.

Damn it.

Normally, washing her long hair made for a frustrating chore, but she had to eradicate all traces of that last encounter with Jerahmeel. Had to try to forget the hell that awaited her.

Dunking her head into the water, she enjoyed a moment of muffled, watery silence. Weightless for the smallest space of time, she pretended to have no stress, no need to kill, and no pressure to worry about Barnaby. Nothing but warmth and stillness.

The cooling water reminded her that the peace never lasted.

Once she finished rinsing her hair, Ruth stepped out of the tub, a towel wrapped around her head. Then she dried off with another plush towel. Such indulgence using two towels. No other guests apparently used them here, so she might as well take advantage. Opening the door, she peeked out into the hallway. The sounds of a television drifted up to her from the first floor.

She found her luggage in a well-appointed guest room that featured a beautiful oak sleigh bed with detailed scrolling at the head and foot. A dark blue duvet was folded back to reveal cornflower-blue sheets, fine Egyptian cotton if her fingers detected correctly, and down pillows. The enticement to get in the bed and rest was obvious. She would indulge in relaxation later this evening.

Pulling on khakis and a silky maroon shirt over her underwear and bra, she toweled her hair as best she could. It would take hours to dry, but at least she now smelled like flowers, not rotten eggs and suffering. Finally feeling, well, not actually human but the closest she could be, she girded herself to face Odie. She had to be honest with him and honest with herself; it was the right thing to do.

No more pretense, no more costumes, no more hiding.

It was time to share her carefully guarded story for the first time in forever. Even Barnaby didn't know all of the details of her shame and pain.

But Odie had been honest with her. She could do the same.

If only sharing her innermost pain didn't make her heart feel like a buggy wheel rolled right over it.

Alert to an intriguing aroma emanating from the first floor, her nose distracted her from the depressing thoughts. She strolled downstairs in bare feet as the scent of vanilla and strawberries drifted into the foyer. As she entered the kitchen, Odie plated what looked like crepes with strawberries and cream. After dusting the pastry with powdered sugar, he brushed off his hands, stiffened, and turned around. He had replaced the denim shirt she shredded with a snug, gray Henley. He left the top buttons undone, revealing a hint of pectoral muscle and a light dusting of dark hair – the image served as a cruel taunt to her resolve and equilibrium.

"You're a gourmet chef?" She forced her gaze to his face. The folded crepes with strawberries peeking out constituted a work of art.

"I dabble. If I have a good reason."

"When is that?"

"Never. Until now."

He brushed a thumb across his lower lip. That single tiny gesture set her ovaries on virtual fire. Damn. He was good.

"You have some powdered sugar on your face."

"What should we do about it?"

Ruth shocked herself by licking the spot of sugar from his cheek next to his nose. When she leaned back, he followed her. His pale green irises were turning black again.

"I should cook more often," he said.

"I agree. This smells delicious."

"That's not what I was talking about, *chère*."

She would not go back down this oh-so-tempting path. Not right now. Not with him. Although she didn't want to hurt him, she needed some emotional distance if she was going to get through her own story.

"I know." Taking a few steps back, she added, "So, um, can anyone have one of these treats?"

He blinked, like a sleepwalker waking up, and his pupils constricted back to normal size. Glass green colored the irises again. His lips thinned. Good. Message received.

"But of course, *madame*. If you'll allow me to part with formality, we can eat these on the front porch. I do love the night air and the quiet."

"Polite society would be scandalized by such barbaric behavior."

"You're exactly right. And that's why we're going to do it. Grab both of those plates along with the forks, please. I'll bring dessert wine."

They settled on the second to top step of his grand porch. Tree frogs chirped so loudly, it sounded like a crowd of people talking all at once, in a singsong rhythm. The cool, damp night air calmed Ruth as she inhaled the scent of soil and autumn leaves and sighed. Even a few stars were visible tonight, their tiny lights wavering in the humid atmosphere.

She cut into the still-steaming crepe and took a bite, savoring the sweet cream, the slightly tart strawberries, surrounded by the vanilla crepe.

"Amazing."

"Glad you like it." His fork glinted as he cut a piece of dough.

"Thank you for cooking. I know it's not your top priority."

"I'm glad I had a reason to cook." In the shadows, it was hard to make out the details of his face, but she felt him studying her nevertheless. Her mouth went dry.

"I should call and check on Barnaby," she said.

She jumped when he stilled her with a warm hand on her knee. Damn that reaction. And damn how his hand heated her entire leg.

"I called Peter while you were upstairs. Barnaby is unchanged. Peter and Dante are taking turns spending time with him. And two Indebted have joined them and are keeping tabs on both Barnaby and the mortals."

"They don't need me, then."

"Of course you're needed. But it's okay for you to rest as well. It's no use if you're constantly on vigil. You won't think as clearly if Barnaby needs you later."

"You're right." In the moonlit glow of the well-kept lawn, the grass and trees took on a grayish-blue color. "You've got quite a place here. Such a haven from the world. I remember nights similar to this, sitting on the porch, telling stories, and talking about all manner of things."

"What was your home like?"

"Before?"

"Yes."

"Do you know any of my past?"

He paused. "Only that you were a Civil War nurse from Maryland. Barnaby was very tight-lipped about your history. Said it was your story to tell, not his."

"Sounds like something Barnaby would say."

Barnaby would also tell her to let go and confide in someone.

Over the years, she had helped physicians cut men's legs off, nursed countless people through devastating illness, and killed on command. She was good at everything she did, professionally. But letting down her guard was the one thing she had never accomplished since she became Indebted.

Maybe Barnaby was telling her something, even now. A knot formed in her gut, but she pushed it down, hard. Maybe it was time to try to trust.

"I was born in 1834 in Rockville, Maryland." She began. "I had a typical life for someone with an upper-middle-class upbringing. I played with friends, received education on how to run a house, then attended finishing school in Baltimore to learn how to catch a husband and become a perfect wife and mother."

"You had mentioned your schooling before. Didn't you enjoy the course of study?" He took another bite of crepe, the vanilla aroma drifting around her in the still night air.

"Knowing what I do now? No. But that was the only option for women's education in those times."

"So was school successful? You found a husband, correct?"

It was impossible not to smile in response to his sheepish grin.

"See, now you're joshing. But yes, I did manage to snag quite the specimen: William Coe. William Coe the Third, no less. Most eligible bachelor in Rockville, Maryland. Oh, he was handsome enough, had a golden-brown moustache that made all the ladies swoon. He cut a fine figure in his evening best, too. But what attracted women, or more specifically their ambitious mothers, was his pedigree. Mr. Coe came from a long line of English aristocrats who settled in Baltimore. Despite having moved to this country, his family had the means to continue their high-class ways."

"You sound, how should I say, less than enamored of the lineage?"

"How should I say? I say that the man makes the man, not the money or the breeding. However, as luck would have it, William became infatuated with me during my debutante season. I was eighteen. He was twenty-four. My mother, who always had ambitions of higher status, loved the opportunity to have a descendant of an earl in the family. She jumped at the chance to essentially propel her daughter from landed gentry status to a member of the peerage. Figuratively speaking, of course. Even though it was America, the British Victorian influence remained strong in the upper classes."

"So did you love this man?"

She paused as emotions churned. In her own way, she had loved him. But with the distance of time, it was obvious that he didn't return the love. And the care she had for her husband had only gone so deep. "It was a favorable match."

"That wasn't my question." Odie pushed an errant piece of dark hair back off his forehead.

"I loved the idea of being in love. This was the first man who'd truly been in contention for marriage, and I had no comparison. All I saw was a debonair gentleman who lavished attention on me. With Mother's prompting, I encouraged him, and six months later, we were wed."

"And then?"

"Then nothing. We lived a harmonious, if not dull, society life together. I tried to be a loving, nurturing wife. It was my life's work at the time. Then we had two children, Charlotte and then William the Fourth."

"You and your husband must have been so proud."

Was that a hard tone underneath his words?

"I loved my son and daughter dearly, and they never wanted for anything. William looked at our children more as an outward demonstration of our satisfactory union and a continuation of his lineage."

"That sounds cold."

"It's practical. Based on the era, that sentiment fell well within society's expectations. So yes, he was distant but never unkind to the children."

"And to you?"

"After our son was born, he pulled away from me. My duty to produce male offspring had been completed, right? Of course, in my desire to please and be pleasing to him, I continued to try to love him. And I did love him, in a manner of speaking. But it's obvious now that was a waste of time. Wishful thinking."

"How do you know that?"

"I'll get to that part. The story gets interesting. No more 'poor rich girl' anymore."

He held his hands up. "I didn't say—"

"You didn't have to. I said it." A few steps below her, she crossed her ankles and peered up at the stars. "As the Civil War developed, Maryland mostly went north with the Union. Rockville split more evenly, and each family supported its side as best it could. William took a position of captain in the Army of the Potomac under General McClellan, a big honor. As a dutiful wife, I of course supported my husband wholeheartedly. He had to leave home often for trainings and later to attend strategy meetings. One day in September of 1862, he came home frothing about a campaign coming up soon. He was so excited that he'd lead his own company of the Maryland infantry in a key part of the battle.

I got wrapped up in his excitement and wanted to help in any way possible."

"September of 1862?"

"Antietam."

"Wasn't Antietam a bloody battle?"

"That's an understatement. After he went to war, I disobeyed his express wishes and followed."

"Let me guess. You were to stay home with the children?"

"Yes, but in my mind, that's what their grandmother was for. I had met a woman named Clara Barton a few days prior as she loaded up supplies to help with the wounded during the battle. Her passion and drive were contagious. Right then and there, I realized that she possessed what I was missing: a greater purpose, a mission."

Odie leaned forward, elbows resting on his knees. "What did your husband say when you left home?"

"Well, he didn't know at first. So the battle started. Clara and myself and a few other nurses operated out of a barn set apart from the main battlefield, but close enough that the cannonade and rifles hurt our ears. There's a legend that a bullet passed through Clara's sleeve and killed the man she was tending."

"Was it true?"

"I saw it with my own eyes. She was an amazing woman."

"Sounds like you both were amazing." His warm hand on her shoulder grounded her to the present, even while her memories placed her firmly on the battlefield in the past.

"I took direction well. There was no way I could decide what to do next without her guidance. So in the midst of battle, with all these casualties streaming in, all I could do was fix what could be treated and move on. The surgeons were sawing off limbs faster than I could prepare the men for amputation. The screams, the thick smell of blood, the foul stench of entrails, then later the almost-sweet odor indicating infection. Even now, I remember it like it happened yesterday.

"We worked the day of battle and into the night. The next day, there was a break in the battle, so any able-bodied soldiers cleared the battlefield, dragging in even more casualties. I went from one soldier to another, cataloging injuries, moving each man to the front or back of the surgeon's line, as the injury dictated."

"I can't imagine what that was like." His gaze never wavered from her face.

"Knowing what I do now about modern medicine, the treatment was beyond barbaric. But we did the best we could with what we had."

"How did your husband's company fare?"

Pulling her damp hair over one shoulder, she finger combed it as she stared into the darkness. "Depends on how you approach the question."

"I don't understand."

"Well, from the point of view of following orders, the company performed admirably. William's company held their line and pushed inward toward General Jackson's forces. But in terms of attrition, it was catastrophic. Half of the company was cut down in the field."

"What about your husband?"

"So, the day after battle, I happened upon a delirious soldier with blood-soaked bandages around his chest and belly. There was grime and gore everywhere. Even his trim moustache had been coated. It was William. I was so horrified, I actually vomited. He had that scent of death about him. You know the smell?"

"Of course, *chère*."

Shame coated her like tepid mud. "I'm sorry, I know you've faced death before, too."

"Yes, but this is your story." He placed her hand in his and squeezed gently.

"So when William woke up, his pain destroyed me. All I could think was that my husband lay dying. Who would support the children? Who would be my companion for the rest of my life? Despair is the best word to describe how I felt. No human should have to suffer the way he did. So I yelled out to the heavens, to the stars, the moon, for someone to help me save this man."

"And you got an answer."

"Of course. Jerahmeel. Like you, I simply signed on the dotted line."

"Did it work?" He rubbed the back of her hand with his thumb, the reassuring circles calming her.

She flicked her hair back over her shoulder and stared at him. "William walked out of that dirty field hospital two days later. The surgeon declared it a miracle that his belly wound had closed and sealed without so much as a hint of infection. My prayers had been answered, and William received an honorable discharge from the army."

"So he came home?"

"Yes, and for a week or so, things were perfect. He was a loving father and kind husband. Our life, far from the frontline of the war, rolled on in a perfectly calm manner."

"Until?"

"Until one day, I woke up with a knife attached to my leg and a hunger to kill like nothing I'd ever known before. I thought I was losing my mind. I tried to take the knife off, but the pull it had over me ... It was a part of me."

Odie nodded, a mere movement of shadow in the darkness.

"One day, Jerahmeel appeared again and gave me my marching orders, as it were. I found a criminal in Rockville and killed him, but an acquaintance nearly witnessed the kill." Reclaiming her hand, she dropped her face into her palms and scrubbed, as though she could erase the memory.

"No witnesses, that's the rule."

"I know. Believe me, I know. So every week or so after that, I took a trip to Washington or Baltimore to roam more freely with a larger selection of criminals and more places to keep a kill hidden."

"Wait. You returned home after each kill?"

With her chin resting on her hands, she looked up at him. "So I did two things I wasn't supposed to do. That's what drew Jerahmeel's attention."

"What?"

"I told my husband what had happened and what I was. And then I stayed with my family." Nausea speared through her again, like her transition to Indebted happened yesterday.

Even though Odie knew perfectly well what being an Indebted entailed, she still hated the crimes she had to commit in her new existence. Even speaking the words made her all the more ashamed.

When he rubbed his jaw, the scratching sound made her nerve endings tingle.

"That's bold," he said. "Jerahmeel forbade me to have further contact with my girls."

"That's what he told me, too, but I couldn't do that. I loved my children so dearly. For whatever reason, Jerahmeel made an exception for me to stay with my family. My freedom lasted about a year."

"Wow."

"Unfortunately for me, I believed in complete honesty with my husband. Little did I know that integrity was not his strongest character trait—not by a long shot. Neither was sobriety or fidelity."

"What?"

"I had wondered why William was so accepting of what I'd become, especially given the potential for my Indebted status to ruin his good society name. He encouraged me to take trips to feed the knife's needs. He supported my decision to travel some distance away from Rockville to obtain the kills, even take extra trips if needed. At the time, I thought he was simply helping me with the situation."

"But?"

The worst part of the tale by far, how her trust had been repaid by his cheating. She made a conscious effort to relax her jaw, so tightly did she clench down, almost to hold back her disgrace. But what's done had been done. Might as well share everything.

"But he was slaking his own personal desires while I was gone. Drunk more evenings than not. And enjoying his time with a childhood friend of mine, no less. He told her that I would be out of the picture soon and then he'd marry her."

The grind of Odie's voice contained his anger, but only just. "That must have devastated you."

Unshed tears burned as the memory played in her mind like it had happened yesterday. "I came home one day after a trip to Baltimore and found them together, one room above where my children were playing. I got very angry, angrier than I can remember ever being before."

What went unsaid was how her power had erupted at that very moment. The weird screaming whistle in her mind had threatened to split her head open, tried to rend the humanity from her soul. At that moment when she reached into William's mind and pulled out his carnal sins for examination, her terrible power had fully manifested.

She wasn't ready to share that piece with Odie, though.

"My yelling must have been impressive. The other woman fled, half-dressed. My children were crying. And William cut me to the bone. He told me I was no longer fit to be a mother, much less a wife, and I could never fulfill his needs. Because of the monster I'd become, he said I had to leave for the children's benefit and never contact them again."

"Horrible. Did he recognize the part about how he was the one committing adultery?"

"In his mind, it was but a logical step on his way to replacing me as his wife and securing a more suitable mother for his children."

"You sacrificed everything for him. *These were your children*," he whispered.

Her voice cracked, despite trying to maintain control. "Don't you think I know that? I lost everything. My mortality, my humanity, my soul. I became something I despised. A criminal. I became Death."

Fists formed at his sides. "And he repaid your sacrifice by throwing you away?"

"He threatened to tell everyone what I'd become and why I took trips to the bigger cities. Then he'd publicly divorce me."

"That's cold. What a bastard."

"Yes, but colder still was my death he faked after I left."

"You're kidding." The intensity in his shadowed stare made her insides clench.

"I wish it were a joke. I moved to Pennsylvania, started a new life, and entered nursing school. Months later, I discovered that he somehow got a body that looked like me, mutilated it, and publicly mourned the death of his beloved, precious wife. Complete with a lavish funeral, no expense spared. You know, the funeral seemed so silly. But what wasn't funny was how I never saw my children again."

"Do you know what became of them?"

"It was too painful to find out, so I buried them deep in my heart and then went on with my life, such as it was. Nursing school twenty or thirty times, trying to find a purpose for this hellish existence."

"Awful."

He smoothed a piece of her hair over her back. Whether her shudder came from the fragile trust growing or the frank catharsis that, after 150 years, she could finally tell her story, she didn't know. All she knew was, she needed to finish the hellish tale, get all of the hidden pain out.

"Each time I matriculated, I got split even further into two people: quiet and competent Nurse Ruth and the tempting seductress who killed evil people. Neither person was the real me, but both were necessary for my mental survival. I couldn't allow the real Ruth to be the killer. But I had needs beyond nursing that I refused to explore. So I got very good at hiding, pretending to be what people expected. Or didn't expect, as the case might be."

Odie lifted her hand and brushed his firm lips over the inside of her wrist. A sensation like a shiver wrapped in electricity shot up her arm and down her torso into her core.

"Well, now you know the sordid history."

"You're an amazing woman, mother, and wife."

The weight in her ribcage had disappeared. Although she hadn't cried, she was exhausted, as if she'd wept for weeks. Her head hurt at the memory of her children, but the weight that had been holding her down for hundreds of years had gone. Hope pushed up like a butterfly emerging from a too-long sleep in the cocoon.

She shook the torpid heaviness off her shoulders. The lightness felt like freedom and new life. She had crested a mountain and was peering down the other side. Her history created the person she was today, but her future lay at the foot of the precipice.

Where Odie waited for her.

Could she take the leap of faith with him?

Desire flared. Holy hell, she wanted him more than ever. She glanced sideways at him and licked her lips.

CHAPTER 15

That tongue darting over her lips was all it took to break his dam of restraint. Odie yanked her around the rest of the way to face him, kissing her deeply. He wanted to replace her pain with pleasure. He wanted to commune with her in a way that shared their pain of becoming Indebted and turned that torment into something good and pure.

On the steps of the porch, he poured out his own suffering, his own experiences, his sympathy for her sacrifice, into the kiss. It was meant to be a balm for her, but instead, every press of her lips against his soothed his own battered soul, piece by piece.

She ran her fingers through his hair and over his scalp, sending shock waves right to his groin. The scrape of her nails across his head sent his mind reeling. If she continued, his balls would explode, they were so tight right now.

Desperation drove his hands in a frantic need to touch every inch of her body. He wanted to draw her into himself, take away her pain. Wanted all of that and so much more.

"Ruth, I need you." *Mon dieu*, but his voice had gone ragged, like the words shredded his throat. "But I have no right to ask. After what you've shared with me and all you've been through."

"You have every right and even more reason." When she brushed her breasts against him, it took all his preternatural strength to keep from tearing her clothes to pieces.

"I want you. Here."

He waved a hand to encompass the dark porch, the quiet night, and the rows of trees and acres of land surrounding them. No one would see them, but he had to take Ruth here, exposed, outdoors, in any way he wanted. He wanted to strip away all of her costumes and free the true Ruth. He wanted to be equally as bared to her. No pretense, no roles to play. Just two people. No hiding.

Her breasts heaving, she focused on him for a full minute.

The definition of torture lived in those sixty seconds of silence.

Slowly, she pulled off her top, revealing ample breasts beneath a lacy bra. How could he have neglected this area earlier this evening?

Dropping kisses on the tops of her breasts, he smiled when a shudder passed through her. Excellent. He wanted her to know every bit of his hunger, his desire. He had waited hundreds of years for a woman like this; he was going to savor every inch of her body.

And he was going to enjoy her outside of the confines of polite society, outside of the structure of the house, outside of any pretense.

He pulled her forward by her waist, appreciating how her luscious hips flared below his hands. Sampling her body earlier today had not been enough. An appetizer, really.

When he unclasped the bra and drew it down her arms and away, the sight before him robbed him of speech. In the moonlight, her skin glowed. The darkness of her taut nipples contrasted beautifully with her creamy skin. Rapt, he drew his hand down her breasts, lifting each heavy globe and teasing the tips into hard pebbles until she groaned.

After unbuttoning her pants, he moved down two steps as he slowly removed the khakis. Slow torture indeed.

She lowered herself to sit on the top step, in all her nude glory, luminous in the moonlight. Glorious. Amazing.

"*Chère*, the porch. I don't want to hurt you."

"Will the wooden planks hurt you?"

"No."

The sweet sound of her breathy words caressed his ears. "Then they won't hurt me, either."

She sat forward, her dark nipples tempting him. He climbed the steps to better explore her full breasts. Each time he squeezed and licked, her back arched as a sigh passed through her mouth. An entire lifetime could be gladly spent, enticing those sounds from her lips.

When he trailed a hand over her curved abdomen and lower, he spread his fingers and caressed her curls. As he cupped her folds, she rocked against his hand. She reached for him, but he placed her hands at her sides, and she gripped the edge of the step.

He nudged her legs wide, so she sat, totally exposed, on the top step of his porch. "Stay in this position, *chère*. Please."

He scooted down several steps, not caring how the wood splinters dug into his knees. As he lifted his head up to meet her feminine lips, he inhaled the warm scent of her arousal. He slid his tongue up one side of her soft skin and down the other, then swirled around her nub, sucking until she began to shake.

When he gently nipped the sensitive folds, her hands clenched in his hair. His desire spiked. At some point, she'd given up holding on to the porch, and he didn't care one bit.

Lifting one hand, he parted her folds, exposing her heated core. Her salty taste went straight from his tongue to his hard erection, which strained for release.

As he licked back up to her nub, he slid two fingers inside. Her ragged cry of his name gave him endless satisfaction, and he curled his fingers back and forth while he flicked his tongue and sucked. She shook as her hips rocked against his mouth. She was perfect. Soft, strong, beautiful, tough, vulnerable, sexy. Perfect.

He pushed her until she came apart in his hands and shuddered time and again. The way her muscles clenched around his fingers made other areas of his anatomy jealous.

Time to rectify that situation.

• • •

Ruth knew she would never reach heaven, but if experiencing heaven came anywhere close to this pleasure, then she envied the angels. Odie making love to her on the front porch of his mansion in the clean night air was an act both primitive and beautiful. He had evoked emotions in her she had never thought existed, or at least believed buried forever.

As he twisted his fingers deep inside of her, another tremor passed through her, delicious and warm.

When she reached for him, he slipped out of her grasp and walked up to the main porch, leaving her reclining on the whitewashed wooden steps. She yearned to pull him back to her body. She wanted much more of this man.

"Come here. Please." His words, gravelly and sharp, weakened her knees.

She stood up, surprised that she wasn't shy before this fully clothed man. Even being out in the open didn't bother her. She wanted him to see all of her, wanted to give herself into his hands.

"You're beautiful," he said.

"And you're still dressed."

"I intend to correct my oversight immediately."

He stripped off his shirt, the muscles of his back rippling with the movement. She licked her lips, wanting to nip the skin over those muscles. When he peeled off his jeans, the knife in the sheath stood out dark against his lower leg. Pulling his briefs off, his erection sprung free, touching his belly, a drop glistening at the tip. Her nipples tightened.

"If you might indulge my whim?" he said in a hoarse whisper.

When he motioned toward the porch railing, Ruth hesitated. With caresses that reassured her and made her shiver, he gently turned her around. Placing her hands on the railing, he ran his hand down her back and over one buttock, moving her leg out to the side, avoiding the blade attached there. He did the same with the other leg until she bent forward at the waist, spread open for him. Aching for him to fill the space between her legs.

There was no fear, only trust that he wanted her. She held still as he stood behind her.

"*Magnifique*. You are the loveliest woman I have ever seen."

He stepped next to her, and she began to straighten back up.

"No, please, stay like you were. You are a feast for the senses."

He brushed her long hair over one shoulder, trailing his fingers over a collarbone, down her arm and back up again. When his hand drifted over her belly, the muscles there jumped at his touch. He skimmed over her inner leg, over the heat pouring from the apex of her thighs. Moving to the opposite side, he repeated his touches, drawing shudders from her. But at his encouragement, she held fast to the railing.

"Step back for me, *chère*. *Bon*. Now, legs wider, please."

As she did as he asked, her torso dipped to the level of the railing, her breasts tightened as her buttocks rotated upward. She was completely bared to him, quivering, hungry for his touch, trusting him to bring pleasure. He walked in a semicircle around her. A glance at his large, stiff erection had moisture pooling at the opening of her vagina, cooled by the night air.

Still, he didn't touch her.

Anticipation mounted until she couldn't think.

He finally touched her with the lightest stroke of one finger along her buttock, and she cried out. He continued down to her wetness and dipped a finger inside as she whimpered.

"*Mon ami*, you are glorious," he whispered. "I want to be inside of you. I want to make you scream. *Oui*?"

"Yes."

When he spread her buttocks up and out, exposing her even more, her breath came out in tiny gasps.

"Odie, please."

"Please what, *chère*?"

"Please. Holy hell. Please anything."

"As you wish."

He pressed against her with a harsh moan. The tip of his erection rested only an inch inside of her, tormenting both of them. She tried to lean back, but he held her still. He withdrew, and she clenched her hands around the railing. Suddenly, he filled her an inch more and then out. Each thrust faster and deeper than the last, he continued until he had almost filled her, but not quite.

"Oh God."

"*Chère*, I want you."

He withdrew once more, growled, and plunged in deep, stretching her. Over and over, he drove into her, thrusting harder and faster. His panting grunts encouraged her, and she met him each time. Widening her stance and rotating her hips up further, she seated him even more deeply within her hot core, nearly driving her mad with pleasure.

Still connected, he leaned forward and squeezed her breasts. "*Mon dieu*, you will be the death of me."

How could she not have known it could be like this, so vulnerable, so powerful, so connected? Even his strokes on her hair made her feel complete.

"Look at me, *chère*," he panted. "See what you have done."

She peered back over her shoulder. The image of his jaw set, teeth clenched together in ecstasy, neck muscles straining, pushed her over the edge. As she screamed her way over the brink of sanity, he gripped her hips with one hand and pinched her nipple with the other hand. He sped up his rhythm and drove in harder than was humanly possible. His deep, guttural groans matched her passion as he followed her to a peak, spilling his hot seed into her.

As she put her forehead down on the wooden railing to recover, he slid his hands down to her nub, bringing her to the brink of climax again.

"There is no rest for us. We are not human. I do not tire like other men. And I will never, ever tire of you."

With a roll of his pelvis, he started the hard, hot rhythm up again, bringing her to another crest and proving his point.

The porch rail splintered beneath her hands.

Chapter 16

Rolling over in the guest bed, a plush duvet tucked around her, Ruth shocked herself by yawning. Then she stretched.

Had she actually slept like a mortal?

Early morning light filtered through the lace curtains. She extended a hand over for Odie but found nothing but a cool indentation next to her.

Her night had not stopped at the magical lovemaking on the porch, but continued after he carried her up the curved foyer stairs to this room. Afterward, they made love in the clawfooted bathtub, spilling water over the top and not caring. Then they moved to the bed and slowly explored each other inch by inch. From her toes to her hair, she had been deliciously pleasured.

Sitting up, she surveyed the room. From lace window coverings to a floral patterned duvet, this was a room for a female. Interesting that he should keep a room like this. She spied her clothes lying on a nearby chair. They had been neatly folded. Warmth rushed over her face once more.

She cared for Odie, truly she did. But she couldn't trust herself to pick a good partner, no matter how wonderful the man and his sexual prowess.

Odie had torn down the first several walls she kept firmly in place. The woman in his arms at the end of the night, that was the closest Ruth had been to her true self since she was a wide-eyed eighteen-year-old in Rockville, those 150 some-odd years ago. Actually, no. That woman was the truest to her current self. The Ruth from Maryland in the Civil War? She was gone.

Without a barrier to hide behind, even her skin felt raw, scoured. Alive.

All these years, she had withdrawn into herself and shared little of her inner self with others. The nursing allowed her to care, but even so, compassion filtered through her carefully constructed emotional barriers. Even this long after William was dead, his reach beyond the grave still hurt her.

As she considered getting out of bed, the door eased open. Odie's dark, tousled hair bore sexy evidence of their passionate night together. His eyes danced.

But there was something more in his expression. A tension at the corners of his mouth. He was holding something back. Guarded.

Dread curdled in her gut.

"Good morning, sleepyhead. For a creature that doesn't need sleep, you sure pretend well." His pectoral muscles tightened under the gray Henley shirt in a way that made her mouth water.

"Resting felt wonderful."

He stood at the edge of the bed and wrapped his arms around her. With her face pressed to his corded chest, his warmth penetrated to her core, and his hands sent quivers of pleasure as he rubbed her bare back. His scratchy beard tickled her cheek.

"You feel wonderful," he said.

She smiled, but sensing reluctance in his touch, she couldn't meet his gaze.

When would he betray her?

Stupid question.

He pulled back and peered intently into her face. "What?"

"Nothing," she lied. "I should get up and moving. Can we go back to the hospital?"

He examined the bed covering. Like he was hiding something again. Damn.

"What is it?" she asked.

"Nothing. Sure. We can go back to the hospital." He paused, glanced at her face and then away. "I wanted to share some new information with you."

If someone dropped a pile of bricks into her gut, it wouldn't hurt as much as the sinking feeling when she looked at Odie. "All right."

"Would you tell me about your powers?" At her sharp intake of air, he held up his hands in defense. "The ones Barnaby mentioned yesterday."

After a long pause, she answered him. "Why do you want to know?"

"You're a little suspicious of everyone, aren't you?"

"Wouldn't you be?"

"Possibly. Depends on the situation."

He smiled in a convincing manner, raising his eyebrows to complete the effect.

She returned the smile, but stalled for time, frantically considering the implications of his knowing the details of her power. Would he tell others about her preternatural skill? She'd trusted him with the shame of her husband's rejection. Could she trust Odie with a secret even deeper?

"I would never betray you," he said, staring solemnly.

Tears pricked again.

She hoped like hell that Barnaby knew what he was doing when he dropped that massive hint.

Exhaling, she said, "Basically, I can see into people's minds."

"Like ESP? Telepathy? Can you tell what I'm thinking?"

She ticked off her fingers. "No, no, and not without concentrating." Could she tell him everything? Maybe not. "I can see people's memories."

"That's impressive. How long have you known about these powers?"

"I first discovered a hint of my power during Antietam when I was tending the wounded. Maybe the heightened emotional state triggered it. What I didn't tell you about my nursing work was that sometimes I looked at the memories of the men as they were dying. I'd send letters to their families, describing an image that I saw, and then write that the soldier had told me all about his wife, or children, or brothers and sisters."

"That must have given comfort to the grieving families."

The images of pain, love, betrayal from those soldiers overwhelmed her own memories. She'd had to pick and choose some of the descriptions. Sometimes the letter to the soldier's wife wasn't the letter to his love. Sometimes the last thoughts weren't kind at all. Had she been right to filter the images, to adjust them to give some thin consolation to the families?

"I hope so. It was the least I could do."

She scooted over and tucked the blanket under her arms, over her breasts. The bed sagged as Odie sat on the edge.

"I got better at reading the minds of patients so that I could tell them what they most wanted to hear. Or find out what they most wanted to hide." Rubbing goose bumps on her arms, she shuddered. "Later, I realized I could use my power to find out when people were lying."

Odie quirked an eyebrow. "So, have you read my mind?"

"Don't have to." She crossed her arms. "Seriously, I wouldn't. The power has to be intentionally activated, and I've learned over time that I truly don't want to know what people think about me ... or anything."

"You can't mean that."

"Oh, but I do. After the battle, the next time I consciously used my power was when I caught my husband cheating. That's when the power exploded into full force. I read him through and through and learned far too much about how he truly felt about me. I was but a producer of an heir to his line and a social figure to accompany him to events. That's all. Nothing. I was nothing."

Odie's warm hands enveloping hers fixed her in the here and now.

"That was one bad person. No one sees you like that at all today, I can promise."

"Of course they don't." She flinched as her cynical tone betrayed her. "I only use my power now to verify the crimes before I use the knife."

"That's convenient. Double-checking your kills."

"Convenient but sometimes gruesome."

"I can imagine. At least you know who you're killing and why."

"I try to use the power to pick the worst criminals in the hope it'll get me to the Meaningful Kill faster."

"Interesting."

"You know what was strange? I also got a weird wave of my power when I touched Allie. Might have to do with her own gift, somehow."

"Makes sense." He laced his fingers in hers.

"So why are you asking me about my power?" Her stomach clenched.

"Remember how Barnaby mentioned doing the genealogy search on you?"

"Vaguely."

"Well, I—"

His cell phone rang, the electronic sound slicing through the morning air, shattering the closeness. He released her hands to answer the phone.

After a moment, his brows drew together as his expression grew thunderous, furious.

"All right, we'll be right there." He thumbed off the phone and turned back to her, taking her hand in his and rubbing it against his rough cheek. "Barnaby's going."

"Going where?" she asked. Dumbly, the answer dawned on her.

He cupped her cheek and frowned, those green eyes soulful and sad. "He's passing away, *chère*. We need to be with him."

A black wave of fury smashed into her mind. For a moment, Ruth couldn't speak or move. Then adrenaline kicked in. She jumped out of bed and threw on her clothes.

"Let's go," she said.

Chapter 17

Odie got to the hospital in record time.

At the entrance to the ICU, they met a fellow Indebted, Javier. The swarthy man held Emma, murmuring to her in an old Spanish dialect while she cooed.

"How are you supposed to fight off All Who Is Evil with that baby in your arms?" Odie asked.

"Gene."

He pointed with his narrow chin about fifty feet down the hall where a thin, nondescript black man ostensibly read a magazine. At his name, the man looked up with a grin and nodded at Odie and Ruth.

"Fair enough. I take it everyone else is in with Barnaby?"

Javier nodded and bent his head to continue crooning to the baby.

The scent of death in Barnaby's room hung like heavy, thick cloth blanketing the room. Ruth had smelled it before—a sweaty, exhausted, ammonia tang.

A couple stood on each side of the bed, everyone's expressions stricken. Dante held Hannah in front of him, his great arms enveloping her tiny frame. Allie had tucked in next to Peter, her head resting on his shoulder. Of course, as a physician, she would understand best what was happening here.

"Has he woken up? Said anything?" Ruth asked the group.

They looked to Allie, who eased away from Peter.

"No, just some muttering a few hours ago. Nothing that we could understand."

Ruth's vision faded around the edges as a ringing in her ears squealed louder and louder until the sound pierced her head like a dagger.

Jerahmeel had mortally wounded Barnaby.

Her focus narrowed onto the shriveled figure on the bed. Barnaby. He was as close to a father as she'd had in ages. He loved her unconditionally, never judging who or what she was. Her head ached, and her ears rang.

Through the screaming whistle in her head, she heard Odie speak.

"Is he in any pain?"

"It doesn't appear that way," Allie replied. "But I can't know for certain."

"How long?" Ruth said.

Allie flicked a glance to the monitor. "Soon, I think, judging by the way his vital signs are fluctuating. I wish you all could talk with him one more time."

Peter and Dante looked at the floor while Hannah's sniffle punctuated the silence.

Helpless. Her friend, her mentor. Because of Jerahmeel.

Because of Ruth.

Holy hell, she was going to lose her only tether to the Earth. There would be nothing left.

Something shifted and grew inside of her mind. Like a caged raptor, restless, waiting to be released. Eager.

Terrible. Terrifying. A beast about to burst from confinement.

Her mind shifted, like throwing a vehicle from full throttle drive into reverse.

An idea occurred, right as her world dropped out from under her.

The shrill sound pierced her mind.

"We can talk with him," Ruth gasped.

Hannah winced and stared at Ruth.

Even the unflappable Dante's jaw dropped open.

"What?" Ruth asked.

Peter rubbed at his ears. "Ruth, your eyes. Hell, your voice."

"I don't understand."

Allie's face contorted as she doubled over. Peter held her upright with effort.

Ruth held her hand over her mouth. Somehow she was hurting these people. What in the blazes?

Odie's voice cut through the high-pitched sound burning its way through her skull.

"*Chére*." He grasped her by the upper arms and turned her to him.

Her vision blurred, but she clung to his solid form. Anything to regain control over what was happening in her mind.

"What?" she whispered.

Hannah and Allie cringed. Dante wrapped a hand around Hannah's head and actually growled.

"Your eyes have gone completely black," Odie said.

"That's normal. We get emotional."

At Allie's moan, Peter tucked her head into his shoulder.

Odie paled. "No, black-black. No whites at all. And when you speak, I hear it in my ears and also in my head. It hurts. How are you doing this?"

"I have no idea," she said.

Allie put a hand to her ear; Ruth wished she could reduce the mental volume, but had no idea how. She was barely clinging to sanity with all of the emotions banging around in her head. Her friend was dying. All because of Jerahmeel's sick fascination with Ruth. All because she failed to protect Barnaby. Her fault. The sound had increased to a train whistle. Her ears had to be bleeding by now.

"Turn so the nurses can't see you," Allie said between gritted teeth, glancing toward the central nursing station. "Try to control what you're projecting. Please."

Ruth swallowed and concentrated harder than she ever had in her life. Odie's warm hands on her arms grounded her.

With head-splitting effort, she pressed the swirling emotions and pain into a thin line. And she tethered it to her own consciousness.

"Better?" she asked.

Hannah nodded, but wore a confused expression behind her glasses.

"Let me talk to him," Ruth said.

She actually felt her voice rumbling in her ribcage. Deep. Strange. Amplified.

Allie and Peter stepped aside as Ruth leaned over Barnaby's inert form. She hadn't attempted this particular act since those men died at Antietam. Could she still reach into a dying mind? What would it cost her? Would it hurt him?

This experiment would be so much more than the recollection of memories. She wanted to commune with Barnaby one more time. Was such a thing possible?

Sure enough, placing her hands on the sides of his head, she sank into Barnaby's mind. Thick air surrounded her, making it hard to breathe. He was so tired. His mental curtains were much heavier than with other people, and he had so many layers of them. With sluggish effort, she kept pushing them to the sides until she reached the core of his mind.

All of the other sounds—that shrill scream in her head, the beeps of machines, the whining whoosh of the oxygen—faded into nothingness. Her focused spear propelled her right into the ember of Barnaby that remained.

One last sheer, light curtain, and a weak yellow glow greeted her mental self. She touched it with her mind.

"Hello, my dear." Barnaby's essence lapped over her like the gentle ocean waves, easing away her tension, reassuring her. She relaxed, drifting near the yellow glow. Until the undertones of what he was not saying got her attention.

"Oh God, you're dying."

"I've avoided death for hundreds of years. It's finally time, my dear." His hollow, floating voice came from the vicinity of the glowing light.

"What about those of us you leave behind?"

"I will regret not seeing your lovely face every day."

Her heart squeezed. "What will we do without you?"

"Take care of each other, of course."

"You're the only family I have, Barnaby. There's nothing else in this never-ending hell."

"That's where you're mistaken, my dear."

"I don't understand."

"You have more family than you know."

"That's not possible."

"Ruth, your legacy reaches far beyond your long-lived existence."

"I don't understand."

His quiet voice wavered as the wan yellow light flickered in the depths of his consciousness. "There's something special about you, your power. Jerahmeel is right to watch you and be very afraid. A similar power runs in your family."

"Family?"

"You have family in this room right now."

"Not friends. I mean true family."

"My dear, you're standing next to some of your progeny right now."

"I don't understand."

"Reach out your hands to Allie and Hannah."

Outside of her connected mind, her hands rose of their own volition until she had hold of the two women. Suddenly, they were there, in her mind, watching her interact with Barnaby as they floated behind her shoulder. Hannah's sprite-like, white energy contrasted with Allie's soothing golden-brown light. Ruth sensed the other two women could hear her voice and Barnaby's.

"How is this possible?" she asked.

"Your powers are so much more than you imagined. They've lain dormant all these years, buried deep inside, with the rest of you. Did you think you were the only one in your family with these gifts?"

"Allie and Hannah?" She felt the squeezes on her physical hands.

"They are but two of your lineage who share a measure of your gifts."

"Lineage?"

"Your daughter held the power and passed it along her line. To her however-many great grandchildren."

The brightness from Allie and Hannah flared. A sense of surprise and warmth glowed behind her.

"How do you know this?" she asked.

"You're not the only one with gifts, my dear. My power was a sort of amplified intuition. Kept me out of more scrapes than I can count."

"You've never told anyone?"

"And ruin the legend that is Barnaby? No thank you. Best to let everyone presume I was a smart and lucky guesser." His laugh drifted past her like dust in a wind, thin and fleeting.

"Why didn't you tell me that you'd figured out my powers?"

"You weren't ready to hear it."

True.

Refocusing on his fading yellow glow, she mentally reached for him but grasped air.

"Barnaby?"

"Your legacy was the last thing I wanted you to know. After so many years, I've now finished my work. I'm going to leave now, my dear. I'm so tired. It's finally time to rest."

The two women withdrew as one from Ruth's mind, leaving her with only the sense of Barnaby.

"Please. How do I keep them safe?"

The ember pulsed with his mental chuckle. "Ah, I thought you didn't have anything to bind you to the mortal world."

"There was no reason to care about anyone else before now."

"Remember, it's not even ... about Allie and Hannah. You have other family. It's time for you to fight for them and for yourself. If anyone could make it through the portals of Hell and destroy Jerahmeel, it's you and Odie."

"You can't be serious."

"It's the only way for everyone to be free. Eventually, Jerahmeel will learn of your extended family and come for them. As long as he exists, they are all at risk."

His mind's voice had faded to just a whisper. She had to strain to hear him.

"You can do this, my dear. Trust Odie. Use your powers on Jerahmeel. There are risks, but Odie has the right idea."

"I don't trust anyone."

"Maybe it's time for a change ... go ... protect your family." His voice was a tiny wisp of sound in her mind now. The golden glow faded to almost nothing. "I love you, my dear. If I could have had a daughter, she couldn't have been better ... than you."

The ember went black. Nothing met her but silence so complete it ached in her head. She searched for Barnaby, but the curtains were stiff, immobile. Nothing stirred.

How would she leave his mind? Which direction should she go?

The air in her lungs spilled out as she followed Barnaby into the silent darkness, falling into the deep well of nothingness.

"Ruth? Come back," Allie's voice pierced the silence. Distant. Fading, too.

The voice came from behind her. A direction.

Within the blackness of Barnaby's dead mind, Ruth turned around. Step by exhausting step, she pushed through the sludgy depths toward Allie, squeezed herself back into the real world.

The monitor droned a flat line. Barnaby's ribs no longer rose and fell.

Oxygen hissed into lifeless lungs.

Hannah sobbed into Dante's chest. The big man's eyes shone as he hugged her.

Peter pulled Allie into his arms.

The wry expression on Allie's face over her husband's shoulder caught Ruth off-guard. Her great-great-however-many granddaughter? Was it truly possible?

Ruth stepped back on shaky legs and abruptly stopped against Odie's hard body. He held her up by the upper arms, his warmth and strength flowing through her. "Trust Odie," Barnaby had said. A more difficult proposition than the old man realized.

Nurses bustled into the room, but Allie waved them off.

"Family?" Ruth tilted her head up and back, enjoying Odie's scratchy beard on her cheek.

"I tried to tell you this morning, but we were interrupted." He spoke next to her ear.

Hannah said, "Explains why we got that odd feeling when we saw each other yesterday. And explains the stories of strange family members generations back." She sniffed and motioned toward Allie. "You have weird people in your family? Cousins?"

"Nope, just me, at least as far as I know, but my folks weren't close to their extended family. You know, the first time I touched you a month or so ago, Hannah, there was something different, but I thought it was my death visions going haywire with the pregnancy hormones and all."

Hannah dug an elbow into Dante's ribs. "See, and I thought it was because I'd recently healed Mr. Indestructible here and my powers were still on the fritz."

"Well, now what?" Peter said. He kept one arm around Allie as if unwilling to let go.

Odie took a breath to speak. But before he opened his mouth, a visitor joined them.

"*Très triste*, so sad, our friend finally rests peacefully."

Jerahmeel. Invading the sanctity of Barnaby's final resting place.

Jerahmeel. The cause of Barnaby's death.

Rage built again, like an unending train whistle, and folded in on itself until the thick taste of fury filled her mind. The crescendo of sound focused into a spear of pain until it exploded.

"Get out!"

Everyone in the room recoiled as Ruth's voice split into two parts, the mental portion lancing into each person's consciousness. Even Jerahmeel startled and stepped back.

After recovering, he studied her as one corner of his lip curled. "That's a nice trick, *mademoiselle*. You'll have to show me how you do that. In private. Together. *Très interessant*. Who knew that by inflicting pain on those you love it would create new ... talents? I wonder if hurting others would bring out more of your gifts? Something to explore."

Ruth would have gone for his throat, but Odie kept a firm hold on her waist. His body had gone taut like a rubber band about to snap. If she were mortal, his grip would have hurt. Right now, it felt like kindred hatred barely held in check.

"Get. Out," Odie growled.

"From this gathering of friends for Barnaby's passing? Why, I wanted to give my last respects."

"You're not doing anything of the sort. Leave now," Odie repeated. Although his voice sounded flat and grim, his muscles quivered in hard tension.

"And what about my other friends?" Jerahmeel ignored Odie.

The sharp scent of sulfur invaded Ruth's nose as Jerahmeel seethed. All she wanted to do was kill this creature.

He pointed a perfectly manicured finger at each person in the room.

To Dante: "You're a traitor."

Hannah. "You're worthless."

He pinned Peter with a black glare. "You shouldn't even be alive."

"And my dear, you've broken your promise never to use your power again." Allie recoiled as Peter stepped in front of her.

Never had Ruth been so furious, so powerless, to act.

"Well, then. I will be on my way. For now. I expect to see you," he pointed at Ruth, "very soon. There's nothing holding you here anymore."

"You killed him," she whispered.

"No, I only hastened his anticipated *dénouement*. And remember, I didn't touch him. Rules, I have to stick with the rules." His laugh scraped her ears like nails on a chalkboard. "Ahem. *Pardonnez moi*. I will be leaving."

Another steam of sulfur, and he disappeared. They all stood in stunned silence until Allie grabbed Peter's arm.

"Emma!"

"Hell."

CHAPTER 18

Allie and Peter dashed out of the room, Ruth and the others following closely behind. At the end of the corridor, a stiff and wide-eyed Javier clutched at Emma while he stared down a looming Jerahmeel. The baby whimpered. Gene hovered nearby with an expression of horror.

"Oh, what a precious little one," Jerahmeel said, reaching for the baby.

"No!" Allie dashed forward and grabbed Emma, cradling her daughter to her shoulder.

"No?" Jerahmeel seethed. "You, a mortal, said no to me?"

Smoke rose from his fingertips.

Holy hell.

Ruth felt a surge in her mind like nothing she had ever experienced before. Superimposed on the image of Emma were the faces of her own children as precious infants. She would be damned if he hurt that baby.

As Jerahmeel pointed toward Allie, the woman flinched, still clutching Emma.

Allie's pain echoed in Ruth's own mind. Jerahmeel was burning into Allie's head, but without touching her, damn it. The terror on her friends' faces chilled her blood as each person froze in place.

Desperate to stop the pain, Ruth stepped forward, touched Allie's arm, and entered the woman's mind. There, she found it, a red-hot drill of smoking light destroying Allie's consciousness. Instead of digging deeper like she typically did, Ruth's mental presence shifted sideways and hovered in front of Jerahmeel's piercing attack.

Like a diffusing screen, her power scattered the pain across her mental shield and away. Dimly, she recognized that she had never done anything like this before. The last two times her power had jumped up several notches had been with extreme emotional stress. Could that be what truly triggered the evolution of her power?

No matter, she would hold the shield here as long as it took to dissuade Jerahmeel. If what the Cajun said was correct, Jerahmeel simply showing up here had to have taken an immense expenditure of his power, to say nothing of him using that power to harm others. So, if Ruth could hold on long enough, Jerahmeel should have to stop and regroup. But how long could she endure the fiery onslaught?

God, it hurt as her mental shields heated up, protecting Allie.

Holding still while standing in a blast furnace wouldn't hurt this much.

"*Merde*, this is shit."

Like a vacuum sucking out oven-hot air, he withdrew, leaving Ruth hovering in front of Allie's mind. Then Ruth slipped out, a pounding headache all that remained of her efforts.

"Baby!" Peter said sharply to Javier.

The Spaniard grabbed Emma as Allie's knees gave out on her. Peter helped his wife to the ground.

Odie stepped forward, a look of rage so intense it bordered on deadly. He went toe to toe with Jerahmeel, a dreadful mistake, poking the not-so-sleeping bear.

"I believe I asked you to leave." God bless his courage, but he was foolish. And so brave.

"Don't think I will forget this," Jerahmeel snarled. "Consider yourselves all marked." He grinned at Ruth. "And you, *mon chèri*, are mine. Don't take too long to come to me, or others will suffer."

She staggered a step backward. Hanging out with the Lord of Evil was the last thing in anyone's best interest.

He disappeared, slowly this time. Not the crisp entrance and exit he normally demonstrated.

How much had the attack on Allie cost him? As if to answer, the hunger to kill started up again, almost as soon as he was gone.

"You feel it?" Odie asked.

"Need to kill," she gasped.

Javier and Gene nodded. Already, they searched the hallways for prey. Anything to slake the intense need.

"Is Allie okay?" Ruth said.

Peter helped Allie to stand.

"Emma?" She wheezed and rubbed her temples.

"She's fine, *señora*."

Javier returned the baby to Allie's arms, but he hovered nearby, keeping watch over the cooing bundle. Remaining on guard duty. Odie had picked good fellow Indebted for this assignment.

"This madness has to stop," Ruth said.

"How?" Peter said, his voice hoarse.

"Give him what he wants."

"Absolutely not." Odie grabbed her by the upper arm and shook her. "You don't know what you're offering."

"Well this"—she swept her other arm out to the group of people—"is no option. Should we wait for him to come back? And then what? You think he has pleasant plans for them?"

"So, let's say you give him what he wants. What's to say he won't hurt everyone, anyway?"

God, Odie was right. She had zero guarantee that Jerahmeel would leave her family alone, even if she sacrificed herself.

"What if we did what I originally suggested? What if we went to his lair?" Odie said.

"How will that help?"

"He's weak right now."

"Not after we all kill in the next few hours." She peered out the window into the street, looking for a criminal to feed the knife.

"What if all of us didn't kill?" He pulled her focus back to his earnest face.

"What are you talking about?"

"What if we kept him weak, off-balance, long enough to get into his lair?"

"And then?"

He pressed his mouth into a grim line. "I'll think of something."

"You'll think of something? That's a horrible plan."

"You have a better idea?"

"What if I can get into his mind enough to confuse him or distract him?"

"Could work ..." Odie rubbed his chin.

"*Amigo*, if you do this, we should hurry," said Javier. Already, he and Gene were looking at the exit, right hands stretched down toward their knives.

"I agree. We need to call all the Indebted and tell them to hold out for as long as possible. No kills for at least two days." Odie thumbed on his cell phone. "I downloaded most of the numbers last night. How about you two?" He glanced at Peter and Dante.

"Between the two of us, we'll call anyone in North America, if Javier and Gene can call those outside the continent. How does that sound?" Dante said.

Peter darted a quick nod, still focused on his wife and baby.

"Excellent," Odie said.

Ruth turned back to Allie.

"Are you sure you're all right?"

"Fine now." White lines tensed Allie's shining eyes.

Ruth gazed down at the child in Allie's arms. Emma made smacking noises with her perfect bowed mouth and nuzzled into her mother.

Intercepting a glance between Peter and Allie, Ruth saw a shocking depth of despair. Their expressions, sad and resigned, suggested they didn't believe they'd survive. Fear for their daughter etched pain across their faces.

Dante and Hannah murmured in a corner to each other. By the Swede's wide, tense stance, he would protect her with his last drop of blood. But the normally unshakable man had a furrowed brow that belied his usual brash confidence. He was scared. These mortals could never run far enough. Jerahmeel would eventually find all of them.

This family—her family actually—was in danger. Helpless, they had no way to fight Jerahmeel. Helpless, like Odie's sick children, like those men dying in the Civil War.

But Ruth was not helpless. She had something to give. The years of acting, hiding her true self, using her power, could be the key. Maybe she could use her gifts to fool Jerahmeel. All she needed was one chance.

Ruth turned to the two Indebted, both on their phones already. "Javier. Gene. Can you keep them safe?"

"Until we have to kill, *señora*. But one of us can keep watch at all times. We'll hold out as long as possible." Javier sketched a light bow.

"Good. Odie, let's go. We need to make plans."

His lips pressed into a grim smile, but no happiness reached his eyes. "That's my girl."

Hannah came up and gave her a quick hug. "Come back to us, please. I only just met my multiple-great grandmother."

"Thank you, Nurse Ratched, for trying to help," Dante said, his voice rough.

Peter cleared his throat. "Be safe. For us."

Allie lifted up her baby. Ruth dropped a light kiss on Emma's smooth forehead, inhaling the clean baby scent. The smell of possibilities, of life. Blinking hard, Ruth turned to a silent Odie. The stark, desperate expression on his handsome face frightened her.

As they hurried toward the parking garage, she stopped short.

"Family? You knew? That would have been good information to have."

"You would have known if you'd kept up with your genealogy. The power comes down from your daughter's lineage. There are letters and notes describing unexplained powers in that line."

"So it's from Charlotte?"

"Yes, both Allie and Hannah are descended from your daughter."

"What about William's line?"

He took her hand in his. "He had no offspring."

"Why not?"

Her heart thumped. Ridiculous to be so concerned; he had died over a hundred years ago.

"Mumps in his teenage years rendered him sterile. He married but never had children of his own."

"That's too bad."

"I feel bad for your son, but not for your husband. All he wanted was to continue the male line, and it stopped with your son. Quite the comeuppance for a man as shallow as your husband." He stopped himself. "My apologies, I shouldn't talk poorly about your former spouse. It's not my place."

"But you're correct. He was a real horse's patootie."

He brushed a kiss over her lips. "So?"

"Sounds like we're going to the gates of hell."

Chapter 19

On the flight to Portland, Odie kept reviewing and discarding plans to destroy Jerahmeel. Guns and grenades wouldn't work. Destroying the lair itself wouldn't work. Coercion wouldn't work.

The only option? Going right into the lair and annihilating him directly.

Ruth's job: get Jerahmeel to take her to the lair, deplete his energy, and keep him distracted by whatever means necessary until Odie arrived. The "whatever means necessary" part had Odie worried. But Ruth had refused to back out of the plan.

Odie's job: find the lair, ensure Ruth's safety, and deal Jerahmeel a death blow. Somehow. The research suggested that Jerahmeel could be killed with a thrust of an Indebted blade into his heart, so that was their plan. Then, Odie had to get Ruth and himself out of the lair, alive. Unfortunately, he had zero idea of what to expect in the den of hell.

What had he gotten them into? His plan had an excellent chance of one or both of them dying. Or more likely, in Ruth's case, Jerahmeel could enslave her forever, force her to stay with him by using the threat of harm to her family. She would exist as the gruesome creature's plaything.

Jerahmeel could also go right ahead and destroy Ruth's family and be done with it. The remaining Indebted would be forced to kill even more frequently to maintain Jerahmeel's energy supply.

So many innocent lives were at stake. So much opportunity for failure.

And the plan involved Ruth acting as bait. Even in Jerahmeel's weakened state, he would still be able to maim, torture, and destroy anyone to get what he wanted. If he attacked Odie, fine, Odie expected to be punished for eternity.

But if Jerahmeel focused his fury on Ruth? Odie rubbed his chest to relieve the pressure built up there at the thought of her smooth skin torn into shreds. She'd heal quickly, only to endure even more torment. Jerahmeel was a sick enough creature that he wouldn't destroy her quickly, but drag out her pain until the end of all time.

Their plan hinged on Jerahmeel's obsession with Ruth and Odie's ability to predict Jerahmeel's behavior. Bad odds.

As they drove from the private airstrip in Portland to Barnaby's home overlooking the Columbia River, Odie's mind churned. The ponderosa pines shushing in the breeze should have relaxed him. This trip to Barnaby's immaculate Tudor mansion should have been a homecoming of sorts for Ruth.

Instead, the act of opening the heavy wood door unleashed a firestorm of emotion. They were about to spring the trap.

How could he ask her to climb into the devil's den?

Odie wanted only to destroy Jerahmeel and exact retribution for his daughters. He had what he wanted—a partner in the plan and a sexy romp in the sheets. Exactly what he wanted, right?

At what point had she become more to him?

The moment he had first met her.

Oh, no. He wouldn't name that emotion, but his feelings for Ruth made him want to lock her safely away and insist she didn't partake in this dangerous plan.

Odie's plan hinged on timing and luck. Could he fulfill his promise to send her into the pit of hell and then get her out again? He had no guarantees, just centuries of research and a dogged determination to succeed.

It might not be enough.

Jerahmeel was currently weak, though, creating a slim window of opportunity. Odie and his friends had contacted every Indebted they knew; fewer than 100 of them existed now. Each man and woman had pledged to hold out against the urge to kill as long as possible.

But time was running out. They had twelve hours, tops, before an Indebted caved and killed—and Jerahmeel's power surged.

In Barnaby's empty house, all the etched glass, fine furniture, and rare decorations couldn't distract from the fact that the heart and soul of this house no longer lived here. The rich wood and tile floors echoed with a stillness that felt more pensive than peaceful.

Odie found himself yearning for his plantation home in Louisiana. At least the crickets and tree frogs broke up the silence there.

Ruth left him in the sunroom while she changed into an outfit that Odie recommended. She returned in a flowing white skirt and blouse, a departure from the black leather hunting gear and her conservative khaki ensemble. Impractical ballet flats and cascading deep auburn curls completed the picture of innocence and sweetness. The image she presented stole the air from him, she was so impossibly beautiful.

Another costume? Or the real Ruth?

He swallowed the lump in his throat. "Wow."

"Will this do?"

"If Jerahmeel desired you in your plain work clothes, he'll be powerless to resist you looking like this. I almost can't resist."

Her cheeks flushed. "Let's hope he agrees. So when do I need to contact him?"

It should take a little over an hour for Odie to fly to the airstrip in Yreka, California. Thankfully, the pilot from New Orleans remained on standby, ready to leave at a moment's notice. Once in Yreka, he would have to get a loaner car and drive to Mount Shasta.

"Give me two hours to be on my way. Then do whatever you need to do to get Jerahmeel's attention. It'll take a large amount of his power for him to come get you and then transport you somewhere. But he's so proud and he wants you so badly, he'll do it, if only to prove that he can." Simply saying those words put a foul taste in his mouth. "In all my research, the two closest options are Mount Rainer and Shasta, with the consensus that the main vortex is Mount Shasta."

"So I could be going somewhere completely different?"

"It's possible but less likely. If that happens, you'll have to stall until I get it right. I am making my best educated guess."

"How long would I have to stall if you're wrong?"

"Too long for the plan to work. Days."

The gold in her eyes dulled as her shoulders slumped.

She brushed a piece of hair back. "What's he going to do once he has me?"

"I can't say. You'll have to improvise. Maybe use your power to manipulate his mind?"

"So do something I've never done before."

"Basically."

"Will it work?"

"No idea."

"You have such confidence." Her sarcasm made him wince.

"I'm confident that you and I can do this." He projected much more positivity than he felt. All he had was an insane idea and a brash attitude. Nothing more.

But there was no other option, so for now he'd fake his belief in the plan. As long as Ruth believed him, then she'd play her part. Odie prayed he could manage the rest.

"Sounds terrifying."

"If it's any consolation, he has very little reason to kill you." He caressed her cheek as her irises briefly darkened.

"Yeah, but every reason to want to kill other people."

"True. But Javier and Gene will do their best to stay with your family."

"Didn't slow Jerahmeel down earlier today."

"No, but we have to hope it will be enough."

"We have to hope *I'll* be enough." The sadness etched on her face spoke volumes about the pain inside of her.

"You'll do fine. I'll be right behind you, I promise. It's 12:30 p.m., so start making a ruckus at 2:00. Actually, make it 2:30. I have to purchase a few items to climb up the mountain when I get to Mount Shasta."

"I'm getting abducted by the Lord of Hell, and you're going shopping?"

He caressed her cheek, wanting to touch every inch of her skin. "It's not like that, *chère*. The supplies will help us survive in the lair, and more importantly, when we leave it."

"*If* we leave."

"We will, I give you my word." He wanted nothing more than to prove himself worthy to her.

The corners of her full lips turned downward. "You'll forgive me if I don't believe you. But I'll do this for Hannah and Allie and their families. They don't deserve to suffer at Jerahmeel's hands. No one does."

In response to her shining eyes, he pulled her into his arms, kissing her so hard, their teeth met. He buried his hands in the heavy fall of her hair, holding her flush against him. They were out of options, but still he wished there was something he could do to keep from sending this woman into the house of Satan.

She pulled back and laced her arms around his neck. "Can you do one thing for me?"

"Anything, *chère*." Resisting her soft lips became easier when faced with her steady, serious expression.

"If I don't come back—"

"Don't talk like that." Dread churned, slow and steady, like making hellish butter in his gut.

The corners of her mouth turned up. "If I don't come back, I want you to do something for me." She stepped back and took his hands. "Make sure Allie and Hannah and their families are taken care of, both physically and financially. They need to be safe. They deserve normal lives."

The reality of what he had asked Ruth to do finally hit him. He was sending her into the lion's den with only a promise that he would try to rescue her.

But despite the danger, her only thought was for the family she found out about only today. Love and loss flowed beneath her cool exterior. She had sacrificed for her husband and children years ago, and this amazing woman was willing to do it all over again. Because Odie had asked it of her. Because she wanted to keep her family safe.

Would any of his ancestors care if he died? All his talk of tracking down his progeny and helping them, and for what?

What connection had he truly forged with his family?

In twenty-four hours, this woman had gone from isolated and adrift to steely determination and sacrifice.

What had he done?

"If our plan doesn't work, I'll make sure your family is safe. But first, I will move mountains if necessary to get to you."

She ducked her head, and his heart twisted in response. That unnamed emotion reared up inside of Odie.

"Hopefully it won't come to moving mountains." Her lips thinned. She looked everywhere but at him.

"I will come for you, *chère*. I promise."

"I'll hold you to that promise. Now get going, time's a wasting."

She turned as he left, but not before he glimpsed the shimmer in her eyes.

CHAPTER 20

This house seemed so ... wrong ... without Barnaby. Ruth paced up and down the main hallway hundreds of times, checking her watch on every turn.

Seconds crawled by, each one *tocked* by the old grandfather clock at the end of the hallway.

The swish of her skirts and the scuff of her shoes were the only other sounds in the empty house as she turned and continued to walk.

Too much time to think. The heavy sadness weighted her limbs. Barnaby was gone. A sigh turned into a sob. She didn't have enough time with him.

Time. Too much after 150 years, and yet not enough.

And now? Not enough time to prepare for what awaited her in Jerahmeel's lair where she might have to use her power in a completely new way.

That damned power. Why had she not noticed any odd power sensations as she tended Hannah after she'd nearly died? No idea. Maybe it was because Hannah had been in a coma. Maybe Ruth's emotional state had not been heightened at that time, unlike in New Orleans. If someone or something threatened those she cared about, or her emotions got the best of her, those were the times the powers flared. Just like her powers changed with the men dying in the war, and when her husband cheated, and in the last two days with Barnaby's death and Jerahmeel's appearance.

Prior to Barnaby falling prey to Jerahmeel, Ruth had to consciously work to enter anyone's mind. Since then, the power had expanded and become more instinctive, more defensive and more protective. Maybe her gift would calm down after all this was over.

If she survived. If Jerahmeel could be destroyed.

If.

She had walked away from her family in Maryland so many years ago. Never looked back, never put up a fight. Maybe she should've watched over her children, like Odie did with his own descendants. If she survived this ordeal, perhaps she could spend some time with her new family. Her next job might be as a real-life fairy godmother to randomly help her progeny when things got tough. Now that was a pastime that interested her.

If she survived.

How things had changed in the space of a day.

What about Odie? She couldn't deny their connection, but she suspected his ulterior motives. He'd gotten precisely what he wanted: a partner in the plan to destroy Jerahmeel. Certainly, he hadn't caused Barnaby's death, but the timing of Odie's plan, Barnaby's decline, the steamy sex, discovering her lineage—it all seemed too coincidental.

Had he used her?

Images rose before her: her children's smiles, Emma's sweet face, and the horror written on Hannah and Allie's expressions. The decision settled on her like a yoke, and she adjusted her mind to support the extra weight.

Used or not, she'd try to carry out her mission, if only to give her family a chance to survive.

Two thirty. The time for planning and second-guessing had passed.

She squared her shoulders and forced her pounding heart to calm down. Damn, how her hands shook as she arranged her hair in the hall mirror. This might be her last acting job. How would she pull it off?

How could she not?

No more delays.

Then she started yelling. "Jerahmeel! I'm ready for you, My Lord Jerahmeel. Come and get me."

Nothing.

She repeated herself until she was hoarse. No response.

What if Jerahmeel didn't even show up? Odie hadn't entered that possibility into the equation.

And Odie was headed right into Jerahmeel's lair, regardless of whether or not she was there. He would be walking directly into his destruction.

Jerahmeel would still kill all the mortals she cared for.

What if Odie didn't make it to the lair in time? She'd looked up the weather for Mount Shasta, and the forecasters predicted storms on the mountain. How would that change Odie's timing? Could he even get to her?

No time to dwell on what ifs. The plan was already in motion.

Holy hell. Time to take this up a notch. She had to get Jerahmeel's attention.

How did Jerahmeel track her all these years? The knife. If blood flowed into her knife, Jerahmeel arrived. So knife it would be.

Simple enough.

She stepped into the powder room, put her foot on the toilet seat, and pulled the knife free of the holster. Damn, the urge to kill ratcheted up ten times as the naked blade glowed its eerie neon green color. For several long moments, she stared at it, torn between signaling Jerahmeel and heading into downtown Portland to find an adequate kill.

By sheer force of will, she stayed put, bared her arm over the sink, and pulled the knife across her skin. The red blood bloomed from the line of the cut and the knife drank its fill. Unfortunately, the blade found no satisfaction if she provided her own blood. Not only did her hunger to kill not abate, it rose another few notches.

Even as she pressed the razor-sharp edge against her open skin, the wound began to heal, typical for an Indebted. Though the injury hurt like a beast, the gash had already closed. If this injury didn't draw him out of hiding, she'd have to cut again, not something she eagerly anticipated.

Volcanic sulfur odor wafted over her.

Her heart thudded.

Jerahmeel's ash-colored face appeared outside the open bathroom door. He sagged against the doorframe. Her stomach twisted.

"*Mon ami*, you are delectable. I am without words."

She had a few words for him but bit her tongue.

"I didn't know if you'd come." She tried to hit the right tone between coy and awestruck.

"For you, I would travel around the world."

"Doesn't that make you tired?"

Even his unnaturally red lips had paled. "For someone as strong as I? The effort is but a soupçon of my total immense power."

His narrow shoulders sagged. She wasn't buying the tough-Satan act. But he wanted to keep up pretenses. Even better for her plans.

She batted her lashes, ignoring the nausea that came with flirting with evil. "So it won't be a problem taking me with you?"

Flipping her hair back, she avoided dragging the strands through the last bit of blood on her arm.

His narrow glare had her on edge. Even his immaculately groomed eyebrows drew together in speculation as he studied her.

Prickles of heat broke out on her upper lip.

Had she overdone the flirtatiousness?

Did he know about Odie's plans?

Maybe he saw right through her. Oh God, her family. If Jerahmeel knew about the plan, they were all doomed.

A bead of sweat rolled between her breasts.

Why didn't he say anything?

He simply watched her.

She fought to hide her disgust, a struggle when looking at his oiled hair, the way he dabbed a pinkie finger to his tongue and smoothed his brows, and the way he licked his lips. He preened in front of her. The avid, cruel glint in his tiny eyes told the tale.

He believed he was getting his lover eternal.

The mere thought of intimate relations with his red tongue brought a wave of lightheadedness. She surreptitiously gripped the edge of the sink to remain upright. But thanks to her ingrained manners, she kept her face fixed in a polite, bland smile.

He examined his unmarred cuticles. "How do I know you're not leading me on?"

Excellent question. And difficult to answer, since all she'd done for the past 150 years was avoid him.

When in doubt, best to answer a question with another question. "Who wouldn't be intrigued by a man with such power and grace?" Even her words tasted like bile and dishonesty.

"That's true. But you've hated me for so long. Why change now? Is it because your Barnaby is gone?"

"Only partly. After we left New Orleans—"

"We?"

Oh no. Her heart rat-a-tatted like a wild snare drum beneath her ribs.

"Odie flew me back up here and, um, then returned to Louisiana. He probably wanted me to himself, but I sent him away. How could he compete with a man like you?"

"There's no contest, really."

"None at all." Little did Jerahmeel know.

"So prove to me you want me."

How she kept her face bland while revulsion plowed through her like a steamroller was a miracle. Prove it? He would know how much he repelled her the minute she touched him.

Maybe she could use her past to help her future. She poured on the antebellum charm.

"My lord, I'm still a genteel woman of polite society, despite the years of service to you. Any courtship and displays of affection must be in proper order and with decorum."

He immediately exuded an oily, obsequious manner and even sketched her a courtly bow.

"Of course, *mademoiselle*. But surely you wouldn't withhold a small taste."

A taste?

He smacked his blood-red lips together.

Fine. A taste, but not of her mouth.

She kept the knife in her hand and sliced her arm again. With an avid expression in his black leer, his tongue darted out like a red salamander. Probably equally pleasurable to kiss.

With bony fingers, he grasped her arm on either side of the cut and dragged his hot mouth across the gash. The rasp of his tongue on her skin made her shudder.

"So, you like, *ma petite*?"

She swallowed hard to hold back what she truly wanted to say. "Mmm. How could I not?"

"Your skin, your blood. So sweet. I want more than a taste."

"In good time, my lord. Don't we have all the time in the universe?"

Slowly, so as not to give the wrong impression of her enthusiasm, she pulled her arm back and ran water over it, patting it dry on a towel. The cut no longer bled, thankfully. At least she wouldn't ruin her white clothes. Not that it mattered in the long run, but thinking about stains kept her mind off the fear clutching at her shoulders.

She then carefully cleaned and resheathed the knife, all the while aware of Jerahmeel's scrutiny. She tried to put as much reverence into her care of the weapon, knowing that in some phallic way, this blade and her handling of it signified much more to Jerahmeel.

"Well?" She forced herself to meet his lifeless stare.

"Shall we?"

Without waiting for her response, he yanked her flush to his bony frame. His head stopped at the level of her nose and she fought not to recoil from the thick scent of his oiled hair. Thin fingers dug into her ribs right below her breast. Her bland smile froze in place.

Her heart thudded as the brimstone smell increased.

Wood paneling blurred. The ticking grandfather clock faded to silence.

Nothing. She existed in a place with no sound, no light, no gravity. Had Jerahmeel let go of her? She had no sense of his hand on her chest.

Nothing.

Darkness and disorientation swamped her until a wan, unearthly orange glow illuminated what looked like an ice cave. The soles of her feet registered hard ground.

"We're home, *mademoiselle*." He slid away from her.

She turned in a circle, taking in the bleak setting. Winking crystals of light punctuated rough, gray, pockmarked walls. Cold, lifeless air settled over every inch of her body.

Where was she? How in blazes would Odie find her here?

More importantly, how would she keep Jerahmeel's amorous salvos at bay until Odie arrived?

At the edge of her vision, she saw Jerahmeel stagger and put a hand to the wall to steady himself.

Good. No advances from him for a while. One problem solved for now.

Not as all powerful as he gave himself to be.

She'd try her best to exploit that weakness.

Until ...

Chapter 21

Damn it, the snow was deeper than Odie had expected. Not enough time and not enough progress. How could he have known that an early winter storm had dumped feet of snow in the high reaches of the peak?

Mount Shasta City, a quaint tourist village of alpine and craftsman buildings, felt welcoming, even on this overcast day. He had arrived there just after two, right on time, and stopped at a local outfitter. Despite the clerk's attempts to dissuade Odie from heading up the mountain so late in the day, Odie managed to stock up with alpine and survival gear.

The clerk tried to convince Odie that *randonnée* skis would be far superior to snowshoes. But Odie knew himself. This Cajun did not ski up or down a mountain, and he had no plans to start any time soon. Besides, he had no idea what sort of state Ruth and he might be in, if any, upon exiting the lair. He had no idea of the terrain they'd have to cover. He wanted the simplest way to travel. So, snowshoes it would be.

He stuffed the gear—coats and warm clothing, oversize sleeping bag, base layers, dehydrated food, a bivy sack—into a large backpack then lashed an extra pair of snowshoes to the outside. These supplies should sustain them for a time after any escape.

If she was up there.

If they could escape.

What the hell was he doing, attempting to destroy the most evil creature in the universe?

At least he would have tried. At least he had created some meaning from his cursed existence, from the horrible choice no parent ever wanted to make. He would sacrifice part of his being if it meant no one else would have to experience hundreds of years of hell on Earth.

Satisfaction was knowing that he'd found an amazing woman to cherish, even for a short period of time.

Satisfaction was knowing that he could govern some portion of a life that had been filled with helplessness.

High reward, higher risk.

Unfortunately, that risk involved Ruth. He had wanted to order her to stay home and not attempt to attract Jerahmeel's attention.

But the only way this plan would succeed depended on his tenuous plan and her power. No other options existed.

In the loaner sedan, he headed up the only road on the mountain, a narrow road full of tight switchbacks. As he climbed from the base elevation in town of 3,000 feet, he scowled at the drizzle that turned into thick, fluffy snowflakes. After a few miles, the snow built up on the road, challenging the stamina and stability of the vehicle's front-wheel drive. Normally he wouldn't care, but he could scarcely afford to waste time dealing with a disabled vehicle. He skidded through the snow, working hard to keep the vehicle on the road.

Finally arriving at an open parking area at 9,000 feet on the flank of the mountain, he discovered that a forest service gate blocked the way. Five feet of snow piled up on the road beyond the gate. He would have to travel the rest of the way on foot, through the forest and in deep snow, in the waning late-afternoon light, to reach the lair entrance and find and extricate Ruth.

It seemed like such a simple plan when they hatched it in Louisiana.

He was wasting time. Time he didn't have.

Time he and Ruth and every other Indebted didn't have as their killing urges grew.

Once someone killed, Jerahmeel would regain enough power to fight back.

How long could Ruth keep up the farce with Jerahmeel before forfeiting her soul, her life, or her family's lives?

Hurry.

Scowling at the massive amount of snow, Odie strapped on snowshoes and slung the backpack over his shoulders. He needed to find Panther Meadows, a large natural spring area on the mountain. Easier said than done, since the springs would be covered in snow. From there, the entrance to Jerahmeel's lair shouldn't be far beyond.

If his research was correct.

If he had picked the correct vortex.

Damn the word "if."

Striding up the mountain, he ate up the additional miles he had to travel on foot. Instead of following the blocked road, he cut straight up the mountain to where the GPS indicated Panther Meadows's location.

He struggled to focus on the GPS readings, but he kept imagining Ruth by herself in the devil's den.

Ruth, his fierce, sensual woman. Such an enigma, from controlled caregiver to sexual wildcat. Her appetite for him—and vice versa—had been near insatiable, and Odie liked her that way. He would gladly spend a lifetime or more devising ways to satisfy this woman.

A lifetime? Like a brick to the head, that unspeakable emotion slammed into him.

Later. He would examine his feelings later. If there was a later.

There hadn't been time to see if her interest reflected his, either. If she survived, he'd bet on her staying in Oregon with her newfound family, and that didn't include him.

Disappointment hit him like a kick to the gut.

How selfish could a guy be? The woman had discovered that she had surviving family. She'd committed to risking her life to save them all. How could he fault her for wanting to spend time with them?

He refused to press her. If, after this was all over, she wanted nothing to do with him, he would let her go. It would hurt like having his guts ripped out and stomped on, but he'd do it to bring her happiness. Odie would be damned if he'd ever betray her trust as her bastard husband did.

Which was why Odie stepped up the pace to climb the mountain in the increasingly deep drifts and waning light. He'd made a promise to come get her, and he intended to fulfill the promise, no matter what it cost him. He would do anything to keep her safe.

He almost tripped over the trail sign for the turnoff to the upper meadows as he stepped right on it. Kneeling in the snow, he dug it out to confirm, then punched in the coordinates on the GPS.

Following the directions, he traveled past the first set of springs to the upper meadow and then deeper into the woods. Caved-in pockets of snow indicated the path of each flowing spring, burbling water muffled beneath the thick blanket of snow. He passed the main springs, looking for a smaller, hidden spring that marked his proximity to a particular opening in the Earth.

Mount Shasta enticed numerous sorts of people to visit. Some folks loved the year-round adventures here, but others came for the vortex, the spiritual energy emanating from the mountain. Still others traveled to the mountain to discover the Lemurians, a mythical race who reportedly had hidden villages inside the mountain. According to legend, the Lemurians sometimes came down to the town below and swapped mortals for their kind, leading to the idea that these creatures walked among humans and influenced events on mortal Earth.

If people only knew that these sightings and legends all had to do with Jerahmeel's activities on this mountain. Over the years, the native peoples worshipped this site as the source of their spiritual power. Yet *they*—in fact, all humans—provided power to the corporeal form of Satan. But the legend grew and took on a life and mythology of its own. Thankfully at this time of year, Odie didn't have to dodge tourists or spiritual wanderers to reach his destination.

Hearing a new tinkle of water, he walked up a steep hillside. Here, the fir trees were twisted into unnatural, grotesque shapes. Again, it was said to be due to the vortex's energy warping the life fields nearby. That much was absolutely true. The power of Jerahmeel's travel would change the structure of any life form if exposed long enough.

Digging in the snow, Odie saw the water coming out of a breach in the rock. Close. Very close. Mon dieu, *please let this be the right vortex.*

Voila! There, a small slot in the side of the rock face, twenty feet away from the spring, exactly as his notes had described. There was barely enough space for one person to fit, so he stashed the pack under a nearby contorted spruce.

He squeezed through the entrance and paused.

There was little data as to how far into the mountain he would need to travel. No one had gone this far before and survived. But he could leave a trail. He tore off a piece of neon orange duct tape every ten feet or so and pressed it to the wall. As long as nothing else disturbed the tape, he would find his way out, hopefully with a light, but if need be, he could feel his way from piece to piece.

The thin passage widened to the width of two people. Rocks littered the floor, some as big as a hope chest. The wall sparkled with water seeping through the rock. Shining his light upward, he couldn't see a ceiling.

At a rumble under his feet, he froze. The sound of rock fall in the distance had cold sweat stippling his neck. Despite wanting to check his escape route, he gritted his teeth and continued onward.

After walking for an hour through the damp darkness, he heard a chuckle.

Odie stopped dead in his tracks.

Crouching down, he turned off his flashlight and let his vision adjust. A faint glow of light filtered back to him. He resisted the urge to sprint headlong toward the laughter. If Ruth was anywhere near, his rash actions could risk her life.

But hope leapt in his heart, and he slunk toward the source of the evil laughter.

CHAPTER 22

Ruth had ended up in a red dress. Not just any red, but a fires-of-hell red.

She hated red clothing. Never wore the color. Black, brown, maroon even, any pigment but red. But when Jerahmeel had invited her into the bedroom and insisted she pick out something more comfortable to wear, she couldn't refuse the request. At least if she mooned over fashion selections, she could get away from Lord Slime for a few minutes.

Damn, she had done everything imaginable to stall his disgusting advances.

First, he gave her the grand tour of the cavern, hewn from within Mount Shasta's volcanic rock itself. Mount Shasta. Upon hearing that tidbit of information, she almost cried.

Odie's guess had been accurate. Now if only she could buy him time. The storm outside had worsened, according to Jerahmeel, who used the weather forecast as an opportunity to emphasize how cozy he and Ruth would be, cuddled up here in the lair.

How much longer would she have to put Jerahmeel off? How much longer could the other Indebted resist killing? And how quickly could Odie get here, with the worsening weather? He was unhuman but not magical. He still had to fight through the snow and terrain.

It was bad timing and bad luck converging onto one place: here.

Too many variables, which depended on too many uncontrollable factors.

They'd created a house of cards. One whiff of a breeze, and it would all come down.

At least she could play her part to the best of her ability and pray that she and Odie could do the impossible.

She had to succeed. The lives of so many people now hung in the balance.

To succeed, she had to win the Oscar for best actress in a romantic drama/horror film. Easy enough.

So, as Jerahmeel proudly escorted her around the extensive cavern, she *oohed* and *aahed* appropriately. Truthfully, she didn't have to playact; the catacombs in this place amazed her. The interior walls of the living space were polished and cool like glass. Even the floors were smooth and perfectly flat. Something powerful had created this unnatural structure out of solid rock.

According to Jerahmeel, this site had been in use long before he had manifested into Satan in the twelfth century. What kind of man was he before the creature that stood before her now? Who came before him?

At the center of the structure was an unnaturally fueled fire that glowed with a sick, melon-colored light. No wood touched the fireplace, no coal. As he explained, the energy from the humans whose lives bled into the cursed knives provided the fuel.

The slight whine she heard from the flame? Voices screaming in eternal torment.

The flames were living souls incinerating.

Nausea stopped her cold. She'd helped to put souls into the fire.

She couldn't stop staring at the jumping flames, imagining desperate, reaching hands in each flicker of light.

Arranged around the hellish fireplace were cozy chaise longues with burgundy velvet upholstery and ornate wooden detailing. As though Jerahmeel expected guests, maybe to chat together around the soul-fed fireside. Bizarre.

Another large room held a pool of boiling water that the mountain itself heated—oh yes, the lair sat on a volcano, albeit a supposedly dormant one. It was in this steamy bathing room that Jerahmeel had begun his advances, which became more overt as they stepped into the bedroom. Or what passed as a bedroom. The giant cavern with glassy walls reflected the glow of flames in recessed sconces. In the exact middle of the large room sat a round, red velvet–covered bed.

Disgusting.

Unfortunately, at this point, he dropped all decorum. Although she demurred, citing tradition and modesty, her mistake had been continuing the ruse and asking if he had warmer clothes for her to wear.

Licking his lips, his ember-red eyes glowed as he opened a giant wardrobe where every manner of sexy, seductive, and slinky clothing—all red—hung, ready for her.

They were all in her size, too.

Not only did Jerahmeel have a hang up about the color red, but he clearly possessed even more of a fixation on her than she'd originally believed. So, much to his glee, she made a great show of examining several different outfits to determine which one would be perfect for him.

As he left the bedroom, she caught how he briefly staggered against the doorway. Good. Now, to run down his hellish batteries even more.

Unfortunately, that meant modeling the least racy of the ready-for-sex-with-the-devil collection of clothing available in the wardrobe. She rejected the majority of the outfits due to the fact that they were little more than tiny strips of crimson cloth. Finally settling on a floor-length scarlet satin number with cap sleeves, she sighed as she studied herself in the mirror. The neckline on this outfit plunged, drawing too much attention to her ample bosom.

Too bad he hadn't stocked the wardrobe with coats. Damn, in the cool air, the shape of her nipples showed through the silky fabric. Her comfort was not the priority—only the display of her assets.

Holy hell, Odie needed to get here soon. How long could she carry out this farce to convince Jerahmeel of her interest?

As long as it took.

Odie and Hannah and Allie and their families' lives all hung in the balance, depending on how well she played her role. All right. What was one more pretense?

Peeking out to the—what? the living room, the den, the conversation pit of hell?—she spied Jerahmeel resting on a couch nearby. Maybe she could wait until he woke up and burn more time.

"*Mademoiselle*, are you dressed yet?" He called to her from the couch, waving his thin fingers in the air.

Her stomach sank.

"Of course I am, my lord," she cooed in what she hoped was a winning manner.

"Come out and model for me which garment you selected."

She shuffled in her ballet slippers to the center of the room. Judging by his avid leer and red tongue darting over his thin lips, he approved of her selection. He sat bolt upright and stared at her until she squirmed.

"Does this please you, my lord?"

"I've never seen a more tasty morsel."

"Thank you." It was all she could do to keep a smile pasted on her face. *Stay professional and pleasant.*

He patted the padded velvet next to him on the lounge. She rejoiced a little bit that he did not get up and approach her. Hopefully his energy waned even further.

"Come closer so I can look upon you."

"Of course."

Instead of walking the few feet directly, she strolled around the far side of the room, circling all of the furniture first. She kept her gaze downcast, watching him beneath her lashes as she trailed her hands over the furniture. With the fire directly between them, obscuring his view, she chanced a glance around the room, studying the opening in the rock he said led to the outside world.

At first, shadows flickered over the passage. Looking again, she spied a figure hidden within the darkness of the opening—Odie. Her heart beat a staccato. She'd recognize his broad shoulders, even in a crouched position. Her knees wobbled and she grabbed the edge of the chair in front of her.

He'd come for her as promised.

Her heart leapt, and it took all of her strength to maintain an impassive expression.

For the first time in 150 years, her trust had been rewarded.

Don't look at Odie. Give nothing away.

Holy hell, they still had a chance.

Stay calm, stick to the plan.

Hopefully Odie could strike before Jerahmeel's power returned.

Another glance into the corner, where Odie's face glowed in the eerie firelight, and a terrible realization hit her like a bucket of ice water: if Jerahmeel looked in the right place, he'd see Odie.

"Well, what do you think, my lord?" She purred and stopped just beyond his reach, drawing his attention away from Odie's hiding place.

"You are a delicacy, to be sure. Sit."

"Don't you want to stand?" she ventured.

"May I tell you a secret?" At her nod, he said, "I'm feeling a bit ... depleted ... this evening."

"Like, unable to perform?" she blurted out.

"Very tired, through and through. I'm waiting for my employees to provide some fresh souls to replace my energy stores."

"If you need me to leave and go kill someone, say the word."

"No, *mademoiselle*, I want you right here so I may feast my eyes ... and more ... on you. As soon as someone provides me with a soul, my stamina will quickly return." He licked a thin fingertip.

Hiding a grimace, she perched on the edge of the lounge. He reclined against the cushioned back, his oiled black hair framed by the intricate carved wood framing the chair.

"Better. I can see you properly now."

Judging by the direction of his leer, it was obvious which parts of her body he could see properly. Out of the corner of her eye, she spied movement in the shadows, and her heart pounded.

Forcing herself to stay calm, she cleared her throat. "My lord, you mentioned the twelfth century. Would you tell me how you came to power?" She prayed this was an acceptable topic. If not, his rage could be considerable.

"Certainly, anything for you, my lovely. I'll regale you with many tales of my life. If we have an eternity together, you will hear all of my stories."

Sounded like the opposite of heaven to Ruth.

He lifted a manicured finger to slide down her bare arm. The contact felt like hot slime on her skin. Thankfully, he dropped his hand to his lap, as if it took too much energy to raise. This could be the time to act.

If her own hunger to kill was blinding her, then it was only a matter of time before another Indebted caved in and acted on their all-consuming knife lust.

"Let's see. I was born just before 1200 *anno domini* in Narbonne, in the southern part of France, very near the sea. Beautiful town, God-fearing citizens, as people were meant to be. Until the holocaust."

"Like in World War II?"

"The world had two horrible holocausts, the first of which occurred from around 1200 until 1240 or so."

"I don't understand." Why was he discussing God? Jerahmeel was the manifestation of Satan.

"I grew up devout in the true Christian faith. Catharism."

"You mean Catholicism?"

"No!" he roared. "That is precisely what it is not." Steam trailed from his fingertips.

Misstep. She gulped and remained perfectly motionless.

Odie's shadow appeared on the wall behind Jerahmeel. It took all of her concentration not to glance over her shoulder.

"We believed in the true faith. Catharism. Two Gods. The good God of the New Testament and the evil God, Satan. Both are real. This is the divine truth, and no torture could drive that from me." His thin fingers fluttered over his arms and neck.

"All right," she said carefully. He might be weakened, but he could still inflict great pain.

"Yes, so when Pope Innocent, that blasphemous heretic, sent his inquisitors to Narbonne, we tried to hide, all of us, my entire family, other families. But our evil neighbors paid their way to false absolution by witnessing against us. Although they brought my family in to the inquisitor with the false charges they laid against us, our faith remained strong.

"To try to get us to confess and declare our conversion to Catholicism, the inquisitors used torture. My younger sister, aged fifteen, went to be a *seraglio*, a sex slave, for an inquisitor. Each evening, the unbeliever would describe in detail to my brother, youngest sister, and parents what lechery he forced upon her and what evil was yet to be done to her." Spittle formed at the corner of his blood-red mouth, his glowing eyes focused on the ceiling.

"That sounds awful."

"Worse. They then racked my father. He was the strongest man I'd ever known, but he screamed like a suffering animal as his shoulders dislocated. I can recall the cracks of the sinews releasing his bones from the joints and finally how his skin tore open."

"Oh my God. How old were you?"

Was that a tiny bit of sympathy seeping into her mind? Impossible, considering the heinous acts Jerahmeel had committed, the threats to her family. But what person wouldn't change after witnessing the torture of their family members? Wasn't that exactly what she feared for her own family?

"I was twenty. The inquisitors made me watch everything, hoping to get a confession out of me. They burned my older sister alive at the stake, scourged my brother, and mother received the iron slipper."

"What in heaven's name is that?"

Contorted features creased his face.

"They tied my mother to a metal chair and encased her foot in a red-hot iron shoe. The flesh burned away to bone. She passed out before they applied the second shoe."

"What did they do to you?"

Even though her job was to keep him talking and distract Jerahmeel, his story, whether true or not, had her riveted.

Another glance confirmed that Odie inched along the wall. If Jerahmeel looked in the right place, he would see him. She had to keep her erstwhile suitor occupied a little longer.

She brushed her fingertips over Jerahmeel's dry hand. His reptilian stare locked on to her.

"What did they do to me? Nothing." He laughed mirthlessly. "They did nothing. Except continue to demand my confession while my family suffered. So I called out to the two Gods I'd dedicated my life to worship. Called out for help and salvation from this hell on Earth. The second God answered."

"Which one?"

"Satan. It so happened that he needed a new human to take over his worldly affairs. His only desire was to consume energy from human souls. Satan employed an immortal human to collect the criminal souls to feed his hunger. After he made me his pawn, my only job was to use wiles and trickery to recruit humans to keep me supplied with power. As I thrived, then Satan, who possessed my soul, would thrive and carry on the Cathar traditions."

"Did it work?"

"Aside from Hitler's brief interest in Catharism during the Jewish extermination, no. The religion faded into obscurity. No one worships the two true Gods anymore. I was betrayed. But I toil alone in my mission."

"Mission?"

"To revive the true religion, of course."

"By tricking people to become immortal killers?"

"You wouldn't understand," he growled.

He straightened up and flicked a glance around the room.

Keep him distracted.

"So, how will you bring about the revival of Catharism?"

"Starting with you, I plan to create a new breed to lead the people back to the true religion."

"You know Indebted cannot have children, right?"

"All things are possible with the true God."

Horror turned her gut to cement. Breed? Have children? With her? *This* was his master plan? Madness.

"What about all your threats against mortals?"

"Anyone who crosses me is eventually destroyed."

At a scratch on the rock floor, Ruth coughed, trying to cover the sound.

Did Jerahmeel notice? Sweat cooled on her skin.

"So did you destroy the people who hurt your family?"

A reptilian smile crossed his thin face, and she rubbed her arms, shivering.

"Of course. Once I become the manifestation of Satan, I had no trouble acquiring more employees. In those times, people frequently called out to the heavens for help. I gave each person exactly what he wanted, and in turn, my employees served me well, providing me ample power."

He stretched his smoking fingers and then curled them into fists. When he rested his hand on the back of the lounge, he unwittingly pointed directly at a shadowed Odie.

Jerahmeel's ember-red eyes glowed.

"Did I destroy those that hurt my family? Oh, my lovely, yes I did. I annihilated those corrupt inquisitors and the Catholic criminals. My power then was vast. Unfortunately, in recent times, fewer individuals seek divine intervention. My power has waned. But soon, it will be time to revitalize the true faith."

Odie had crawled to within a few feet of Jerahmeel's chaise.

Ruth held her breath and struggled not to look in Odie's direction.

As Odie rose up, blade in his hand, Jerahmeel lifted his head. Ruth froze.

"Ah, ah, my child. You almost had me."

A twisted smile corrupted his angular features.

Flicking a finger, he blew Odie back into the wall with a blast of lightning.

Odie didn't move.

CHAPTER 23

"Even in a weakened state, I still have more power than you." Jerahmeel turned on Ruth and snarled. "This is the thanks I get for everything I have done for you? Ah, but like Barnaby, perhaps this idiot is but another obstacle in my path to possess you. I will simply rid the world of him as well."

"That makes no sense, my lord! You need Odie to feed you!" She slid away from him.

"You know nothing," he seethed, his voice now booming off the stone walls. "I would *like* to feed on souls, but I do not require it."

Holy. Hell.

Massive underestimation.

He pointed a finger at Odie, who writhed in pain on the floor, holding his head. His body contorted as if the muscles would tear apart.

Jumping over the lounge, she leapt in front of Odie and the power smashed into her, knocking the wind out of her lungs.

"No, my lord! You will not do this."

Pain receded when he dropped his smoking hand.

Jerahmeel panted but stood and walked around the chair. "You cannot stop me. I am the second God of the true faith."

"You're his puppet."

"Lies! Heresy! You'll see. Together, we'll rid the world of scourge like this man and the inquisitors. You are mine. I will have you. We will rule the world together, along with our offspring."

Odie groaned. "Ruth, get out of here." Then he whispered, "Miscalculated."

The front of his forehead had a burn mark, like a cigarette had been extinguished there. Only it continued to smoke. His eyes rolled back in his head.

When she turned toward Jerahmeel, he raised his other hand, and she staggered backward like a sledgehammer pounded her chest.

All right. She couldn't confront him directly. He still had too much power. If Jerahmeel attacked Odie, that assault would sap the pawn of Satan further. But he would destroy Odie in the process. Unless ... could she absorb some of Jerahmeel's power? Diffuse it again?

Remembering how Hannah had bought time for Dante to kill the minion, Ruth knelt and put her hand on Odie's head, pretending to check for injuries.

"Stay back!" Jerahmeel howled.

"I'm only making sure your power is indeed destroying him, my lord," she said.

"Stop lying, you Jezebel. You're trying to distract me, but it won't work. I am focused on my goals. You will soon be unfettered by such banal distractions as worldly companions and family."

Threats motivated her.

White-hot rage, like what she experienced in the hospital, erupted from her mind and spread out until it consumed every inch of her body. That steam whistle started to lacerate her ears again. Good. Let the power build.

Able to touch Odie and make a connection, she slipped her mental self into Odie's mind. The amount of torture he'd already endured shocked her. Red slices from Jerahmeel's onslaught steamed on the surface of Odie's mind. Thankfully, the psychic gashes knitted even as she watched.

Sliding in front of the essence of Odie's soul, she extended her consciousness, like earlier when she had protected Allie. But this time, she kept the shield light, airy, and wide. Maybe Jerahmeel wouldn't detect it while she leached some of his power.

She spoke to Odie within his mind, like she'd done with Barnaby. "*Pretend you're dying.*"

Even his mind's voice had the sultry Cajun accent she loved.

"*Not hard to pretend. But thank you for taking away some of the pain.*"

"*I don't know how long I can hold him.*"

Jerahmeel's forehead creased in concentration. Odie groaned and clutched his head with a rictus of pain that appeared one step from death. Jerahmeel pulled his lips back into an eerie grin.

"*How much longer? I'm not healed yet,*" Odie sent.

"*Another minute, maybe. Then what?*"

"*We take him. He'll be at his weakest. Any longer and someone's going to give in and get a kill, powering up his batteries. The instinct to kill has gotten bad.*"

Like a shield dissipating a blowtorch flame, she absorbed all the fiery anger pounding against Odie. Her own mind wavered as the pain grew. She had to hold on long enough to give Odie a chance to attack.

"Have you had enough?" Jerahmeel asked. The glowing finger dimmed and smoke trickled off the tip.

"Never." Odie flew to his feet.

Ruth wanted to help, but she couldn't make her legs move. Her head throbbed, but at least the hellfire had stopped.

Jerahmeel raised his hand again, but only a tendril of smoke came out. He gripped the back of the chaise, his bony knuckles turning white.

"This is impossible. Where are my kills? What happened to my powers?"

"We abstained," Odie said with a pained smile. "You know, like a religious fast, very good for the soul, don't you think?"

"Damn you."

"Too late, you beat me to it, my Lord of Pestilence."

Odie whipped his knife out of the sheath and plunged it into Jerahmeel's gut. The mountain around them rumbled and creaked as the knife drank its fill.

Instead of crumpling to the ground, though, Jerahmeel began to get stronger, like a snake eating its own tail. He wrapped his long fingers around Odie's arm and pulled the knife back. It was almost entirely out of his body.

"Ruth, quickly!" Lines creased in Odie's face as he struggled to hold the knife inside of Jerahmeel.

Her limbs had turned to rubber. Trying to stand and failing, she did the next best thing. Hitching up the blood-red satin dress, she dragged herself over to the men. She pulled her own knife out and stabbed Jerahmeel in the back of his knee, buckling it and bringing him down him to the floor.

As he fell forward, she plunged the knife into his upper back, pushing until she felt a pulse thumping against the blade. Funny, she never considered that he had a heart.

"My Ruth, I wanted to rule with you."

His fingers glowed brighter, becoming stronger as his own life fed the knife. Smoke poured out of his hands.

No. They couldn't fail. Her stolen life, stolen family, fear, death all created an explosive mixture that propelled her to shove the knife in harder.

What a waste. Jerahmeel had taken everything from her. She'd only just met her family, and now he intended to kill them all, too.

As she turned the knife, he hissed. But he couldn't move. For now.

She leaned forward and studied the face of the Lord of Evil. Needed to watch, to know if he could be destroyed, or if she needed to brace for her annihilation.

"You can't succeed! I'm one with the true God, Satan. His power will always inhabit this Earth. Even if you destroy me, you'll fail."

Did he speak the truth, or were these the words of a desperate being? Would there be further punishment for the Indebted?

For their families? As her resolve wavered, her grip on the knife loosened.

Jerahmeel lunged, his clawing, sizzling fingers outstretched.

Aimed at Odie.

Odie. The man who had helped her reconnect to the real world, who had peeled away the layers to find the real Ruth, a woman worthy of giving and receiving passion. Worthy of someone's care.

Jerahmeel planted one foot then the other beneath him.

His hands continued to reach for Odie.

Jerahmeel rose to his feet.

The knife she'd sunk in Jerahmeel's back began to glow red and burn her hands.

As Jerahmeel stood, he pulled up Ruth, still holding the handle. Despite the firm grip she refused to relinquish, he took one heavy step, then another, toward Odie, and success slipped away as each movement became stronger than the last.

He was getting more powerful.

How?

The siren scream in her head started up again, canceling out Odie's yells, the cracks of the mountain around them, her own harsh wheezing.

She heard nothing but that wail, a cyclone of hell in her head, spinning louder and louder.

A rivulet of deep red blood flowed from Jerahmeel's smiling mouth. However, tall and larger now, he raised a glowing fingertip and pointed it at Odie.

Fire burst from Odie's chest, but he didn't let go of his knife. With a guttural moan, his lips thinned to white lines, and he jammed the blade back into Jerahmeel's gut and then angled the blade upward.

She concentrated until she could hear Odie over the shrill noise beating against her skull.

"That's for Ada and Vivienne, you monster." He choked.

"You can't win. I will endure." Jerahmeel's shriek echoed through the cavern.

Ruth's hands trembled with effort to keep the knife lodged in his back, fighting the blade's impulse to fly out of Jerahmeel's body.

Holy hell, he wasn't dying.

Steam rose from of every inch of Jerahmeel as his howls joined the sound in her head and pierced her eardrums. His demonic laugh raked over her as surely as his clawed hands.

"Give up now, and I'll kill this man quickly. Otherwise, it could take decades for him to die."

Odie's green eyes widened as he stared up at Jerahmeel.

Ruth couldn't see all of Jerahmeel's face, but she could see reflections of embers in Odie's horrified expression. He huffed against the hole burning its way through his torso. Oh God, he couldn't heal fast enough.

"I'm well versed in the language of persuasion, *mademoiselle*," Jerahmeel howled at the ceiling, shaking stone. "First this man, then those two useless relatives of yours, then that delicious baby! Look what pain you have brought down on your loved ones. Your fault."

White-hot fear roared in an inferno of rage. Her head would splinter into pieces unless she released the fury.

No more death. No more torment.

She twisted her knife deeper and sent all of her power down her arm, spearing into his back.

He shuddered.

"Again." Odie gasped.

With a yell that came from a world other than this one, she released the critical pressure of that steam whistle in her head. Odie grimaced as her yell split into audible and mental resonances, but she couldn't control the explosion of power.

She screamed and shoved every last bit of her gift into Jerahmeel.

And twisted the knife again.

Deep inside of Jerahmeel's torso, the two blades brushed by each other. A blinding spark of clear light exploded out of Jerahmeel's chest. Pain lanced up her arm, and she almost dropped the weapon.

The hole opening in Odie's ribcage had receded. Either he healed faster or it burned slower now.

He gritted his teeth. "Do that again. Touch blades."

"God, it hurts."

"It hurts him more. Do it!" Odie said. "Your power is the key."

"Fools! You'll be destroyed," Jerahmeel screamed. "You have no idea what will happen."

Odie squinted at Jerahmeel. "You don't know either, do you?"

With a sick calm, Jerahmeel twisted his head unnaturally far around and pinned her with an evil glare, almost as if memorizing her face. "You kill me, and I will unleash every ounce of Satan's evil onto your family. I vow this to you."

"Ruth, don't listen to him."

She no longer cared if he destroyed her. There wasn't much left. *Just a newfound family*, a small voice whispered in her mind.

And Odie.

Whom Jerahmeel now tried to annihilate.

Another wave of screaming anger flooded her vision, her mind, her limbs. Sound blended into an indistinct whirlwind as the well of power rose up again inside her body. This time, she wouldn't check it, but release every ounce, bleed her power dry, no matter how much it hurt.

The confident smirk on Odie's face wavered as Jerahmeel leaned forward again.

No.

No more destruction.

Barnaby was correct. Her power was the key.

Squaring herself to stand directly behind Jerahmeel, she avoided his hands flailing backward to reach her. She turned her head to the side, couldn't watch. Shoving the blade in further within his chest, it grated against Odie's knife with a shriek of metal on metal that set her teeth on edge.

The moment of solid contact exploded like a supernova. Light poured out of the center of Jerahmeel's body as beams spilled from his eyes, his nose, his ears, and his mouth. Even while she squinted, the brightness blasted through her eyelids.

Shaking beneath her feet and between the two knives increased.

He was vibrating apart between their two knives. A desperate scream rattled the walls of the cave. Hers? After a hard pop in her right ear, hot liquid dripped down her jaw. Her eardrum had ruptured. Couldn't care less.

Jerahmeel's unnatural howl mixed with her split voice keening 150 years of anger and pain. The two sounds swirled like a furnace-hot wind, flying in all directions, battering against Ruth's mental shield. The shrieks hit her so hard, her mind compressed, like a window about to shatter.

"My lord, Satan, why have you forsaken me?" he yelled.

"Sorry, you're not a messiah. And you were forsaken from the moment you were created." Odie twisted his blade again to scrape metal against metal in the center of Jerahmeel's body.

"How much longer?" Ruth yelled to Odie. Her mind couldn't take any more psychic onslaught without imploding.

"Keep going," Odie called back. Determination lit up his face. Flickering shadows created ghostly shadows as he pushed harder.

The pain etched on his handsome face mobilized her into action. She shoved the knife in with her augmented strength, willing all of her power to discharge through her arm into the blade.

Jerahmeel swiveled his head around again, the unnatural movement making her stomach churn.

"I loved you. I would have given you the world. Why did you betray me?" His eerie ember stare bore into her.

"You do not deserve love, only death, for a horror like you," she said.

"Enjoy true hell." Odie grinned.

The explosions coming from within Jerahmeel blasted through Ruth's bones and into the mountainside. Rocks fell all around them. One glanced off her arm, drawing blood.

A few seconds later, she looked down. Still bleeding.

She no longer healed. Oh, no.

"Almost there," Odie called out.

With one final, horrible, percussion of pain and light, Jerahmeel disintegrated into a giant cloud of dust. With a vacuum like whoosh, the cloud shrank into a tiny pile of ash. Her ears rang with the sudden eerie silence.

Their breaths rasped harsh in the empty cavern.

She searched the structure.

Nothing.

No movement, no nasty laughter, no glowing fingers. Nothing.

"Did we—" she said.

An expression of wonder transformed Odie's features from pain to happiness. Did he have a few more lines around those pale eyes? Was that a streak of gray in his beard?

"We did."

He pulled her into his arms, the movement stirring the ashes in the slight breeze.

Breeze?

Deep rumbling began up high. With gut-wrenching cracks, rocks began to fall.

A few feet away, a car-sized boulder crashed into the floor, pulverizing lava rock into gravel.

"Odie?"

The light from the fire area had dimmed to the faintest glow.

A deep, grinding sound like a locomotive engine driving into a wall of ice came from high above them.

"*Mon dieu*! Run!"

CHAPTER 24

Good news and bad news: they were no longer immortal. Odie winced as a rock glanced off his back. The injuries they were taking on could no longer spontaneously heal. He should've factored that possibility into his plans. How were they going to get out of this disintegrating death trap alive?

Grabbing Ruth by the arm, he dragged her away as another huge block of stone exploded on the floor. He dodged falling rock to reach the opening to the passage out of the cavern, finding the flashlight where he had laid it a few feet into the tunnel. Clicking it on, he shone it down the passage as smaller rocks fell in the tunnel. Ruth sagged against the wall as she bled from cuts on her arms. She panted in the gritty air.

"We'll die if we stay here," he said.

He pulled her along as he scanned for the orange tape on the walls. A few pieces were missing or covered in dust from the rock falls, and he cursed every time he had to search for a marker.

Ruth yelped behind him and yanked against his arm. When he turned around, the sight of blood running from a cut on her forehead stopped him.

"Can you keep going?"

"Yes," she yelled over the din of rocks falling.

The entire world flew apart around them.

It had taken him nearly an hour to get into the cavern. No way did they have that much time to make the return trip. They would be crushed and buried long before then, at the rate this place was crumbling.

Orange tape, orange tape. He stumbled on the heaving floor and endured impacts by rocks raining down. *Keep going.*

Endless side passages presented themselves. He kept searching for the proverbial trail of breadcrumbs as he maintained a grip on

Ruth's wrist. She grunted every so often when she would trip or hit the wall. He knew rocks struck her, but he had no choice. They either had to get out of here as fast as possible or die. There was no middle ground.

The rumbling deafened him until his world boiled down to the roar of the mountain collapsing on them, the flashlight shadowing the passage, and Ruth's hand in his.

Faster. Go faster.

He had to get Ruth to safety. She had risked everything to help him fulfill his plan. He refused to let her perish because of her efforts.

Fresh rock fall blocked the passage, and he skidded to a stop.

"Oh God," she said.

When she panted, puffs of vapor came out in the cold air. She clutched at her arm, staunching a wound, but blood oozed through her fingers.

"Can we go another way?" she asked.

He spied a small orange tape about a foot away from the rubble.

"No. We have to go through it."

Frantically, he began digging through the pile as Ruth held the flashlight. His hands were bleeding, but he no longer cared. All he wanted was to be out of this tomb.

More rocks fell behind Ruth and the rumbling increased in intensity.

"Odie!" she screamed.

"Come on."

He shoved her through the small opening he created in the pile of rocks. Continuing up the tunnel, they dodged more falling stone. With a crash, the entire passage right behind them exploded in a blast of dust. Too close.

Keep following the orange tape.

Refusing to let go of her hand, he dragged her along the passage. She was his lifeline to sanity. He was her lifeline to escape this tomb.

Suddenly the ground gave way and they sank up to their knees.

In snow.

In snow?

They were out!

His ears rang in the open air. He heard the faint sounds of rocks falling back in the passage.

And then silence in the bone-chilling night.

The snowy weather from when he entered the passage hours earlier had given way to a cold, clear starlit night on the mountain.

Ruth shivered in her torn red gown. The flashlight beam caught snow settling in her dust-covered hair. Trails of blood dried on her arms and face. She never looked so beautiful.

He pulled her into his arms and kissed her hard, loving how their skin had cooled to normal temperatures.

"We made it. *Mon dieu*, we made it!" He whooped.

"Oh my God," she said. "Is it real?"

"No more slavery as an Indebted. No longer will we be forced to do things no person should have to do."

She sagged in his arms, and he held her until her shivering got his attention.

"You need to get warm."

He pulled gear out of the large backpack stashed nearby. A pair of boots, snow pants, and a sweater for her. Hats and gloves for both of them. The extra pair of snowshoes. She wouldn't be completely outfitted, but it would to be enough to get them off the mountain.

"What's that?" Ruth asked as she tucked her dress into the waistband of the insulated pants. The lumpy fabric and her dirty face made for an endearingly sweet mess.

"What's what?"

Concentrating, he heard it. A rumble in the distance, steadily growing louder and deeper. The ground shifted beneath his feet.

Mount Shasta was a snow-covered dormant volcano, housing the portal to hell.

They had just torpedoed the portal to hell.

Inside a dormant volcano.

Covered in snow.

"Let's go. Now!" he yelled.

"What?"

"The mountain's going to blow!"

"What—"

He cut her off with a slash of his hand, shoved boots on her feet, and strapped on the snowshoes. Cramming a toboggan on her head, he turned downhill and shined the flashlight into the darkness that had fallen.

"What?" she yelled.

"Something bad is coming. Run!"

They ran awkwardly in the gear, both of them tripping a few times until they got the hang of the movement. He could have used that Indebted strength and endurance right about now. Damn, how his thigh muscles screamed as he paused to use the GPS to retrace his steps to the main meadow.

Upon arriving at the open meadow, a recent avalanche of snow and torn-up trees had settled across the expanse. He motioned for her to follow him as he traversed below the worst of the slide. Too long, they were wasting precious time. Although he struggled for oxygen at this altitude, he didn't dare stop moving.

The sounds of disaster continued all around them. Some rumbles were close by, some on the distant peak high above them. When he looked back up the mountain, an eerie glow emanated from its moonlit tip.

Glow? What would glow on the mountain?

Not a mountain. A volcano.

Lava.

Mon dieu.

Lava plus snow.

A deadly combination.

Jerahmeel's death had woken the sleeping mountain at the worst possible time.

"Ruth, go faster. You have to move faster."

"I'm trying." She panted, her quick puffs of vapor punctuating the cold air.

She galloped along in the snowshoes, off balance as she stepped into a soft snowdrift, then moving faster on packed snow. The glow behind him had changed. Sparks flew off the mountaintop behind him.

Sparks?

Not sparks. At this distance of a vertical mile below the summit, those were actually car-sized chunks of molten lava ejecting from the bowels of Mount Shasta.

What happened when superheated tons of rock met massive amounts of snow?

They had just run out of time.

Gasping, they struggled down the mountain. The GPS signal put them very close to where he had parked the car, but could he find it in the darkness?

He scanned the snowy landscape, frantic to find the vehicle.

Damn it, where was the parking area?

Distant detonations evoked images of a Vulcan hell rupturing behind him. It no longer paid to look; survival hinged on getting out of here.

Ruth stumbled and landed on her face with a hard *oof.* As he turned to pull her back to her feet, the sight behind her turned his blood colder than the snow beneath his feet.

The entire top of the mountain slid in slow motion toward them.

Clouds of glowing ash poured out. Foreboding orange light illuminated the slowly moving wall of ... everything.

That mass of destruction might be a mile away, but it was picking up speed, coming right down a natural alley carved into the mountain.

The alley ended below where the car was parked.

"Go! Go!" he shouted.

He left her behind as he sprinted straight down the snow-covered road until he saw a glint in the darkness. The car, parked right where he'd left it, right in the path of liquefied molten death.

Reaching the car, he flung open the back door, threw his pack inside and kicked off his snowshoes. He dug around the front floor mat until he heard a clink. As he grabbed the keys, another rumble sounded, this time very close.

When he looked back, Ruth clambered across the snowy parking lot, awkward in the snowshoes. Right behind her, a wall of snow piled behind the forest service gate began to move.

Hot lava contacted the icy rocks, causing surreal pops of boulders bursting. Massive tree trunks snapped under the weight of ice, lava, rock, and mud. A wall of liquefied debris headed right toward them.

She kept a few feet ahead of the steaming mountainside, her face the picture of terror with death literally nipping at her heels.

"*Mon dieu*, come on, come on! Get in!"

He reached over, opened the passenger side door, and turned the key in the ignition.

Click.

True panic, more than anything he had felt before now, fisted his heart in a grip that took his breath away.

Sweat prickled his forehead.

"Start," he whispered.

Click.

Damn it.

It wouldn't matter if she made it to the car; they were about to be buried alive inside of it.

He pumped the gas pedal a few times, trying something, anything, to help.

The image in the rearview mirror reflected a giant moving wall of darkness closing in.

He turned the key and sent up a prayer.

The vehicle turned over, almost begrudgingly.

It finally caught, and then purred.

Ruth dove into the front seat.

"Go, Odie!"

Before she could get her feet properly in the car and the door closed, he took off down the mountain. He grabbed her coat and hauled her back into the vehicle when the snow yanked off her snowshoe. Half lying on the seat, she heaved her one remaining snowshoe-clad foot into the passenger side. She slammed the door closed and shot him a wild-eyed look of terror the likes of which he had never seen.

In the red illumination of the brake lights, the snow moved in a muddy, piping-hot wall behind him. He was barely staying a few feet away from the leading edge.

If the lava caught so much as a back wheel, they were dead.

Pushing the woefully inadequate car to go faster, he sped down the treacherous switchback road.

Ice rimed the windshield, rendering wipers useless. He could see nothing.

"Put your seat belt on," he said between gritted teeth.

Of course the seat belt wouldn't matter if the lava and snow engulfed them. But if he somehow avoided the avalanche of mud and debris sliding down the mountain, he didn't want her injured by something silly like a vehicle crash. Mortal danger. Something he hadn't thought about in over 250 years.

"You too."

"No time. Do me a favor. Hold this."

He unclenched one hand from the steering wheel, fished in his coat pocket, and handed her the GPS. Gripping the wheel again, he skidded down the road. Unfortunately, the rock fall was so bad that he continued to dodge large chunks of mountainside that littered the pavement.

One good collision and the car would be destroyed. He struggled to avoid the largest boulders and winced at every jolt as they plowed over smaller rocks. The worst of the flow had diverted down a chute on the mountain to his left, though some of the slushy death still flowed in his direction.

Damn this horrible windshield. He was driving blind, going too fast for what little visibility he did have. Veering around a hairpin turn, the downhill front wheel slipped off the road. With force of will, he pulled the car back onto the pavement and hit the accelerator once more.

Rolling down the window, he stuck his head out. The ice-cold air stung, but he could at least see where he was going.

"Ok," he yelled. "There's an area to our right that makes another natural gulch for water and avalanches to flow down the mountain. Can you see it?"

"Yes."

"Can you follow it on the map all the way to the bottom of the mountain?"

"Yes."

"We have to outrun anything coming down that gulley. I'm sure that mess is picking up steam. This road crosses that gulch a few more times. At the bottom of this road, near town, there are side roads we can use to get out of the lava flow path. Can you find them?"

"I'll try."

She tapped on the screen while he continued to drive as fast as he dared. The road snaked to the right around the front of the mountain and then zigzagged down the face. The switchbacks might be dangerous, but it was at the bottom of the hill where death would collide with them.

At the base of the mountain, the road had been built over a chute where the folds of the mountain naturally funneled water. That was the alley he desperately wanted to reach before the avalanche did. On one switchback, he glanced up the mountainside only to see glowing mud, entire trees, and hot ash rushing directly toward them.

He had to go faster. Speeding up, he fishtailed down more switchbacks, at times only mere feet away from the roaring flow and inches away from a sheer drop-off.

The right back tire lifted as the leading edge of the liquefied mountainside caught the wheel.

Ruth. After everything she had sacrificed, he had to get her down this mountain alive. He couldn't fail.

How could he come this close to having a normal mortal life with a woman he loved and not survive?

Loved?

Damn it. No time to contemplate that conclusion.

He needed more time with her. Their lives couldn't end like this, buried on Mount Shasta.

The defroster finally caught up with the ice on the windshield, and he flipped on the wipers. Recklessly, he applied brakes and accelerator, nearly running them off the road as they careened around yet another corner. How many turns were on this road? Ridiculous.

In the valley, he saw the brighter lights of the town below. Almost there. The terrain had relaxed into a long, rolling stretch of road. Maybe they would make it after all.

"We just passed McBride Springs campground," he called out. "You see it on the map?"

"Yes. Get ready to make a right turn."

A wall of ice and debris coursed next to the road. Everything was funneling to the same point. He had to get there first. He accelerated through a dip in the road, only to see the molten mountainside cross behind him as the two chutes merged, cutting off the road up the mountain. One more gully to avoid.

"Turn right—now!" she yelled.

He slammed on the brakes and skidded the car onto a gravel road.

"Oh God," Ruth whispered, her voice barely audible above the destruction only feet away.

She pointed. A house's light flickered and went out. He cringed, hoping no one was in the structure as it had been either buried or pulverized.

They jolted down the gravel road. Unfortunately, the road angled directly into the path of the flow.

"We're getting close," he warned her.

"I see that."

Tap, tap on the screen.

"Can you go faster?" she said.

"I can, but the car might not make it."

"You should probably try." Her voice was much too calm.

The sweat on his damp skin turned to ice.

He accelerated, and the car bottomed out, scraping the oil pan against a rock. Not caring how badly he jarred them, he sped up again. Twice, he caught air as they sped downhill. The mixture of liquefied mountainside and ice rushed next to them, now only about ten feet away and quickly closing the gap.

"We're too close, Ruth. Get us out of here."

"Ok, there should be pavement soon. When you hit it, go faster and turn right onto the next road."

She studied the illuminated GPS. The bumping ride abruptly smoothed out, though the sludge now licked at the left side of the vehicle, lifting the back tire.

"Right turn, now!"

He swerved, almost missing the turn. After a dogleg through a residential area, she navigated them to a final right-hand turn onto a frontage road that led them uphill and out of the path of destruction.

He exhaled and eased off the gas pedal.

Braking at a turnout several miles up the road, far away from any ice flows, Odie slammed the car into park. The tapping, spent engine, their sharp gulps of air, and the muffled rumble in the distance met his ears. His arms shook as he forced cramped hands to let go of the wheel.

Silence settled over them.

"You're alive. We're alive!"

He pulled her across the seat to him, kissing her lips, forehead, and cheeks. Her whole body quaked, so hard did she tremble. He tasted salt and pulled away.

"Tears, *chère*?"

"We almost—"

He clutched her to him, unwilling to let go. From start to finish, they had cheated death in the most improbable way. Only fitting, since death cheated them so many years ago.

She startled as fire engines with sirens blaring sped past them down the frontage road, toward the destruction.

"The people back there? That avalanche, the volcano ..."

"I know. I'm sure people were hurt and possibly died. *Mon dieu*, those poor people. Family members lost. I know how that feels, without a doubt. But what we did saved so many more people from centuries of pain, death, and suffering. Jerahmeel's dead. We just rid the world of that evil. And we survived."

"I can't believe it's really over." She sniffed.

Easing back into her seat, she unbuckled the remaining snowshoe. He walked around the car and opened her door. At his offered hand, she stepped into his arms and clung to him. He pressed his lips to her forehead, inhaling her sweet lavender and mint smell, now combined with a scent of sweat and dust. She was so very alive.

He turned so they could both see the spectacle occurring on the mountain. The top of the massive peak flickered as lava ejected thousands of feet into the air. The ground still moved beneath their feet, though much less at this distance.

"Wow," she said.

"You've got that right."

"All of our loved ones ..."

He tightened his arm around her shoulders. "You know what? As Jerahmeel was exploding, all I could see were the faces of my dear Ada and Vivienne smiling at me. Now, some day when my natural life ends, I might see my lovely daughters again."

"Of course you will. You were a wonderful father."

"And you were a loving mother."

"I should have done more. Like you did."

He dropped a kiss on an uninjured area of her forehead, then pressed his face to hers. "Well, now you've found your family again. I'm sure you'll want to be with them, learn more about the family you missed out on having."

"Yes, but—"

"All that catching up doesn't leave a lot of time for other things."

"But—"

He pulled back to appreciate her beautiful face, possibly for the last time. "I understand if there's not a lot of room in your life for anyone else right now."

"Odie—"

"You have a new life to live."

She stomped a booted foot. "Odie, stop talking. We are both very old people now. We've lived for hundreds of years enslaved to evil. You're right, I've found my family and I do want to spend time with them. But ..."

Irrational hope welled up as his heart flipped over.

She sniffed again. "It's taken hundreds of years to find someone like you. I don't intend to walk away now. Unless you want me to leave so you can have your own human life?"

It took several seconds for her words to sink in. The roaring of the mountain coming down nearby receded into a low resonance behind him.

"There's nothing I want more in this world than you in my life. Every day. I love you more than my own life," he said.

Damn it, if his chest didn't threaten to explode. That's right, he was susceptible to cardiac arrest as a human now.

She flung her arms around him, and he returned the embrace with interest.

"I love you, Odilon Pierre-Noir."

"I'm no longer that man. I'm Odilon Martin Turcot. My given name, not that killer's name. Ruth, you are more precious to me than the air in my lungs and the blood in my veins, and it would do me the greatest honor if you'd agree to be my partner for as long as the rest of our lives are meant to last."

"Oh, yes. I want to be with you, Odie."

She paused, her dusty face lit by the glowing mountaintop.

"But?" he asked.

"I like how you have been a secret sponsor for your family. Maybe I can become a covert fairy godmother. I'd love to find out more about my extended family, possibly visit some of them. Maybe I can still bring some happiness to the world. What if there are others in the family with similar gifts who could use guidance?"

"I think that's a wonderful use of your mortal life."

"Would you be my genealogy guru?"

"At your service, *chère*. Now and always." He captured her lips in a searing kiss that heated the cold night. A kiss that demanded to be repeated for the rest of their lives.

Chapter 25

The scent of turkey and all the trimmings wafted into the living room of Allie and Peter's home in eastern Oregon. Bouncing baby Emma in her arms, Ruth inhaled the smells of good food and sweet baby. Behind her, the low voices of Peter, Dante, and Odie blended with Allie and Hannah's higher tones.

Ruth could remain here forever, surrounded by newfound family and loved ones.

Minus Barnaby. A bubble of sadness lodged in her throat, but she pushed it down. No, she would relish her mentor and friend's memory. He had completed a long, rich life and lived it to a natural if not abrupt conclusion.

And she would live her life like Barnaby, enjoying every human moment.

With Odie at her side.

Emma's silky, fine hair reminded Ruth of her own babies. The aroma of a home-cooked meal hearkened to family gatherings in Maryland before the Civil War.

It was as though she'd lived the past 150 years in black and white, and now sudden color flooded her entire existence.

Relief meant relaxing with a baby in her arms. Relief meant no more looking over her shoulder and no compulsion to kill.

She was free. Odie was free.

And her family was now safe from Jerahmeel's spindly, fiery fingers of death.

"Ruth?" Allie had quietly entered the living room.

Ruth turned away from the living room window and offered Emma back to her mother.

"She likes you." Allie slid her arms under her daughter and cradled Emma. "You're the best great-times-six grandmother."

"The *only* one in existence."

"You might be right." She rubbed her cheek against Emma's soft forehead. "Any thoughts on what you'll do with your whole life ahead of you? Maybe I could see if there's a nursing position open at the hospital here?"

"Thank you, but no." Ruth studied the pine trees and mountains outside the window. "Being a nurse? That portion of my life is over, and I'm satisfied."

"So what will you do?"

"She will make this old man happy for years to come, that's what she'll do." Odie slid his arms around Ruth, making her shiver. Every time he caressed her, the sensations were so real, so vivid, it felt like the first time they touched.

Ruth leaned back into his chest and smiled over at Allie. "You know what I'd like to do? Odie's family tree program has revealed some interesting branches. I'd like to meet a few of my descendants."

"Sounds like fun," Allie said.

Odie tightened his arms around Ruth. "Anyone going with you on this wild goose chase?"

"Me and one other goose."

She sighed and relaxed, surrounded by the man she loved and the family that grounded her and added meaning to her life. Just knowing these people satisfied the gnawing emptiness that had consumed her entire soul. She didn't realize she'd been starved for human connection and warmth until now. Now, the hunger had abated and was replaced by love.

"Hey, old fogies, dinner's on."

The boom of Dante's voice startled Emma from her slumber and she fussed.

Dante raised one arm in defense as Allie stalked toward him, brandishing the crying baby. Hannah nudged him out of the way with her hip. Peter guided his wife and daughter into the dining room.

"Was it worth it?" Odie's tenor voice next to her ear sent frissons of desire straight through her body.

"What?"

"Giving up everything." He kissed her temple.

"I gave up nothing. We had hell to pay. The tab is settled. I'm looking forward to some peace and quiet. No killing, no pain, no evil."

He nipped at her neck, drawing goose bumps. "Not even a little evil?"

"Maybe a tiny bit of evil."

"Come *on*, you two love birds, I'm hungry!" Dante shouted.

Emma wailed as Allie shushed her.

Peter muttered a curse.

Hannah giggled.

Home. Ruth had found her way home.

The real Ruth had found love and discovered her true self.

About the Author

Jillian David lives near the end of the Earth with her nut of a husband and two bossy cats. To escape the sometimes-stressful world of the rural physician, she writes while on call and in her free time. She enjoys taking realistic settings and adding a twist of "what if." Running or hiking on local trails often promotes plot development.

She would love for readers to connect on Twitter @ jilliandavid13 or on her blog at http://jilliandavid.net. Readers are always welcome to e-mail her at jilliandavid13@yahoo.com. If you enjoyed this novel, please consider posting a review at the site where you purchased the book or on Goodreads.

More from This Author (From *Relentless Flame* by Jillian David)

Dante entered his seventh bookstore to case since he'd arrived in Portland, Oregon. Smoothing his Armani slacks, he folded himself into the worn reading chair at Cover to Cover Books and fingered the worn chintz fabric. He relaxed, taking in the clusters of scarred wooden chairs around oddly paired tables, several upright upholstered chairs like the one he occupied, and three threadbare loveseats. The smell of old books and wood polish lulled him into a state of nostalgia for quaint shops from his homeland, Sweden. The images almost distracted him from the mission. Almost.

Of course, he could have telephoned each store, but a strange man asking for Jessica Miller might have driven her to ground. That might not even be her name anymore. With what little he knew about her past, he wouldn't blame her if she tried to disappear.

So he'd been patient and systematic as he performed this different kind of stalk, but a stalk well within his forte. He'd honed his tracking skills over centuries of hunting devious criminals; finding a woman trying to hide in plain sight would take only a fraction of his talent. And time? Who cared how long it took to find her? He had all the time in the world. He was an Indebted—cursed and long-lived. Weeks, months, or years meant nothing to him.

In response to curious glances from customers, he rotated his wrists in his lap to hide the shiny gold cufflinks. He needed to blend into the population, quite a task for such an impossibly sexy man like him, standing at over six and a half feet tall. He didn't even have to be dressed to impress, come to think of it. Thankfully, modesty was one of his many exceptional traits.

Exceptional traits like killing? *Kristus*. He forced himself to relax his hand, lest he splinter the arm of the chair like he'd splintered the limbs and heads of criminals for centuries.

Thankfully, the citizens didn't realize a murderer lounged among them in this genteel business establishment. An Indebted killer. Quite the title to go on a business card. Despite his expertise with his weapon of choice, that godforsaken foot-long knife, truth be told, he'd prefer to have a luscious *flicka*'s legs wrapped around him any day of the week. Thankfully, he was proficient at both activities.

Clenching his hands into fists, Dante fought the urge to stretch his fingers toward the handle. For 300 years, whenever he killed a vile criminal, he supplied the energy needed to feed his boss, Jerahmeel's, soul. He'd have to find a criminal soon and satisfy the blade's hunger, or innocent citizens would begin to attract the weapon's attention.

A few sideways looks from customers of the female persuasion reminded him that he was, as usual, looking spectacular today. He flexed his shoulders, pleased when several sets of eyelashes batted. Not that he doubted his charm. A particularly luscious blonde and long-legged *flicka* had casually dropped her card off at his table at a restaurant yesterday. He licked his lips, anticipating a rendezvous this evening. Par for the fantastic course of his unnaturally long life.

Recently, though, his powers of attraction did not satisfy like before. What was missing? He patted his shirt pocket, reassured to feel a heavy bond paper still stored there.

Too bad the thought of a tryst didn't hold his interest right now. Since when was he indifferent to sex? Since never. Maybe he had fallen ill?

Flipping through the Bedier translation of *Tristan and Iseult*, one of his favorites, Dante glanced around the store. Despite the modest street entrance, the comfortable bookstore sprawled into a labyrinth of stacks, which enticed him to wander and explore. They even used library ladders here, which added to the shop's charm and reminded him of bookstores long gone. But that wasn't why he sat here, near the hissing espresso machine as an aproned worker brewed another cup. It was all about his objective.

Jessica.

And then what?

He'd decide later. Improvisation was one of his strong suits. Well, improvisation, a massive physique, and sexual magnetism, of course.

When a customer entered, the breeze wafted a scent of early fall trees mixed with the coffee and musty books, lulling him into a rare state of calm. He would sit here for hours if necessary.

A diminutive woman appeared at the register and murmured in a low voice to a customer. How had he not seen this worker before? It was as if she'd materialized out of the bookshelves, with a dull, gray sweater that hung off her frame and allowed her to blend into the walls. She kept her movements understated, wary, like a mouse trying to remain undetected. It was this deliberate effort to disappear that caught his attention.

Dante sat up straight when she spoke. Something about her rich intonation that flowed like silk across his face, the smooth sound at odds with her bland appearance, sent a frisson of excitement into his chest. He glanced at her over the top of his book.

Her strawberry blonde hair brushed her shoulders, and freckles dotted a cute button nose. She ducked her head shyly at the customer and bit her lip. When she made eye contact to run the credit card, those soft lips tensed. But then she smiled at a comment from the customer, and her entire face lit up, transforming an average countenance into a radiant one. A jolt of longing froze Dante in place. *Where had that emotion come from?*

Soulful chestnut eyes behind black frame glasses flitted toward the door. That warm gaze slid over him like she didn't acknowledge his presence.

Vad i helvete? What the hell? Since when did a woman not stare at him or resist his beauty? It must be because her glasses weren't calibrated properly. No other explanation made sense.

When the door opened, she startled like a frightened deer and pulled the gray cardigan around her. He tensed, ready to dart over to her. How odd. In his hundreds of years on this Earth, he'd never experienced that strong of an urge to safeguard someone, especially not a woman he hadn't even properly met.

What would she look like beneath that shapeless sweater? The alabaster skin of her neck was cruelly hidden from his view by the sweater's modest neckline. Were her curves lush or subtle? Would her breasts fit easily in his hands or did she hide more bounty? Damn it, he couldn't tell, and that limitation only made him grit his teeth in frustration.

Another customer, a middle-aged man, wandered between Dante and the cashier. No longer able to hide behind the book, Dante craned his neck to continue studying the woman.

Her delicate hands as she worked the register made him wonder how those hands would feel on him. Would they drift like silk against his hard lines and angles? Desire tightened his groin, and he shifted to relieve the unexpected pressure.

How could he be this interested in a woman without her reciprocation? Yet here he sat, responding like a randy schoolboy. Was this the woman he searched for? Or was he just on another of his *kvinna* hunts, led by his overactive libido?

If this twenty-something woman was Jessica, she stood in stark contrast to her stepfather. Raymond Jackson had been large boned and full of burly cruelty. Sharp rage speared Dante. *Ja*, if this were Jessica, she wouldn't have stood a chance against that monster.

When she slipped out from behind the counter, Dante nearly missed the movement. He couldn't resist following her thin frame, clad in a flowing pale pink skirt, as she floated down the aisles.

She sidled around customers, adroitly melting into the bookshelves to avoid contact. When she took several swift steps, her hips swayed unevenly and one foot scuffed against the hardwood floor.

As she stopped and cocked her head to the side, he dove into the next aisle and grabbed a book at random. Opening it, he flipped through the pages, pretending to study the content.

From a row over, her smooth voice rolled over him as she directed a customer. The soft rustle of her skirt brought back unbidden memories of homespun cloth and whispers of parishioners in his village's Lutheran church. So strong was the memory that he smelled tallow candles and wood polish. He blinked.

As he heard her walk away, he inhaled the faint scent of coffee, flowers, and book pages.

When he stepped out of his aisle to follow her, she ran into his leg, squeaked, and stumbled. Dante wrapped his hand around her slim upper arm to keep her from falling. Her head didn't even come to his shoulders, and he fought an overwhelming need to fold her into his arms.

When she tilted her head up, the color drained even more from her pale face, enhancing the delicate freckles over her nose. He devoured the view of her alabaster skin from her cheeks, over her jaw, and down her neck—until that damned sweater impeded his ability to explore further.

She tugged against him again, and when he let go, she darted away like a frightened rabbit, her hands fluttering as though she couldn't decide where to place them.

"Can ... can I help you?" Her soft voice, laced with a hint of a quaver, couldn't have shocked him more if she had yelled.

As her warm espresso gaze darted to him and away, her cheeks reddened beneath the freckles. There, that response was more like it. Now that he stood close enough for her to see him properly, she was clearly overwhelmed by his handsomeness, like every other woman.

"Just browsing the *stacks*," he said.

He gave his suave words just enough innuendo and mentally patted himself on the back when the red flush crept down her creamy neck. *Fullstandig*. Perfect.

For someone more than 300 years of age, he still had the goods to impress the ladies.

"Did you find something interesting?" Her voice cracked as she indicated the book he held. She must be overcome with nerves, so great was her attraction to him.

"Oh, yes, I did find something interesting. And some books, too."

Most women batted eyelashes and swooned at this point. In control, in his element, he created a seduction—a work of art. Truly, he was a maestro. She only had to absorb his charm, and then the pump would be primed.

"Hmm, well. You've picked out an interesting topic." The corner of her pink, moist mouth rose, and those impish brown eyes widened. Her tongue darted out to wet those soft lips.

She most likely imagined his masterful kisses and caresses. Her attraction to him was obvious. He had her. Dante straightened to full impressive stature and stood poised to reel her in.

Until he noticed the book in his hands: *The Woman's Guide to Successful Breastfeeding*.

Air whooshed out of him like a rapidly deflating balloon.

He would salvage this one. He was Dante. Women never said no to him.

"I, um, like to be well read."

She quirked one fine eyebrow above her glasses rim and wrinkled her nose.

What? Was she poking fun at him? At *him*? How did his never-fail charm become a train wreck in the space of two breaths? Inconceivable.

"Well, then, any other books I can point out for you? Maybe understanding your body during menopause? Or perhaps getting in touch with your inner Earth goddess?"

When she didn't quite hide another grin behind her hand, his jaw clenched.

That comment hit below the belt, but it was well played. Beneath that shy exterior, she had spunk.

He studied the shapeless sweater that hung from thin shoulders. He considered her twinkling eyes hidden behind rectangular lenses. Flecks of gold swirled within the irises, and he swore that a glimmer of interest, replaced by fear, crossed her features. Then she bit her lip and glanced away.

He had to know more. There was something oh-so-tempting about her but also something broken. A mystery. As he replaced the book that had cruelly betrayed him back onto the shelf, he powered up his never-fail megawatt smile and extended a hand.

"My name's Dante."

"Hi, Dante."

Her hands remained at her side. He groaned. But all was not lost. Time to go to the next level of seduction. He puffed out his massive pectoral muscles and gave her his best rakish grin. This maneuver always succeeded.

"And your name is?" He leaned forward, undoubtedly impressing her with his overwhelming masculinity.

"Not interested."

A bucket of cold water couldn't have shocked him more. Did she truly rebuff his advances? Impossible. Had never happened before. She definitely wore deficient glasses.

She turned away, spine stiff. "I'm sure it's mutual."

Off balance, he stammered. "I'm not ... no I just—"

"It's okay, Dante," she said. Her pronouncement of his name left him with a taste of whipped cream in his own mouth, her voice was so soft and sweet. "Please let me know if I can help you with anything else. In the bookstore."

She glanced back and away, but not before he caught the downturn of her mouth. For the space of a split second, he wanted to touch her lips with his, to take away whatever caused that sadness. *Vad i helvete?* Since when did he desire anything besides his base carnal needs?

With a rustle of cloth and a whiff of flowers, she disappeared into the maze of shelves. Fascinating. Unsettling. If this were Jessica, then he understood her fear. If this were Jessica, he'd have to figure out a gentler, subtler approach.

Gentle? Subtle? Those two words had never inhabited his vocabulary, ever.

What if this weren't Jessica? Who cared? His curiosity was still piqued. This woman still intrigued him. Something about that sweet mouth, the shy glances behind those practical glasses, the flit of her hands to brush back orange-gold hair captured his interest with laser-sharp focus. At minimum, she would provide some welcome diversion while Dante completed his work here in Portland.

Game on.

His jaded heart actually skipped a beat in anticipation of their next encounter. At that next meeting, he would use a different tactic to weave his web of seduction. He wouldn't fail.

He'd confirm if this was Jessica Miller and deliver his message. And then what? Once he delivered the message, he'd be persona non grata. *Hi, I killed your stepfather, want to hang out?* A hell of a pickup line, even for him.

But if that *oåkting* was the bastard Dante suspected, maybe Jessica's gratitude would drive her into Dante's arms. Ah, yes, of course she'd want to repay him for ridding the world of the disgusting Raymond Jackson. And Dante could think of numerous ways for a woman to demonstrate gratitude.

First, though, he really needed to take care of that damned knife lust and go kill a criminal before Dante's mind exploded. The blade pulsed in its hidden sheath on his leg, demanding attention, demanding that he kill again. He hadn't fed it in a week because he'd been too focused on finding and delivering his message to Jessica. Damn technology. His boss, Jerahmeel, had finally crawled into the cellular age and used text messages to divvy out special assignments these days. For standard kills, all Dante had to do was find a criminal and drive the blade into him, which typically slaked his need.

Speaking of exploding, it had been far too long since he'd had sex. Time to rectify that situation. And finally, if appropriate, he'd try again with his advances on this woman and, of course, succeed. Of course. He was Dante.

Very well. His foreseeable future included espresso, death, sex, and browsing books. *Spektakulår.*

In the mood for more Crimson Romance?
Check out *The Cougar's Trade by Holley Trent* at
CrimsonRomance.com.

Printed in the United States
By Bookmasters